DESERT FLAME

AUSTRALIAN SUPERNATURAL - BOOK THREE

NICOLE R. TAYLOR

Desert Flame (Australian Supernatural - Book Three) by Nicole R. Taylor

CHAPTER 1

It was a searing summer morning, and Eloise Hart sat on a battered camp chair, surveying the main street of Solace, Outback Australia.

The verandah of Hardy's opal shop sheltered her from the scorching rays of the sun as she sipped from a stainless-steel tumbler full of ice water and glared viciously at nothing in particular.

Live in the Australian Outback, they said. It'll be fun, they said. Who 'they' were was irrelevant. It was way too hot. Even her brain felt like it was melting, which made thinking hard.

She supposed she had a choice—get back in her motorhome and keep driving—but whoever had sealed that ancient magic underneath the town probably hadn't spared a thought about future generations and climate change. They probably hadn't bargained on anyone finding it at all.

Then there were the Exiles—the supernaturals who lived in Solace—who she'd found love and friendship amongst. They were the things she never thought she'd have until her motorhome broke down five kilometres out of town. She couldn't just leave them and the responsibility of protecting the seal because it was hot enough to cook an egg on the highway.

Trouble was everywhere, and no one was immune from encountering a little now and then.

Eloise sighed at the thought and tightened her grip on her tumbler. Was a fight with a gang of biker dingo-shifters considered 'little'? What about possessed witches and dark spirits?

It'd been three months since the Nightshade had taken over Vera and terrorised Solace with an arcane tornado, and red dirt still kept showing up in the most unlikely spots. Like in the crevasses of the driver's seat in Eloise's van, inside her kitchen cabinets, in her shoes, in her underwear drawer. Somehow, it'd even made its way into her bellybutton. How it got in there of all places, was a mystery for the ages.

It didn't help that Kyne had taken it upon himself to stir up even more. He'd promised to build them a home, and he'd done just that.

The coolest place to ride out the summer in the Red Centre was underground. At the right depth, it was a balmy twenty-five degrees Celsius all year round.

That's why everyone lived in dugouts—underground homes—if they wanted to remain uncooked. The only other option was to head towards the coast to ride out the season, but that wasn't an option for the Exiles. Their watchful presence was always needed...so underground it was.

They'd picked a spot on the ridge behind the pub and got to work.

Being an elemental who loved rocks, Kyne had made short work of the excavations, carving out the hallways, rooms, and ventilation shafts inside a fortnight. With the help of Drew and Hardy, they'd hooked up electricity, plumbing, installed a bathroom and kitchen, and unveiled a hardcore air-conditioning unit that had made Eloise's heart sing.

Since Drew had forbidden Vera from decorating his dugout, the witch was excited to help Eloise and Kyne with theirs. Eloise suspected she was still trying to avoid her own remodelling—considering that Rosheen had destroyed her altar with dark magic—but they'd had a great deal of fun searching for furniture and homewares, most of which would arrive on the next delivery truck out of Lightning Ridge.

Eloise's van was parked underneath a newly built carport beside the front door. Kyne was making good on his promise that they weren't *really* moving in together, even though they actually were. Things had moved so quickly between them, and her gaze kept moving towards the solitary freedom her van had provided. Kyne knew and understood, which was what made him so easy to be with, and after her tumultuous life, she really needed some easy.

The distant rumble of an approaching vehicle drew Eloise's gaze south. A white and yellow truck shimmered through the mirage on the horizon as it crawled along the asphalt.

Kyne and Wally had gone on a mystery errand to Lightning Ridge for the day, and as she sipped her ice water, she hoped this wasn't the fruits of their labour approaching.

It looked like a crane, but as the truck drew closer, Eloise realised it was a drill—an enormous one at that.

It drew to a lumbering stop outside the opal shop, and the air brakes hissed loudly as Kyne turned off the engine. The miner jumped out of the cab, slamming the driver's side door closed, and crossed the highway. He had a huge smile on his face and a pep in his step that she hadn't seen before.

Eloise stared up at the bright yellow machinery. "What in the world is *that?*"

"This," Kyne said, spreading his arms wide, "is a giant drill."

"I can see that. What's it for?"

"It's a Caldweld drill," the miner explained. "It'll help me sink a new shaft out at Black Hole Mine. See this?" He pointed to the drill bit on the back of the truck. "One metre in diameter. It'll chew the ground up and spit it out. Add a little elemental juice, and I'll be down to the level in no time."

"So, you're going back out?" Eloise's heart sank as she looked over the machinery. She was getting used to having him around every day, which was a feat for a solitary soul like herself.

He nodded and leaned against the verandah post. "I thought I'd get things started while there was a lull in life-threatening situations."

She set down the icy tumbler and stood. "But isn't it too hot?"

"Yeah, but the season starts in March, and there's only a four-month window before it gets hot again."

Eloise hesitated. "Only four months? I thought it was six?"

"March through May, if the going's good." He looked over at the drill and grinned. "This beauty will get me going in no time. Still gotta get a tipper, though."

"Tipper?"

"The hoist and bucket," he replied. "You know, the one you crumpled with your mind?"

Eloise groaned and pinched the bridge of her nose. "Don't remind me."

"Maybe you can un-crumple it?"

Could she do that? She looked up at Kyne, who laughed at her hopeful expression.

"Yeah, nah," he said. "Just playing with you."

Eloise rolled her eyes as Wally's ute zoomed into town and hurtled off the highway and into the yard behind the garage. The wheels kicked up a cloud of rust-coloured dirt, the cloud billowing into the still air.

It was a reminder of what they'd been through, and not even the holidays had dulled the memory of the nightmare the Nightshade had risen amongst the wind—*kadaitcha*, the shadow spirits of vengeful souls.

And the seal loomed, as it probably always would.

"What?" Kyne asked, stepping into the shade beside her. "This is my job, Eloise. You gunna miss me that much?"

"Well, the last time you were in a mine to work, it was with me...and it collapsed on us."

Kyne grimaced and rubbed his palm up and down her arm. "How could I forget?"

"I know I never will."

"There's more black opal in that lease," he went on, "and I intend to get it out. Gotta give you something to polish, hey?"

"What about our lessons?"

"We've been working on your power for months now, and you're good, Eloise. *Really good.*"

"Are you sure?" She was starting to sound whiny, and she winced.

"Elemental power is natural," Kyne told her. "You've been doing it all your life, and now you know the difference, so there isn't much to learn."

"You say it like it's so easy," she complained.

"It is." When she scowled, he wrapped an arm around her shoulder and rapped a finger on the brim of her hat, knocking the front down over her eyes. "I'm not leaving you, if that's what this is all about."

Eloise scoffed and set her hat right. "*No.*"

"Then what?"

She sighed and looked away from him, shooting a filthy look at the drill. "*The seal.*"

"What about the seal?"

"Things are only going to get worse, and..." She shrugged. "I dunno, I guess I'm anxious about it."

"The seal will do what it's always done. We're all on the lookout, like we've always been."

"But—"

"*Eloise.*" Kyne grasped her shoulders. "Life has to go on. We have to work and survive. The seal has a whole town full of supernaturals watching it. We've got it covered, *trust me.*"

He was right, but she wasn't fully admitting everything. She was anxious about him leaving to go back into that mine. He had magical powers that could melt rock, so she shouldn't worry, but she couldn't help it. After a lifetime of separation from people, Kyne was...well, he was *important.*

"G'day," Wally called as he strolled across the highway. "What a beaut!" He pointed to the drill. "The best money can rent in all the Ridge!"

Eloise pursed her lips as Kyne attempted to wave him off.

The old werewolf looked between the two elementals and pulled off his hat. Rubbing his temples, he grimaced. "I've a feeling I've stepped in something."

"No, not at all," Eloise said, picking up the tumbler of water off the ground. "You boys have fun playing with your toys. I'm going back inside where there's air conditioning."

She wrenched open the door and stepped into the cool showroom, the sounds of Hardy using the grinder in the workshop drifting out to meet her.

"You didn't discuss it with her?" She heard Wally say outside. "That's the first rule in a relationship, mate."

Maybe that's why it bothered me, she wondered. If that was a 'rule,' then she needed to order a copy of that book...for herself as much as Kyne.

Coen looked out over the vast expanse of the Australian outback, his starlit eyes taking in the layers of earth surrounding the iron ore deposit. It sat north of Solace, on a remote swathe of land once owned by no one but traveled by many mobs, which was now claimed by white fellas living in a place called 'Walawala Station.'

Walawala was a word in one of the many

languages of the first peoples of Australia that meant 'storm.' The iron ore gathered in the edges of the ancient coral reef was just that—a tempest of nature coiled into the ground like a snake warming itself in the sun.

He looked to the sky, studying the blue, and acknowledged the omen. His own name meant 'thunder,' and Drew, the dingo-shifter, was the lightning, though his name didn't bear the words.

How Coen hadn't seen the iron ore before now was a curious circumstance. He travelled the Dreaming and followed the trails woven by the songs of the Ancestors. Something had concealed this place from his sight.

"It's not meant to be here," he said to the dusty brown kangaroo sitting beside him.

Marlu looked up at him, her warm, chocolate eyes full of curiosity. Her joey stirred in her pouch, its gangly legs wriggling in the air. They baby would remain inside for eight months, then stay by her side for another three or four before it was time for him to brave the world on his own.

And what a world he would see.

Magic stirred in this isolated place. Magic like Coen had never seen before, and he'd travelled far and wide. He spoke to mobs in all corners, heard their stories, and listened to their memory. He felt magic all over, but not like here—not like Solace and not like this iron ore.

"An ancient shadow looms over this place," he murmured. "It wakes."

Coen thought of Solace and Eloise Hart with her shiny white van. And Vera, the witch with fire for hair who commanded water. They had been tested, but the iron ore would bring a shadow that stretched over the ages. Coen wasn't sure he was supposed to be a part of this story.

He thought of all the people in Solace and their task deep into the afternoon. He thought so long that the sun began to sink, casting the sky in amber flame.

Stroking a finger over the *marlu's* long silky ear, he sighed as the first stars of the coming night appeared through the sapphire flame of sunset. The planets emerged around the moon—Venus and Mars—and he looked to the dark places between.

His task was to watch the Dreaming and follow his walkabout. He was stepping too far off the trail. He knew this world, but beyond it...? Those were places for others to walk.

Marlu lounged beside him, her eyes drooping as sleep beckoned her. Coen said nothing, letting the kangaroo doze. Her joey was hard work, and their task was even harder. She must sleep if she could.

Coen pressed a finger into the ochre dirt that was still warm from the day and drew. The lines were straight and the corners sharp, the strange language holding magic that was unknown to him or this world. Like others, *she* came from other places, other trails.

Their songs were different from his but wove into the land with a comfortable harmony.

With his drawing complete, Coen looked back to the iron ore and began to hum, his voice echoing softly down the rise.

It was time for the Druid to wake.

CHAPTER 2

Hardy sat at the bench in his workshop, tilting his latest polished opal back and forth.

The light of the lamp bounced off the smooth surface and flashes of red, blue, green, and purple ignited in a kaleidoscope of brilliant colour. The black only emboldened the rainbow, the iron-rich earth deepening the hue of the potch—colourless opal—to create the most valuable opal in the world.

As a vampire, he had an enhanced talent for seeing more than the average human. Things an otherwise experienced cutter would miss—the fleck of colour within a smoky piece of potch, or a streak of imperfection within the stone, or the gentle touch required to get the best cut.

There'd been times he'd let the grinder buff off his fingertips rather than let go of a good piece. One long movement made for a spectacular stone, whereas two would have spoiled it. Pain was relative for a vampire—

considering his fingers healed mere moments later— and the wound was always forgotten in the wake of the finished opal.

The stone was exquisite, but as he set it down on the workbench, he realised something was missing. His wonder and joy had left him.

Hardy had been in Solace longer than he'd settled anywhere as a vampire. It was the first and only pace he'd been accepted for who he truly was. He should be thankful, but his heart was heavy...and restless.

It happened from time to time, and was to be expected given his long life, but a strange shadow loomed behind him. A shadow that he could never quite see, no matter how quickly he turned around.

The showroom door opened, then slammed shut, and footsteps echoed through the shop. The familiar scent of vanilla and black tea proceeded Eloise Hart, and Hardy glanced up as the elemental barged into the workshop with a stainless-steel drink bottle in her hand.

She sank into her usual chair and sighed a rather dramatic sigh, setting down the bottle.

"What chaos has Solace dished up this afternoon?" the vampire asked. It must have something to do with the truck he'd heard pull up outside, because nothing else happened in Solace. Well, outside of dingo-shifter biker gangs and cursed tornado-summoning witches, that was.

"Kyne and Wally went into Lightning Ridge to get a big arse drill and didn't tell me about it."

"Ah, I see." For a moment, Hardy's sadness seemed to lull, and he was grateful for something else to worry about. Something *normal*.

"I just..." She let out a frustrated groan. "Does he have to start right now? It's still forty degrees outside!"

"He is an elemental miner," Hardy reminded her. "He's at home underground, scratching for opal. Besides, he was an eternal bachelor until recently. Discussing things was never his forte, I'm afraid."

Eloise blinked. "Well, that was bland of you."

"Bland?"

"Your tone," she explained. "It was very...*old world*."

"No more than usual." He chuckled, well aware he spoke much more formally that the other Exiles, despite his upbringing.

She looked at him, her eyes narrowing. "Are you all right?"

"Yes," he replied. "I'll have more opal to cut in a few weeks."

"That's not what I meant."

He *was* attempting to deflect, but Eloise was more preceptive than he'd expected. She'd likely prod him until he gave in. He'd give her an inch and hoped she wouldn't take the whole mile.

"It's common for people to go through periods of melancholy," he told her. "Especially in times of prolonged extreme weather, and even more so for vampires. I'll be all right."

"Is that your overblown way of saying you don't like the sun?"

Hardy smirked. "I *am* a vampire."

"*Okay.*" She didn't sound convinced by his explanation, but she turned to her work and began fussing with setting her latest cut onto a post.

He watched her for a moment, then picked up his jewellers loupe and pressed it against his eye. Studying the opal he'd been working on, his vampire sight picked up on a small imperfection flecking through the red flashes. He weighed the pros and cons of buffing it out and decided to let it go. It was undetectable to human eyes, and he risked losing the trace if he fell into the trap of perfectionism. The value was in the colour of the opal, especially anything red on black.

"Hardy?" Eloise's voice rose again.

He turned, sensing the irregularity in her heartbeat. "Hmm?"

"Were you English before?"

He chuckled and set down the loupe and slipped the opal into a small plastic bag.

She wrung her hands together. "It's just... Well, we work together every day, and we've fought some crazy stuff, but I hardly know anything about you. Not that it matters..." Her gaze lowered as she fussed with the opal in her palm. "I'm just being nosey, is all. I'd like to know more about you and be here to listen if there're things you want to talk about. God knows you're done that and more for me and I was a stranger..."

Leaning back in his chair, Hardy smirked. He watched her as the words tumbled out of her mouth, the hole she was digging herself getting larger the more circles she turned herself in.

"It's just, you seem as solitary as I was, though you found yourself here in Solace. And I know how tough it can be on your own, and—"

"Eloise," he interrupted. "You're rambling."

She blushed, the blood rushing to her cheeks. "I-I'm sorry."

"Don't be. When you first walked in here, it was difficult to get you to say an entire sentence. A whole monologue, no matter how rambling, is a remarkable achievement."

Her shoulders relaxed and she let out a thin laugh. "If you say so."

"And to answer your question, yes, I was born in England," he went on. "I had a family like all people do. A younger brother and two sisters. As the eldest male, I was responsible for them."

"Your parents weren't around?"

"No. Times were difficult, and we were simple people. We had to make do."

"What happened to your brother and sisters?"

Hardy's heart twisted as regret pulled at what was left of the reanimated organ. His sister, Mary... Without him there, Tom would have had to take charge, but he was only thirteen. *Still a child.* And Elizabeth was sixteen with the prospect of marriage in her near future. He should have been there...

"Hardy?"

He looked up at and felt the warmth of Eloise's gaze as her elemental power attempted to reach out to him. Whether she was conscious of it or not, was another matter. Her gift for the fifth element—spirit—was an intuitive one.

"I don't know," he murmured.

"You weren't there?"

He shook his head. "I was in Australia...when *it* happened." He gestured to himself. "I couldn't go back."

Eloise's expression faded as her mind began to do the math. Depending on whose history books one read, Australia was 'discovered' by European nations in the mid-to-late-eighteenth century and first colonised a mere decade later. The British staked claim in 1788, to be precise, and that claim was for the nation's first penal colony.

"You had to leave them behind..." she murmured, "for their safety."

Pain, blood, and darkness. Hardy tried not to wince at the uncomfortable memories, more for Eloise's sake than his own. "It's rare for someone to choose to become a vampire, though I'm sure it happens."

"You didn't..." She swallowed hard. "You didn't choose?"

"No." He shook his head gently, turning his gaze back to the opal. "It's never easy, and almost always tragic, but it's the past...and the past should remain there. A memory scarcely thought about."

"I'm sorry," she said. "I shouldn't have asked."

Hardy smiled, though his heart remained heavy. "It's fine. I understand you're curious. I know all about you, so it's only fair."

"No," she said, edging her chair closer. "It's not fair. Your story is your own, and you don't owe it to anyone. I won't ask, but I'm here if you want to tell."

Hardy had always seen what Kyne and the others had in Eloise, but the more her powers began to emerge, the more empathetic and wise she seemed. Was it her elemental ability or her years of isolation that gave her such insight? Maybe it wasn't for him to know.

"How old are you?" she added. "Would you tell me that?"

He exhaled long and slow, the years falling from his breath like ashes in the wind. He was young for a vampire, and had certainly known others who'd lived two, maybe three times longer than he had, and still, he didn't understand how they could bear it. The constant need to adapt, reinvent, and remain hidden was exhausting. He was glad he'd found Solace.

He didn't see the harm in telling her. "211 years from the day I was born."

"You were born in...1810?"

He turned back to his workbench and began sifting through the bag of rough-cut opal he'd bought from Kyne all those months ago.

"The turn of a new century," he murmured. "Or near enough. A Hanover king was on the throne, England had already become the United Kingdom of Great Britain and Ireland, the American Revolution had long ended, the Napoleonic wars were raging, and Britain was stretching its might across the world, colonising the far reaches with its iron fist." *No matter who got in their way.*

"And you came to the colonies?" Eloise asked, awestruck.

Hardy selected a good piece of opal and held it up to the light. "One hundred and fifteen days aboard a tall ship."

"What was it like?"

"Horrible," he replied, turning on the grinder. "Absolutely horrible."

Finn Oreah'anza sat beside a glowing campfire, a bottle of red wine in his hand. It was made in the Yarra Valley, in the southern part of Australia, a thousand kilometres south of the patched-together camp he now called home.

A dozen fae lived here, all beholden to the seal, its magic the only thing keeping them from withering away and turning into monsters. They were tied to it, dependent on the ancient magic like they needed air to breathe.

Finn tightened his grip on the bottle of wine. Were they any better than the creatures who had already attempted to claim it? A time would come when he would have to face his past—and his part in the despair—just as Vera had faced hers. Would this story be his, or would it belong to someone else?

A presence loomed beside him, but he didn't look up. It was probably another attempt at guilting him into sobriety.

"*Finn*."

"*E'dreha,* Siora," he said, lifting the bottle to his lips and drinking.

"*Addrei*, Finn," she said. "Don't talk to me as if I was a stranger."

His gaze lifted and he acknowledged her, his magic greeting her as a friend. "Happy?"

Siora sighed. Her long straight hair shimmered with threads of powder blue and sea green, marking her as an Unseelie fae like Finn. There were two kinds of magical fae that came from their world. The Seelie, those considered to be made of light and goodness, and the Unseelie, who were made of darkness and evil.

They were part of the factions known as the *Shri'danann*, who were the Higher Fae...the elite or ruling class. The other faction was the *De'ashlide*, the non-magical fae, or better explained as the equivalent of humanity. Though, in his world, they had been squashed down by the *Shri'danann* until they were little more than working-class slaves, unable to rise or take titles, govern, or become wealthy. The fae who'd made it to Earth, however, were all *Shri'danann*.

Finn narrowed his eyes as Siora sat beside him, her disapproval of his drinking habits clear.

"I see you've begun on the red," she stated.

"That's because I was finished with the white." He offered her the bottle, but she pushed his hand away. It was a poor imitation of the wine—or *aru'de* in his language—found in his home world, but it was all they had. For a thousand years, they had to make do with the washed out colours of this Earth, unable to return.

Siora looked to the sky, her silver gaze watching the stars. "The magic here is becoming unsettled."

Finn said nothing. He'd felt the flow of power from the seal. The Nightshade had forced him to be a conduit to it, feeding the leaking magic through his body. It was restless, eager to emerge from its prison.

If he were asked, Finn would say that it was sentient and calling out to the weak-minded and the power hungry like a siren. It whispered promises it had no intention of keeping. It wanted to be set free...but no one had asked him.

"Finn," she went on. "You give so much for them and this isn't even your world."

"You don't even go into Solace," he seethed. "Why do you care?"

"Have they come to see how you are?"

Finn scowled. She knew they hadn't, but the other fae hadn't made this a welcoming place, despite Kyne trying to unite them all. One too many rebuffs had forced the elemental to resign to the fact that the fae would not join the Exiles. He was the only fae who went into town, let alone speak to the other supernaturals.

"You grow too close to them," she murmured. "While they call to us for help, they leave you to carry the burden of their actions alone."

"That's not true," he hissed, turning on her. Eloise cared, and the only reason she hadn't come here was because the others had made it clear that outsiders weren't welcome. Siora's heart had become clouded.

"The danger the seal brings will only become worse," the fae said, ignoring his tone. "With each attempt, death creeps closer...for all of us."

In that, she was right. First, it was the Dust Dogs, then it was the Nightshade. The fae's story was deeply intertwined with that of the Irish witches, and Finn had learned the hard way that old hatreds weren't so easily forgotten.

"It's been months and you still haven't fully recovered," she told him. "Think about that, Finn.

Think of what you're sacrificing for a world that is not our own."

"We have no world," he hissed. "Or have you forgotten?"

Her silver gaze met his. "No, I have not."

"But if you were given the chance to return, you and the others would leave me without a second thought."

Siora rose, her movements graceful as her powder blue hair fell about her shoulders. She looked down at him, her expression closed and cold.

"Some things are greater than loyalty beyond blood, Finn," she murmured. "You would do well to remember that."

He watched her walk away, the wine bottle heavy in his hand. "How *Unseelie* of you, Siora," he whispered.

Finn drank again, the alcohol dulling the pain from the fractured connection to his magic. Healing was slow, but Siora's indifference wouldn't be his problem.

"*Rir de'ash zalde*," he declared, waving a drunken hand in her wake. *I set you free.*

CHAPTER 3

Drew sat behind the till at the *Outpost,* his face screwed up in thought.

He flipped the page of the book he was reading and resisted the urge to hurl the bloody thing across the room. *What in the world did auriferous mean?* Vera's shop had a lot of random junk for sale, but the one thing she didn't order was a dictionary.

Having a book at all was anomalous behaviour for the dingo-shifter, but one on mineral exploration and mining was off the charts.

This was more Kyne's department, so why was Drew the one recruited to watch over the iron ore deposit? Coen always had a reason for the bizarre things he did, but never cared to share why—that's *why* they were bizarre.

Coen was teaching him to 'see,' whatever that was supposed to mean. When he shifted, Drew's senses were heightened and he noticed more than he would as a human, so he reckoned that's what the Indigenous man was getting at. The guy had a habit of being airy, like a stiff breeze had blown away his thoughts before he could speak all of them.

Drew flipped to the back of the book, found the unknown word in the glossary, and snorted.

"Auriferous," he read aloud. "Having gold content."

Dingoes and iron ore didn't mix. He was made for wandering the outback, sniffing out dangers above ground, not beneath it. Still, the looming presence of the massive iron ore deposit north of Solace was a pressure point for their ongoing protection of the seal.

The multi-billion-dollar mining conglomerate *EarthBore* was interested, but Hardy had already looked into it. Permits could take years, and the red tape for a project of the size they were projecting wouldn't see them on site for years. Kyne said they'd have to test the ground first and that mean exploratory mining.

If Coen wanted Drew to 'see,' he wanted to make sure he understood what he was looking at. As it turned out, exploratory mining was a lot more complicated than sticking a drill into the ground and seeing what would come out, especially for big companies that wanted to dig a ten-kilometre-square pit in the middle of Outback, Australia.

The door opened and the bell rang as a customer walked in. Drew hadn't noticed the car pulling up out front, but he saw it now. A silver sedan coated with a thick layer of red dust that reached the windows. It was a bit fancy for out here.

A man stood just inside the door, and he looked around the *Outpost*, taking it all in.

Drew took the opportunity to do a bit of looking himself. The guy was definitely not from around here. He wore a short-sleeved khaki shirt with pockets on both breasts, dark-coloured jeans, black boots with rusty toes—courtesy of the Outback—and a wide-brimmed brown fedora.

Other than that, he just looked like a regular bloke. He was a little on the short side, though.

The customer peeled off his aviator sunglasses and turned his attention to Drew, who wrinkled his nose.

Who did this joker think he was? Indiana Jones? He was only missing a whip.

"Hey," the man said, approaching the counter.

"Can I help you?" Drew eyed him, studying his chiseled features and green eyes, but didn't 'see' anything special. Coen's lessons hadn't sunk in at all.

"Just passing through, seeing the sights." A tourist, then. Sounded a little British. "What's north of here?"

It was a loaded question for the supernatural, but Drew shrugged. "A lot of nothing until you hit Longreach. There're a few small towns along the highway, but they're low on amenities."

The man grimaced and looked down the aisle.

"Solace is the last fuel stop for three hundred kilometres that way," Drew added. "If you're running low, then you better fill up. We also have bottled water if you're interested. Three litre jugs." He nodded to the stack at the end of aisle three. "It's on special."

The water had a rough, hand-drawn notice sticky-taped on the front that said, 'One for $5, two for $10.'

The man raised his eyebrows. "What's so special about it?"

"It's in stock."

He smirked and picked up the one shopping basket in the entire store, the one Vera had 'borrowed' from the supermarket in Lightning Ridge. "What's the deal with this place? It seems so out of the way."

Drew narrowed his eyes and studied the stranger. He was asking a lot of questions for a tourist.

"Solace started out as a gold mining settlement," the shifter rattled off. "Some guy found a speck of gold in a dried-up creek and sparked a rush. Turned out to be a fluke, but then some other guy found opal. More people came, but they found out the hard way that opal mining is tough business. There's a cemetery just past the windmill full of the crackpots."

The tourist's gaze moved to the book on the counter. "People still mine out here?"

"Yep."

"How many people live here?"

The shifter's hackles rose. "Enough that we get a postcode."

"That tree is impressive."

"It's a boab tree," Drew told him. "Don't ask me about it. I'm not a botany, or whatever they're called."

"Botanist," the tourist said. "It's called a botanist."

"Whatever." Drew picked up his book and began to read. He hadn't even been to school, and it was a miracle he could read, so how would he know what a botanist was? Like it was important information, anyway.

The man walked down the first aisle and fussed around the shop while Drew continued reading.

The shifter looked up now and then, checking on his progress, and had reached the chapter on core samples when the man returned.

He set the basket on the counter and added a jug of water to his haul. "What's the damage?"

Drew rang up the items, picking up each from the red basket. A box of Band-Aids, a packet of salt and vinegar chips, a box of Tiny Teddy biscuits, vanilla air freshener, toothpaste, a high-vis work vest, and a packet of party poppers.

"Forty-two-fifty," the shifter said, with a raised eyebrow.

The man handed over a yellow fifty dollar note with a low whistle. "Expensive living out here, eh?"

"Party hard," the shifter drawled, tossing the party poppers into a biodegradable plastic bag with the other stuff. Handing over the guy's change, he smiled. "Have a nice day."

The man chuckled and turned towards the door

just as Vera opened it. The witch stepped aside, smiling at the customer, but as the man brushed by her, she jerked back.

The guy didn't seem to notice and continued on his way.

"What's up your arse?" Drew asked.

Vera let the door close and stared after the tourist.

"Don't tell me you've got the hots for him, too," he went on, rolling his eyes.

Drew still hadn't gotten over his jealousy of the last guy who came in here, frothing at the mouth over the witch. Vera said it was just his alpha dingo trying to control a substitute pack since Eloise had made the Dust Dogs disappear. He was still adamant it was because he simply cared about her—not in a romantic way, but the brotherly kind. She'd taken him in when he was nothing but a ragged whelp on the run.

"What are you on about?" Vera asked, blinking.

Drew nodded to the window, where the man had gotten back into his car and was reversing onto the highway. "Aren't you busy with Sergeant Clarke?"

"This has got nothing to do with Andy," the witch huffed. "You didn't feel that?"

"Feel what? Annoyed?"

Vera sighed. "Sometimes you act like a teenage girl, Drew, you know that?"

"*You're welcome.*"

"That guy..." She looked out the window again, but

the car had already driven away. "There was something about him…"

Drew hesitated. "You think he was supernatural?"

"Yeah. Other supernaturals have passed through before," she explained. "Most don't notice what we are, let alone what lies beneath. What did he say?"

"He was asking a lot of questions about the town."

"And what did you tell him?"

"The usual bland speech."

"What did he buy?"

"Random shit." He ticked off the list on his fingers. "Tiny Teddies, chips, a high-vis vest, party poppers, toothpaste… Oh, and Band-Aids."

Vera laughed. "Party poppers? Quit pulling my leg."

"At least he was smart enough to buy water."

"Well, random shit aside, keep an eye out for him," the witch said, picking up the book from the counter. "He might come back, judging by what he bought." She scanned the cover and her eyebrows rose. "What in the world are you reading?"

"Hell if I know," Drew told her. "I don't understand half the words in it."

That night Eloise ventured to the pub early, keen for a drink and some air conditioning.

The short walk from Hardy's was brutal. She dodged between each patch of shade, carving a zigzagging path across the yard. Sunburn was far from a picnic when there was little to no ozone layer.

Once inside, she breathed a sigh of relief.

"There she is," Finn said.

He'd chosen a seat at the Exile's usual table instead of keeping to his perch at the bar. The change made her pause for a moment, but she decided not to bring it up, lest she scare him back to the corner.

"On the wine already?" Eloise sat beside him and nodded to the red liquid in the only wine glass Blue seemed to own.

The fae lifted it up. "McGuigan Black Label shiraz. Want some?"

"I'm not into wine," she replied. "It's too bitter for my taste. I'll stick to cider."

"Suit yourself. More for me."

Blue stuck his head out of the kitchen. "Did I hear you want cider?"

She lifted a hand in a wave. "Please."

As Eloise settled and Blue got her a glass of sweet apple cider, Kyne and Wally wandered in, shortly followed by Vera.

"How's things with your cop?" Finn asked as the witch sat down. "Get some yet?"

"Finn!" Vera exclaimed. "Can't you just say hello for once?"

Kyne and Wally sniggered, earning themselves a glare from Eloise. It was great that Vera was trying to patch things up with Clarke. Not that he remembered anything about Solace, the seal, or the Exile's supernatural status, but the witch deserved some happiness. They all did.

"Valentine's Day is coming up," Blue said. "Got any plans?" His gaze moved from Vera to Eloise and Kyne.

"Uh..." Kyne squirmed.

"He's too busy with his big yellow drill," Finn said, smirking.

"Finn!" Vera shrieked.

"Can we change the subject?" Eloise asked, her cheeks heating. Kyne had been her first kiss and anything other than that had been a no-go considering her powers. One touch was all it'd taken for her to screw up someone's mind, but now that she had a handle on things, the door leading to more was open. *Wide open.*

"I was talking about a nice romantic dinner and some stargazing," Blue grumbled. "Some us don't live in the gutter, you know."

Wally coughed loudly and turned to the miner. "So, when are you breaking ground?"

"Tomorrow," Kyne replied. "I went out today to check where the seam starts and picked a good spot. Oh, and thanks for letting me park the rig behind the servo. I didn't want to leave it out on the lease where someone could see it."

"Who do you think is going to see it out there?" Finn asked, rolling his eyes. "The boogie man?"

"Ratters," Blue told him.

The fae snorted. "Ratters?"

"Thieves. You'd be surprised how far some people go to steal opal."

"Hardy's been selling a lot of black lately," the elemental added. "People talk...and they ask questions. Wouldn't be surprised if a few more leases open up this season."

"Is that wise?" Eloise asked. "I mean, with the seal and all."

"We've dealt with it before," Wally said.

"Yeah, but not with the level of chaos we've bene experiencing," Vera told them. "It'll be trial and error, I suppose. We can't stop people from coming here."

"There's those pesky questions again," Finn drawled, raising his glass.

The pub door opened, and Drew came in, followed by a gust of hot air.

Vera kicked out a chair for him. "You lock up?"

"Yeah," he drawled, flopping into the seat, "I remembered to lock the doors and turn off the lights."

Vera kicked him under the table, causing him to yelp. "Any more visitors?"

Kyne narrowed his eyes. "What visitor?"

"Some tourist rubbernecking at the stupid people who live out in the boonies," Drew told him. "He had a look, rolled his eyes, then drove off like they all do."

"What did he buy?"

The shifter began ticking off items on each of his

fingers. "Band-Aids, toothpaste, air freshener, a high-vis vest, some other stuff, party poppers…"

"Party poppers?" Finn asked, looking perplexed.

"Why do you even stock them?" Wally wondered.

"They had a fine layer of dust on them *before* the tornado," Drew said. "Maybe the bloke wanted to celebrate leaving the hottest arsehole on the face of Australia."

While the Exiles were laughing about the party poppers, Eloise leaned towards Finn. "How are you?"

"Me?" He smirked and waved a hand through the air. "I'm just *lishri*."

"*Lishri?* What does that mean?" Eloise always found the snippets of his language intriguing. Each little word sounded like a magical spell compared to English.

"It means that I'm fine," he told her. "Good, okay, well, *indifferent*."

"How *are* the fae?" Kyne asked, giving away that he'd been listening in. "It was a close call after what had happened with the Nightshade."

Finn narrowed his eyes, his displeasure clear. "How are the fae? How do you think?"

"Pissed off, I'd say," Drew drawled.

"You'd know if you came to ask," Finn went on. "But you haven't, have you?"

"Your people have made it clear that they don't want anything to do with us," Kyne said, his tone turning serious.

Eloise put her hand on Kyne's leg and turned to Finn. "If there's something going on, you can come to us for help, you know that right?"

Finn said nothing for a moment, his silver gaze not moving from hers. "The fae are restless," he finally said. "They don't care. If you want their help, they won't give it anymore."

"That's not—" Eloise bit her tongue as Kyne grasped her hand.

"Turning me into a battery was the last straw." The fae lifted his glass and Blue grabbed it out of his hand before the whole contents spilled across the table. "If you get lost again, you're on your own!" He sliced his hand through the air. "*Ash'au li ak'ande du!*"

"Right, I reckon you're had enough for one night, mate," the publican said, confiscating the wine glass.

"Sober to drunk in ten seconds flat," Drew muttered.

Eloise didn't take her eyes off Finn. She suspected the fae had been drinking well before he had arrived. Could she blame him? What he'd been through was awful, and by the sounds of it, his people hadn't made things easy for him. They didn't like the Exiles, no matter how hard she or anyone else tried to bridge the gap.

She wanted to say something to make it all better, but that was easier said than done.

Before the conversation soured any further, the door opened, and Hardy arrived.

"Sorry I'm late," the vampire said, taking a seat. "Did I miss anything?"

"Did he miss anything," Finn exclaimed.

Kyne coughed loudly and shook his head.

"Well, I have some news," Hardy went on, trying to cover the awkwardness.

"Look out," Wally said. "It ain't anything bad, I hope."

"I don't think so, but I'll be heading into Brisbane tomorrow," Hardy said. "I'll be gone for a few days."

"It'll take you a few days to get there," Drew muttered.

"Why?" Kyne asked, ignoring the shifter. "Have you heard something?"

"Maybe," the vampire told him. "I'm meeting with my contact. She says she has some news on those *EarthBore* permits."

Eloise's heart dropped. It was too soon... They'd been happy for the past few months—the seal was dormant and trouble was a distant memory.

Hardy's gaze moved to her, and she swallowed hard. She'd forgotten that he could hear her heartbeat.

"Here," he said, fishing in his pocket. He pulled out a set of keys and slid them across the table towards Eloise. "Keys to the shop. You can keep cutting while I'm gone if you'd like. It's still too early for the shopfront to be open, so it won't hurt to keep that shut up for now."

She reached out and picked them up. "Wow...really?"

Hardy chuckled. "Sure. You've earned it."

"If Hardy trusts you with the keys to his castle, then you're so in," Vera told her. "Welcome to the inner circle."

"*Pfft*," Finn spat. "What inner circle?"

"It's a joke," the witch fired back. "Don't get your fairy wings in a twist."

"I don't have wings, I cast illusions!" He leapt out of his seat and raised his hands.

Eloise felt magic in the air as a brown snake slithered out of the wine bottle, growing as it wriggled from the small opening. It plopped onto the table and began to glide around the pint glasses.

"Finn!" Vera shrieked, recoiling. "Do you have to summon snakes at the dinner table?"

After dinner, Eloise and Kyne walked back up the hill to their dugout. The sun was still a way off from setting, the long summer days stretching well into the night.

"Hardy has been a little distant lately," Eloise said.

Kyne glanced at her. "How so?"

She frowned, trying to think of how to put it. "He's been...sad."

"I wouldn't worry about him. Hardy's always been the strong and silent type. Stoic is his middle name."

"Did you know he's over two hundred years old?"

The miner paused, and they stood together on the side of the road. "Shit. You don't say?"

"He never told you?"

Kyne shook his head. "Hardy isn't one to talk about his past."

"I get where he's coming from, I guess." She remembered how he'd told her that not all vampires had chosen to become what they were. That their pasts could be tragic. It felt like he was trying to tell her to leave off in his own subtle way.

"He gave you the keys to his workshop, and he confided in you," Kyne went on. "A vampire's trust is a big deal, and you have his. It's more than he's given me, and I lived with the guy up until last week."

Eloise was still confused. "So, I should be flattered, not worried?"

"No, not about Hardy. Finn, on the other hand..." He sighed. "I'd like to understand him and the fae more than Hardy's past."

"Finn will always be eccentric. What happened to him..." Her heart ached knowing what he must have suffered in the water tank. "He needs time and to know we're here for him."

Kyne looked off into the distance towards the fae camp. Well, at least that's where Eloise thought it was.

"I think they're telling him things," she went on, "and he doesn't know who to listen to."

"I have the same feeling," Kyne said. "At least he's sitting at the table with us. That's a start."

"Yeah." Eloise smiled and wrapped her arm around his waist. "It's a start."

CHAPTER 4

Hardy stood on the balcony of his hotel room and looked out over the Brisbane skyline. His gaze followed the curve of the muddied Brisbane River as it snaked its winding path through the centre of the city, and he studied the beige buildings on the opposite shore with a resigned sigh.

The sky was bruised black and purple, the tail end of a cyclonic weather system passing by to the south. A heavy burst of rainfall grazed across the horizon, blurring the sharp line between land and sky.

After spending so much time in Solace, being in the city again was a deafening experience. With his enhanced hearing, every noise was amplified tenfold—sirens, traffic, people, music, and even the rattle of trains passing by in the tunnels underneath the CBD.

And it was humid. The breeze stirred by the unstable weather was doing nothing but swirl the already murky air around and around. It stifled him, and he longed for the dry heat of the outback summer.

He dabbed at the corner of his mouth. Pulling his fingers away, he frowned when he saw a red smear of blood coating them.

As the years progressed, he'd grown better at feeding, and leaving less mess behind. He'd learned how to cover his trail and avoid detection, while being as humane as possible towards the humans he had selected. Modern times had seen the invention of blood transfusions and specialised banks to keep donations fresh and secure. This leap in the medical field had also provided him a way to abstain from directly feeding from others...human or otherwise. However, it wasn't nearly as satisfying as the old way.

"Hardy?"

At the sound of his name, he wiped his thumb across the stain on his mouth and sucked the blood away. He turned and stepped inside the room, making sure to close the sliding door. As the glass hit home, the abrasive sounds of the city reduced to a dull roar.

A laptop sat open on the table in the corner. Beside it, a rolled-up map had been spread out, the edges held down with a coffee cup and two glasses from the room amenities. The fourth corner was pinned in place by the elegant, manicured fingers of Emmaline Montgomery—Hardy's contact within the Queensland Government's Department of Natural Resources, Mines and Energy.

She was a beautiful creature—tall, dark-haired, pale, pink lips, with dazzling hazel eyes—and they enjoyed each other's company a great deal. So much so, he could still see the fang marks on her neck.

Hardy sat on the chair beside her and bit his thumb. A drop of blood pooled on his flesh and he reached towards her, tugging the collar of her black silk blouse.

"Oh, thank you," she said, her accented voice soft against his poor, abused eardrums. She was French, and even though her English was impeccable, she still sounded every part an elegant Parisian woman.

He stroked his blood over the wounds in her flesh, smiling as they healed. "What have you found?"

Emmaline blinked, her expression dazed for a second, before she tapped her finger on the map. "This is the preliminary geological survey conducted by *EarthBore*."

"They've been out to the site already?"

"Not in any official capacity. This is a simple topographic view of the land, some data from ground penetrating radar, LIDAR, and some small core samples."

"It sounds a lot more than preliminary to me," the vampire mused.

"It's all standard." She let go of the map and the corner flicked upwards, rolling in on itself. "There is much more work that needs to be done before the mine can officially break ground."

"What kind of work?"

"They have yet to complete an environmental survey. A mine this size would have a significant impact on the surrounding land, including the water table and wildlife."

"What about the cultural walk through?"

"Vetoed," she replied. "There won't be one."

Hardy leaned back in his chair. "They're cutting corners..."

"Which means this iron ore is serious business." Emmaline shook her head and began to type on her laptop. "I'll send you everything I have."

He moved closer to her and tucked a loose strand of hair behind her ear. "What's wrong, *mon amour*?"

Her hands froze at his touch and her eyelashes fluttered. "This... This deposit is like nothing I have ever seen. If it's passed, it will rival even the Carajás mine in Brazil."

"Carajás?"

"You've never heard of it?" When Hardy shook his head, she grimaced. "Carajás is the biggest open-cut iron ore mine in the world. It's estimated to contain over seven billion tonnes of iron, copper, nickel, gold... This mine *EarthBone* is proposing..."

"Shh," Hardy murmured, pressing his finger over her lips. "No need to worry about it, Emmaline. I'm working on it."

"Then you're not doing a very good job of it." She spun the laptop around. "Their permits were granted."

Hardy straightened and wrenched the laptop towards him, his heart beating double-time. "When?"

"*Yesterday.*"

He scowled and snapped the lid of the computer shut. This whole business stunk of bribes and corruption, but there was nothing he could do about it now. The permits were issued and *EarthBore* was on the move. He'd have to try to stop them on the ground.

"Well," he mused, "then I have my work cut out for me."

"You intend to keep pursuing this?"

"To the bitter end, *mon amour*." The vampire nodded, his mind firmly on Solace and his family.

"And right now?"

He met her gaze. "Now?"

"Yes," she murmured, unfastening the top button of her blouse, "*now*. Shall we move onto other business?"

Hardy said nothing as she straddled him...and he didn't move as her lips found his.

"Hardy?" she murmured, reacting to his rigidness. "Is everything all right?"

This was usually the best part of their meetings—and the only part she would remember—but today he felt nothing. His heart was heavy, and he didn't want her. She was a tool for him to bend to his will, nothing more. When had he become so...*unfeeling?*

"You will get up, tidy your appearance, gather your things, and leave," he told her.

She jerked back. "Excuse me?"

"The moment you leave this room, you will forget me," he whispered, loosening his grasp on her hips. "Forget our meeting, erase all traces of my existence from your laptop and your life. I was never here."

Emmaline stared at him with a blank expression, her pupils dilating as his vampiric suggestion sank into her mind.

"Do you understand?" he asked.

"I-I understand," she rasped. Climbing off his lap, she began to move through his instructions with robotic efficiency. She straightened her blouse, slipped on her shoes, and returned her laptop to her leather briefcase.

When she reached for the map, Hardy grabbed her wrist. "Leave that."

Emmaline pulled away, her movement jerky, and turned to face the mirror. She fixed her hair, pinning the loose curls back into place. When she was satisfied, she picked up her briefcase and left.

Hardy returned to the balcony when the door closed, hoping that the noise of the city would drown out his troubled thoughts.

EarthBore and the seal were one thing, but something else was in the air...and it wasn't the tail end of the cyclone.

His melancholy was seeping into his soul and the things that'd once brought him joy only served to show him how damned he really was. His predatory behaviours had delighted him long ago, but age had made him weary, and wisdom had only served to reveal the harsh reality of what he truly was. An undead predator.

His new life had begun in the depths of a mine and now...perhaps, it would end in one, too.

Eloise sat on the step of her van, her toes buried in the red sandy dirt. The motorhome fit perfectly under the awning Kyne had built outside their dugout, and the shade offset the sun just enough that sitting outside wasn't completely unbearable. But the weather wasn't what had her stomach squirming—it was the date.

She'd always longed for and despised Valentine's Day. One half of her broken heart had desired true love—and the flowers and fancy restaurants that went along with the spirit of celebrating romance. The other half was bitter with resentment, her curse keeping everyone away, lest she turn them sour with a simple touch.

That's why she wasn't hoping for much this year, despite everything she'd been through. Solace wasn't exactly the fine dining mecca of Australia, and Kyne was a miner who lived for opal and other precious rocks.

Besides, from the look of sheer panic on his face the other night at the pub, she knew he hadn't planned anything. He probably hadn't realised it *was*

Valentine's Day, considering he'd gone to Lightning Ridge and rented a huge drill. The chaos with the seal dominated everything they did, so she couldn't blame him for taking today to get his mine started again.

How could she be disappointed? Kyne was amazing, kind, strong...*understanding*. Besides, she was the one who'd destroyed his old mine, so maybe this could be *her* Valentine's present to him.

When his ute came barrelling into the yard outside the dugout, she was thankful he parked downwind, so the dust cloud that followed the car didn't blow into her van. She made a mental note to add considerate to the list of his endearing qualities.

As he got out, he saw her on the step and strode over with a massive grin on his face. He'd obviously had a good day, considering his clothes were coated with rust-coloured dirt. A matching layer smeared his face, except for the outline where his safety goggles had sat. He shook, sending a cloud of dust into the air, and Eloise made a face.

She waved the debris away. "How did your hole go?"

"Got down to the level. That drill is a *beast*. Chewed up everything in its path and spat it out."

He looked extremely pleased with himself, and she couldn't help it when her heart softened. She was going to hate it when he was out at Black Hole Mine for days on end, but seeing how happy it made him, she knew she had to stop giving him a hard time about it. Kyne was an earth elemental and being underground was like oxygen to his powers. How could she keep him from that?

He sat on the step beside her. "How was the workshop without a vampire hovering over your shoulder?"

"Quiet," she replied. "Weirdly so."

"You miss Hardy that much?"

She shrugged. "I kind of got used to his silent presence. He's just...*there*. He's the kind of person who doesn't require conversation to be around. It's kind of nice."

"An introvert's dream come true," Kyne said with a chuckle. He reached into his shirt pocket and pulled out a black rectangular box. "Here. Got you something."

She straightened as he held the box out for her. "Huh?"

"Take it." He pressed it into her hand. "It's no big deal."

Eloise looked down at the box, realising it was of the jewellery variety. Considering it was Valentine's Day, it was a massive deal. She tried her best to play it cool as she eased the lid open, but she could already sense the precious metal and stone that lay within—a side effect of being an elemental.

A silver chain snaked across a black velvet pad and flashes of red, purple, and blue caught the light. She gazed at the pendant, recognising the circular piece of black opal within the simple swirled, polished silver setting. It was the first *proper* bit of opal she'd cut and polished besides potch, and the same one Kyne had given to her the night she'd decided to stay in Solace. Not knowing what to do with it, she'd kept it hidden in her van...or so she'd thought.

"What's this?" she asked, confused.

Kyne laughed and shook his head. "You didn't realise it was gone, did you?"

"You stole it from me?"

He plucked each end of the silver chain out of the box in her palm. "Only to have it set. Here..." He motioned for her to turn around.

Eloise scraped her hair forwards over her shoulder as he lowered the necklace over her head. Her heart fluttered as the opal settled on her chest, and she felt her powers respond to the stone.

His fingers brushed her skin as he fastened the clasp. "How's that?"

"Perfect." She lifted her head and ran her fingertips over the opal. "You didn't forget, did you?"

Kyne ran his thumb over her cheek. "Not for one second."

"Thank you. I love it." Her smile widened. "What now? Are you hungry?"

"Yeah, but first things first, I need to change out of these dusty clothes."

She mussed her hand in his hair, sending grit flying. "And wash this mop of yours."

"Got a bucket?"

She leaned back. "A bucket?"

He unbuttoned his shirt and wiggled his eyebrows. "The plumbing's not hooked up yet, and I don't want to fill your grey tank with dirt. Just splash me with a bucket of water and she'll be right."

Eloise laughed. "You're so low-maintenance."

Kyne wriggled out of his shirt and smirked as her gaze moved downwards. "Like what you see?"

"Happy Valentine's day..." She laughed again, but as he moved to the button on his jeans, she felt heat rush to her cheeks. She hadn't seen him naked before. Well, all the way down to his boxers, but not the rest, and he'd definitely not seen any of her... *Uh...* They'd kissed and slept together, but not *slept together*.

"Get that bucket, would you?" he asked, not noticing her embarrassment.

"Gimme a sec." She went to the back of her van, glad for a little cover, and opened the rear doors. Finding a bucket, she slammed the door closed and hopped back inside, where she turned the shower on and propped the bucket inside the little cubicle.

Get a grip, Eloise, she thought. *It's Kyne. There's nothing to be embarrassed about. He'd never hurt you.*

Once the bucket was full, she turned off the tap and took a deep breath. Turning around, she faltered, her eyes widening as she copped an eyeful of Kyne's bare arse shining pale in the afternoon light. It hadn't seen a lot of sun, that was for sure.

"Bloody hell," she cursed.

The elemental turned, giving her a direct view of his front. He grinned at her, enjoying the flush on her cheeks, and spread his arms wide. "Well then, do your worst."

Eloise grimaced and pushed her embarrassment down. She stepped out of the van, brandished the bucket...and hurled the contents at him, adding a touch of elemental magic for good measure.

As the water flew through the air, the wind lifted it high and her power increased the volume, so when it smashed into him, it was a torrent that coated the miner from head to foot.

"Bloody hell!" He stumbled a step and wiped his eyes. "That was a tsunami, not a little splash with a bucket."

"You said 'do your worst,'" she told him with a shrug.

"Eloise Hart, you're full of surprises." Kyne ran his hands through his hair, then he laughed and launched himself at her.

She dropped the bucket with a squeal as the naked, dripping miner gathered her into his arms. "Kyne! You're drenching me!"

"And who's fault was that?" They laughed as they embraced, and his hand settled over her thrumming heart. "*Eloise...*" His smile faded and a look she'd only ever dreamed about filled his eyes.

He kissed her, his touch deepening as her fingers

threaded through his damp hair, but she was awkwardly aware of his current state of undress and tensed.

"We don't have to if you don't want," he murmured, picking up on her unease.

Her gaze lowered. "I-I don't want to disappoint you…"

"Disappoint me? Jesus, Eloise…" Kyne pressed his hand underneath her chin and forced her eyes to return to his. "You could *never* disappoint me. *Ever*."

She studied him for a long moment, frozen on the precipice. It wasn't *just sex* to her, and it wasn't because it was her first time. She was an elemental who could manipulate *spirit*. She'd caused so much trouble simply because she hadn't understood or been able to control her powers. Things had been going great. She was learning. But sex…? Maybe it was a step too far.

"If you're worried about your powers, don't be," Kyne murmured, holding her close. "We're both elementals, and you haven't done anything to me."

"So far," she whispered.

"Don't underestimate me…or yourself." He smiled and kissed her again.

Eloise breathed deeply. She wanted to. She was ready… If it was going to be anyone, she wanted it to be Kyne.

"Okay." She placed her hands on his chest and moved them downwards, growing braver with every inch. "But I've never done this before."

"I know." He lowered his lips towards hers.

"Kyne?"

"Yeah?"

"I love you."

He smiled and ran his hands through her hair. "I love you, too."

CHAPTER 5

Vera stood behind the counter at the *Outpost*, mobile phone in hand. For once, everything seemed to be going well. The town was quiet, Drew wasn't being insufferable, and the seal had been dormant since Christmas. No bleeding magic, no crazy conspiracies, just...*summer romance.*

She grinned as her phone pinged with a new message. It added to the already long thread that she'd been chatting on all morning, and her heart fluttered.

Holy, Sergeant Andrew Clarke, she thought. *You naughty boy!*

Just as she was trying to think up a new adjective to put in her reply, the door opened and sent the bell ringing.

Kyne strode in, followed by a gust of hot air. His blue eyes sparkled as he took off his hat and set it on the counter. He had an aura around him that made her smirk, and she fired off a quick reply to Andy.

He looked her over. "What's that sly grin for?"

"I'm texting Andy."

"Ah, I see. The guy still clueless about his adventures in Solace?"

She glared at the elemental. "He is, thank you very much for the reminder."

"Just checking," he fired back. "Hardy's so secretive about his vampire-ness that it wouldn't surprise me if his mind control trick had an expiration date he didn't tell us about." He nodded towards her phone. "Did you do anything for Valentine's?"

Vera shook her head and slid her phone into her pocket. "No, we decided it was too soon for that kind of mushy stuff. We're being casual."

"Cool." Kyne jammed his hands into his jeans pockets. "So…"

Vera looked him over, her magic tingling as his power crackled like an empty chip bag. "You're being…*awkward*."

"*Am not*." He pouted.

"Are so," she retorted. "I can feel your magic, and it's all crinkly. *Out with it*."

He grimaced and squirmed, shifting his weight from foot to foot. "Last night…" He couldn't seem to get it out, but Vera already knew. It *was* Valentine's Day yesterday, the prefect time for new lovers to have a roll or two in the proverbial sack.

Her mouth dropped open. "You and Eloise—"

"Shut up," he snapped, his scowl deepening.

"Why are you so antsy?" Vera scowled and shook out her hair. "Let me guess...you had...*performance issues*."

"I did not!"

The witch laughed at his pouty reaction. "Then what's got you so worked up? You're a man, take it like one."

Kyne ran his hand over his face as his cheeks reddened. Vera had never seen him embarrassed before, and it was cute and hilarious all at the same time.

"Bloody hell, just spit it out already," she exclaimed.

"It was good. Great actually... But, uh...at the end..."

Vera made a face. "Maybe I shouldn't have asked."

"Eloise had a vision," he blurted. "Well, we both had it."

"A vision brought by orgasm, interesting." Vera raised her eyebrows. "And you both climaxed at the same time? I thought that was a myth. Usually the man goes first, then forgets about the woman. Did you know—"

"Bloody hell, *Vera*." Kyne ran his hand over his face again. "I know what I'm doing. I—"

"I'm thrilled for Eloise. She needs some thoughtful male attention in her life."

"*Vera*. I came to you about the vision, not sexual education." He narrowed his eyes and leaned over the counter. "And not a word about this to Eloise, you hear?"

She looked him over. "You should've led with that."

"She's your *friend*."

She rolled her eyes and dismissed him with a flick of her wrist. "I'm just playing with you. Get a grip, Romeo."

"Are you going to help me or not?"

"Okay, okay." She waved her hands at him, her silver rings clacking together. "What was the vision?"

Kyne leaned back and glanced out the window. He was making sure no one was coming, and she had to give him points for trying to protect Eloise's modesty.

"It was that black mountain she told us about," he said.

Vera straightened, the tone of their conversation doing a complete one-eighty. She'd seen it too, back when Eloise had first arrived in Solace. She and Drew had broken into her van so she could trigger a vision of her own.

"What was it doing?"

Kyne snorted. "It...*loomed*."

"Loomed?"

"It bore down on everything around it like some sort of poisonous beacon. It was black, like...*nothingness*. The sky was blue and the trees around the mountain were so green... All the surrounding colours were so intense, it was like nothing I'd ever seen before." His frown deepened. "It was like I could reach out and disappear inside the darkness of it."

"When I saw it, it looked like volcanic rock to me," Vera mused.

"Yes." Kyne snapped his fingers. "Like lava that bubbled up out of an ancient volcanic vent and solidified there."

"A lava tube…"

"The mountain wasn't just a heap of rock," he went on. "It was alive. The darkness grew tentacles that stretched into the sky."

"Tentacles?" Her eyebrows rose and stayed elevated. "That's some serious porno vibe."

"*Vera*."

She made a face. "Well, it is."

"Do you think it could be another entity?"

She hesitated. "We don't even know if there is one underneath the seal. We don't know *anything* about it."

"Except what Andante told Eloise about the heart of the ocean."

Vera sighed. *Not this crazy old woman again.* "I know Eloise vouched for her, but she's never made herself known to us before. I'm not buying what she's selling."

"Eloise wouldn't lie."

"No, she wouldn't, but it's not her I'm talking about. This isn't something I'm willing to take on faith alone, Kyne."

"Coen saw her, too," he went on. "At least, he implied he did."

She was tired of talking about the old woman. She wasn't here, but the Exiles were. Whatever reason Andante had drawn Eloise in for, she didn't seem to care about following through, so Vera didn't see the point of believing in her ramblings.

"What did Eloise say about the vision?"

Kyne shrugged and glanced outside. "Nothing. She was embarrassed, I reckon."

Vera leaned against the counter and rubbed her temples. No doubt about it. As far as she reckoned, it was the elemental's first time—considering how her power had screwed up all her relationships.

Vera winced, remembering her first foray. Sex was another thing about the world that wasn't always so magical.

"Her elemental magic is strongest with ether," she said, steering the subject to safer waters. "It's no wonder she has visions in her dreams. That's what ether is. Spirit." She waved her hands through the air. "The cosmic juju that binds us all together. The topmost point of a pentagram."

"Yes, I know what ether is," Kyne complained. "Just because I'm good with rocks doesn't mean I've got them in my head."

"In a moment of heightened emotion," she went on, ignoring his attitude, "she was able to share it with you, and..." Vera realised Eloise wasn't just having a dream here and there.

"And what?" Kyne asked.

"How often does she have these dreams?"

The miner shrugged. "I dunno. Not often?"

Vera shook her head. "I think she's having them more than she's letting on." She stood and grabbed her sunglasses.

"Where are you going?" Kyne demanded.

"To talk to Eloise." She went to step around him, but the elemental grabbed her arm.

"Let me. If she knows I told you…"

"Kyne, I'm not going to hurt her feelings."

"It's not about her feelings," he argued. "It's about her trust. She…" He hissed and let her go. "It takes a lot for her to open up, let alone for things to uh…*progress*. Let me talk to her about it."

Vera stepped back, her heart softening. He had a point. Eloise had spent most of her life hiding from the world, and not just physically. Emotionally, too. She'd made a lot of progress since she'd arrived, but old habits die hard, or so the saying went.

"We need to find out what this mountain has to do with the seal," she said. "Three of us have seen it now, and I don't like those odds."

"I know."

"It has something to do with what's going on here, but it could be anything." Vera was more concerned about whether it was friend or foe, over what it was.

"I'll talk to her," Kyne murmured as he grabbed his hat off the counter. "Could you see if you can find anything out? I know you were looking into it, but after the Nightshade…"

"I'm fine with all that," she told him. "My magic has changed, but I'm still the same witch. I'm just… I'm just not in tune with fire as I used to be."

"Still, I know it can't be easy after letting go of your father's legacy."

Vera tensed, her gaze falling. To banish the Nightshade, she was forced to renounce his coven and sever her connection to their magic. It was like he'd died all over again, but it had to be done. For the seal and the town. For her friends. For the world.

"Sacrifice is part of being a witch," she murmured. "I still have the Brinewold."

"Even if you didn't, you'd always have us," Kyne said.

She drew in a deep breath and plastered a smile on her face. Looking up at him, she said, "Go on." She waved him towards the door. "Go have your awkward talk with Eloise. I'll let you know if I learn anything."

Kyne nodded and opened the door.

"Oh! Hang on a sec!" She raced down the first aisle and grabbed a purple and gold Cadbury Dairy Milk gift box. Returning to the front, she gave the chocolates to the elemental and smirked. "Sex vision talks go down a little better with processed sugar."

He rolled his eyes. "You're hilarious, you know that?"

"Of course, I do!" She shoved him out the door, but he turned back at the last second.

Holding up the box, he grinned. "Thanks."

"Anytime, *tentacle boy*."

Eloise was sitting in the middle of Hardy's opal workshop, staring at the wall. Well, she wasn't actually looking at anything; her mind was elsewhere, on other...*things*.

She shivered and ran her hands up and down her arms. Last night was good. It was great, actually...right until the point where her stupid powers screwed everything up.

Thankfully, Hardy wasn't back from his trip to Brisbane yet, so her lack of focus could slip by unnoticed. She didn't want to know what the vampire had to say about her 'escapades'.

She spun in her chair and opened her journal. Hunching over it, she scribbled a new image, the black ballpoint pen etching a rendition of the mountain that haunted her dreams...and now her sex life—because she had one of those now.

Stupid mountain.

Eloise glared at the page and wrote her assessment under the drawing...and underlined it ten times, her pen strokes so violent, they almost ripped a hole through the paper.

A knock at the door sent her heart into her throat and the pen slipped from her fingers. It clattered to the floor as she looked up and saw Kyne.

"Oh, God!" she exclaimed, covering her face with her hands. Her cheeks flamed so hot it was a wonder she didn't burst into flames. "I'm so embarrassed!"

He edged into the workshop. "There's nothing to be embarrassed about."

"I knew you were going to say that!" she wailed. "It doesn't help!"

"Here." He set something down in front of her, and she eased her fingers apart just enough so she could see. It was a purple box of chocolates with a big golden bow. "This might."

Her shoulders sagged as her hands fell into her lap. "I'm so embarrassed I can barely look at you."

"Why?" Kyne pulled up a chair and sat beside her. "I had a good time. Didn't you?"

She was a ball of emotions, her awkward inexperience trying to force tears into her eyes.

"Whatever you're feeling, don't," he went on. "You don't have to keep anything from me. I never want you to think that. I'll never keep anything from you." He shifted in the chair. "I learned my lesson with that one pretty quick."

Her lips quirked as her anxiety faded. "I know. I just have a hard time breaking through old defences. Talking used to be such an exhausting exercise...and facing stuff. It was easier just to get into my van and drive to the next town."

She felt his hand slip onto her thigh. "I'm always going to be here. For the good and the bad."

Eloise wasn't sure he could make that promise—people fell in and out of love all the time—but she understood the sentiment.

"We need to talk about the vision," he added.

"I already told you about the mountain," she blurted. "That it was in my dreams."

"Yeah, but you didn't tell me you were still having them," Kyne said. "Once or twice is a thing, but continually...? That's *a pattern*."

Eloise shrugged, a little bewildered he was just figuring this out. "I didn't want to keep harping on about it. I didn't know I had to keep reminding everyone. I thought that was the best way for people to brand me as annoying. People don't want to be friends with annoying people who whine about silly dreams."

"It's not a silly dream and you're not annoying."

She snorted. There were plenty of people who didn't get that memo, but there were also plenty of people who enjoyed whining for the attention it got them. She'd known a lot of those kinds of people back when she still tried to fit in with the human race. It gave those who wanted to reach out for actual help a bad name, so it was easier for her introverted self to keep her mouth shut.

"Eloise," Kyne murmured. "How often?"

"I dunno." She shrugged again. "Every other night?"

His eyebrows rose. "Since you got here?"

"Since before...?" Her uncertainty bled through her voice. She knew the mountain was important, but not like this. Kyne seemed troubled.

"Hell," he muttered. "*Eloise.*"

"Vera saw it," she told him. "And she didn't get all worked up about it. I asked Coen and he wasn't, either."

"Yeah, but I'm guessing they didn't see what we saw last night."

She leaned back, uncertain.

"It was different, wasn't it?" Kyne asked.

Eloise nodded. "It's never been like that. It's always just been a mountain. Even when Rosheen and I—"

Kyne jerked up straight, his brows knitting together. "Rosheen?"

"Yeah. Right before I knocked her out." She told him how she'd fought the witch during the tornado the Nightshade had risen through Vera, and how they'd fallen through space and the mountain had appeared.

"Now that you mention it, she did say something..." he mused.

"She did? What?"

"That it spoke..." He grimaced. "No tentacles?"

"No." It was her turn for her eyebrows to rise to

new heights. "Though she did ask who it was. If it said something, I never heard it."

"*Hmm...*" He leaned back and ran his hand over his face. "Can you do me a favour?"

She nodded.

"If you dream about the mountain again, tell me about it? I've got a feeling it's not done with you, and I want to know why."

Eloise nodded again, her heart twisting. She'd become so used to seeing the mountain that she barely thought much of it anymore. How could she be so stupid? If it turned out to be evil, complacency might kill her and everyone in Solace.

"Hey," Kyne murmured, pulling her towards him. "It'll be all right. We'll figure it out. I asked Vera—"

"You told Vera?" she exclaimed.

His cheeks turned a bright shade of red. "*Shit.*"

"I'll say!" She hurled the box of chocolates at him. "I'm mortified!"

He caught the chocolates against his chest. "I was worried about you! You've seen that thing! It's terrifying! It's got tentacles, Eloise. *Tentacles of darkness.*"

She let out a frustrated cry and covered her face with her hands. She knew she was overreacting, but it'd been an emotional twenty-four hours. Add in her expanding elemental powers, and it was a wonder she hadn't short-circuited earlier.

The opal hanging around her neck hummed softly,

warming her skin. Letting her hands fall away from her face, she curled her fingers around the stone and took a deep breath. Her power flowed through the layers of silica and found all the flashes of colour. Much to her surprise, it helped calm her.

Kyne glanced at the door. "Do you want me to go?"

"No." She managed to look at him. "I'm sorry. I know I'm overreacting. I don't mean to, I..." Her bottom lip trembled. "Sometimes I'm not sure I know how to," she waved her free hand in the air, "*people* the right way."

"You're doing great," he reassured her. "No one's perfect. No one at all."

She attempted a smile and scooted her chair closer to him. "The mountain is important, I know that. But it's not like I can ask it what it wants. I don't have any control over the dreams."

"We'll figure it out. It'll just take time." He draped his arm over her shoulders. "There're things Vera can do, and Coen knows about it. Between us, we have to discover something."

"I hope so." She also hoped it was a nice mountain because there'd been too much bad seeping out of the woodwork. No doubt there'd be more, but if there was a way to end the chaos, then she'd be totally down for a happily ever after.

Kyne sensed her relaxing and grinned. "Maybe we can try to recreate it..." Her smile dropped and he grimaced. "Too soon?"

"Maybe..." Her hands trembled and she remembered all the good bits about the night before. And there were *plenty* of those. "Maybe it's not such a bad idea. You know, for the sake of supernatural science."

Kyne chucked and pressed a kiss on her lips. "Well, if it's for science..."

CHAPTER 6

Hardy opened the door to his workshop, glad to be back in Solace. Even though he wasn't bringing welcome news, it was home. Quiet, peaceful, blissful, *home.*

Eloise and Kyne were in the workshop, kissing. They hadn't heard him open the door, and for a moment, the vampire stared at them, an unwelcome feeling pulsing in his cold, dead heart.

Their connection had occurred instantaneously, even though Kyne had been resistant to it in the beginning. They were two pieces of a puzzle that fit perfectly, and Hardy was jealous. He wasn't too proud to admit it, but he'd never say it out loud.

The reality of his life was to live on while everyone around him grew old and died. Kyne, Eloise, and the rest of the Exiles would do the same, and eventually, he'd be on his own out here. Who would help him protect the seal then?

He breathed deeply and realised things had progressed between them since he'd been gone. Another unfortunate and slightly creepy side effect of being a vampire.

He coughed loudly and the elementals broke apart like they'd been hit with an electrical shock.

"Hardy!" Eloise shot to her feet, grinning.

He was so surprised to see her so happy at his return, he faltered.

"What did you find out?" Kyne asked, not getting up.

"It's bad news, I'm afraid." He took off his hat, set it on his workbench, and pulled up his usual chair.

"Crap." Eloise's smile faded, and she fell back into her seat.

"*EarthBore* has their permits," he went on. "They're going to begin testing the ground any day now."

"How the hell did they get permits?" Kyne asked, his anger causing the sound of his heartbeat to deepen. "Have they done the cultural walkthrough? Notified the land owners? No one's said anything to us about it."

"They've bypassed it all," Hardy replied.

Kyne wasn't done. "We're the one's who are going to bear the brunt of the industrial pollution it'll bring, and that's not even taking the seal into consideration."

"Someone has to be paying off the government," Eloise murmured.

"Oh, there's no doubt," the vampire drawled. "This

mine is worth billions in jobs, international trade, taxes...it just sucks for the environment."

Eloise sighed. "And the supernatural wellbeing of the entire planet."

Hardy smirked. "It's a thankless job, but someone's gotta do it."

"How have you guys dealt with it for so long?" she asked. "It's exhausting, and I've only been here six months."

Kyne laughed. "It's been a quiet ten years."

Hardy watched Eloise's expression fall and knew she was overthinking again. She had a good heart but dwelt too much on things that weren't her fault. He knew she believed she was the catalyst for all their recent battles, and it troubled her. But it shouldn't.

"There's nothing we can do about stopping *EarthBore* now, at least not from going out to that ground," the vampire said. "We have to do something here. Bureaucracy was always going to fail us."

Kyne nodded. "Money talks, but we have something better than that."

"What?" Eloise asked. "A ragtag group of supernaturals?"

The miner looked at Hardy. "Compulsion."

"*No*." There was no way Hardy would consider going that far. He wouldn't even entertain discussing it.

"Why not?" Kyne asked. "It would be a simple matter of making the team doing the preliminary work believe the ground isn't viable."

Hardy narrowed his eyes and ran his tongue over his teeth. "It's not simple. This goes deeper than a few people in a truck with a drill. There's been multiple surveys already, government approvals, and an entire company of people who've been working on this proposal for years. Someone has bribed and cut corners not only at state government levels, but federal. This is too big for one vampire to erase."

"He's got a point," Eloise murmured, tugging on Kyne's sleeve.

"We have to do something," the elemental told her. "What else can we do to stop them? It's like you said, we're just a handful of supernatural outcasts." His gaze moved back to Hardy. "What *can* we do, besides use our powers?"

Hardy curled his hands into tight fists, his anger rising. "I won't exploit my vampirism in that way. They're innocent people."

"Innocent until the seal opens," Kyne fired back.

"Then use *your* powers."

He scoffed. "You want me to change the molecular structure of ten square kilometres of iron ore? Impossible. There would have to be a hundred of me, and even then, I'm not sure it'd work."

As Hardy's annoyance at the elemental grew, his teeth started to ache and his vision darkened around the edges. "Then you go out there and screw with their core samples and see how little that'll do to help."

"Hardy…" Eloise's voice was barely audible.

"Then I'm all out of ideas," Kyne retorted. "You're the one who has all the inside information. You tell us what we should do."

"Last time I looked, you were the leader, Kyne."

Eloise slammed her fist on the workbench beside him. "*Hardy.*"

His gaze moved to hers, and he saw fear in her eyes. He pulled back, realising he'd loosened his grip on his control. His fangs had started to emerge and his *eyes*… When the predator inside him took over, they turned completely black.

Running his hands over his face, he said, "I'm sorry."

Kyne frowned at him. "Hardy, *mate*… Did something happen in the city?"

"No, I…" He didn't know what to tell them. Truthfully, he couldn't explain it. "If stopping it at the top was what we should've done," he went on, "I should've gone undercover at *EarthBore* five *years* ago, but we didn't know about them until five months ago. It's impossible. It would've been a long shot, even back then."

"I'll be the first to admit I'm in over my head on this one." Eloise sighed and looked between the two men. "I doubt my power would be able to help, and I know nothing about mining."

"Just the basics," Kyne said with a smile.

"Even so, it's not going to be as easy as it was making the Dust Dogs disappear," she told them. "We need to tell the others what's going on. We should figure this out together."

Kyne's gaze returned to Hardy. "We're stronger together."

"Yes," Hardy said. "I'd like to speak to Finn, anyway."

"Finn?" Kyne asked. "Why?"

"I have a theory I'd like to run by him," the vampire replied. "Eloise, you can close up the shop if you like. It won't hurt to miss a day or two. I gather we're going to get more black opal in a few weeks."

"If there's anyone left to dig it," Kyne muttered.

Eloise kicked him in the shin. "You can keep your defeatist attitude, Kyne Brady!" She smiled at Hardy. "I'll go see Vera and Drew. Tell them what's up."

Kyne snorted. "You really want to go see Vera?"

Her cheeks turned red as the blood rushed to her face. "You want to tell Hardy all about it, too? He's standing right there!"

Hardy had a feeling he'd stepped into something, but he said nothing. Instead, he picked up his hat and made for the door.

He did want to see Finn, but truthfully, he just wanted some peace and quiet. After suffering the roar of the city, and returning to an argument, he was on the edge of something he hadn't felt in a century.

Settlers had called this place Solace for a reason,

and he was reminded of it every time he stepped outside. The stillness calmed the monster that slept inside him. The monster he hadn't seen since… Well, it'd been a long time.

"Hardy?" Eloise called after him.

He turned to find Kyne had already disappeared out the front of the shop. Her sweet, innocent eyes stared at him, and he saw that her concern hadn't abated.

"Are you sure you're all right?" she asked.

Hardy put his hat on and tipped the brim with his finger. "See you at dinner tonight?"

Her shoulders sagged as she realised he wasn't going to open up to her. At least, not any more than he already had.

"Yeah. See you then."

The outback stretched to the horizon, the red earth meeting the cloudless blue sky in a shimmering line. From where Finn sat on the top of the hill, he could almost believe the sunburnt land stretched into infinity. A never-ending circle like the ouroboros—the snake who ate its own tail.

Today, his vision was too sharp for his liking. When he was drunk, his magical nerve endings dulled, and he couldn't feel the ache of his short time as a battery anymore. Being connected to the seal to be able to exist day-to-day was one thing, but being plugged into it was another.

The air stirred around him, kicking up a small cloud of ochre dust. He had a visitor, and it wasn't fae. By the coldness, he knew it was Hardy.

"I'm honoured," Finn drawled, not looking up.

Hardy sat beside him. "You're not at the camp."

He waved his hand along the horizon. "What gave it away?"

"I see the softening up towards us has more to do with the wine than Eloise saving your life."

Finn narrowed his eyes. "What do you want?" He wasn't in the mood for hashing out his attitude problems today.

"*EarthBore* are coming," the vampire replied. "They've got their permits and will be making a move on that land just north of your camp."

"And?" Finn knew where this was headed already. Maybe Siora was right when she told him that the Exiles were taking advantage of the fae.

"This effects us all, Finn. I don't know what will happen to you and the other fae if they green-light an industrial mine. I don't know what will happen to the seal."

"Then we will move someplace else."

"There won't be anywhere else." Hardy grimaced and shook his head as if he knew he wouldn't get anywhere with threats of an impending doomsday. "Whatever... *Can* you go someplace else?"

The fae snorted. Places of power were few and far between, but they'd made the journey here without fading too much. They'd find another if they had to. The internet was brilliant for looking up those kinds of things.

"Finn, Solace has been your home for a long time. I know you can't go back to your world, but don't you want to protect what you have here?"

He sighed and wished he had another bottle of wine. He wanted to do something, but he was bound to his people, and this wasn't their fight. It wasn't their world. Even as he thought it, he knew Siora was wrong. This was all they had and they should be grateful. Still, he didn't know what Hardy wanted him to do about *EarthBore*.

"What would I know about mining and human paperwork, anyway?" he asked. "I know little about the politics of this world."

"It's not about that," Hardy told him. "You have a connection to the Earth that no one else has."

Finn shrugged. "I can see why you'd think that."

Hardy leaned back slightly, his brow creasing. "You don't?"

"It's different here. Always has been." He turned his gaze to the flat, red landscape. Finn was used to dense forests, soaking rain, and grass so thick it was like springy moss. At least, that's how he remembered his homeland, but it'd been a long time since he'd been there. "Wherever I walk on this land, it feels dry."

"Dry? Of course, it's dry."

"I'm talking about magic, old timer, not the desert. Where I come from, the entire world is steeped in the stuff. It's the air, the water, the earth, the fire. It's everything, even to the non-magic folk. If they came here, even they would feel the absence of it." He returned his gaze to the vampire.

"What is it called? Your world?"

"*Lor'Iyslar*," he replied. "In your language, it means something like mother."

The vampire drew in a deep breath. "Mother Earth..."

"I can't help you way the way you want."

Hardy said nothing, but his disappointment was as clear as the sapphire summer sky. The Exiles had no other leads and asking Finn was an act of desperation.

"They're not here yet," Finn said.

"If I'm not mistaken, I think you're sobering up."

"*What a shame.*" Finn didn't want to go into Solace, but maybe he ought to pay Blue a visit. "If you're here asking me about your big bad mine business, then you lot are really scraping the bottom of the barrel. Why don't you use *your* powers for a change? Erase some minds and be done with it."

Hardy's lip curled. "I won't exploit what I am."

"Exploit?" Finn snorted at the irony. "Do you think I'm exploiting the animals I charm with my magic? They haven't got the brain capacity to fight back, is that it? Or is it because humans have worked out numbers and words and are more intelligent?"

"*No.*" Hardy's eyes narrowed and began to change colour. There were even little veins of pulsing blood that ran outwards from his perfect, predator-like bone structure.

"Well, look at you going all angry vamp." Finn reached out and grabbed Hardy's arm. His magic coiled around the ancient power keeping Hardy alive, while the vampire's flesh seeped ice into his own.

Vampirism was a strange concept to the fae. A human body brought back to life by unknown powers. They felt witch-like to him, but not like the witches of this world. This power had the taste of starlight...like the kings and queens of his world.

Wally was a werewolf and Drew was a shifter, both clearly had beasts living alongside their humanity, but so did Hardy. His just manifested differently... Though through his touch, Finn could sense it'd been a long time since Hardy had let it out of its cage, and the beast was restless.

"What?" Hardy asked, pulling away.

"You're on edge." Finn waved his hand at the vampire and pulled a face. "You better not go all Dracula on me."

"How do you know?"

"I'm a beast charmer, and you have a beast inside you, vampire," he stated. "There's a fine line between what you once were and what you are now."

"Could you charm me?"

"No, you've still got too much human in you, but wouldn't that be a sight?" Finn laughed, the sound carrying across the outback. This was the real reason the vampire had come looking for him, not this *EarthBore* business. The vampire was having an existential crisis.

Hardy's expression softened. "I still have humanity? It's a comforting notion."

"Don't get humanity and vampirism confused with good and evil, old timer." He wove his fingers together. "They're not mutually exclusive."

"If that's true, it sure doesn't feel like it."

"From one old timer to another, believe me when I say this won't be the first or last time you question your life and the meaning of it all. It will end for me one day, but for you..." He looked over the vampire and saw his turmoil. "You will go on until someone takes your life, or you end it. *Sucks*, eh?"

Hardy lowered his gaze. "Everyone wants to live forever, but they rarely think of the consequences."

"C'mon, say it straight, vampire," Finn drawled. "You never wanted this."

"How do you know?" he demanded.

"I'm not stupid. That's how I know." He stood and dusted the dirt off the arse of his trousers. "I know a great deal about tragic backstories, vampire. *Sorry to break it to you,* but you're not a unique soul."

"You're so not sorry."

"What gave it away?" He rolled his eyes. "But this is what you are now and have been for *ages*. Get over it already."

Finn walked away, leaving Hardy sitting on the hillside. Whatever they were going to do about *EarthBore*, he didn't know. What was certain was that the fae couldn't do a single thing to stop it.

CHAPTER 7

L *ondon, England, 1831*

Hardy sat beside the fireplace in his sister's room, his brow creased. The orange glow was barely strong enough to light the dank corners, let alone stretch its warmth throughout the house.

Mary lay in the small cot against the wall, her slight frame covered in all the blankets they owned. She coughed, her lungs crackling as her chest heaved.

Winter had been harsh this year, and the spring had brought long days of rain and miserable drizzle—the weather barely broke long enough for the sun to shine. The streets had turned to mush and shite, and there was barely enough to eat, let alone burn for warmth.

Hardy was twenty-one, and a man old enough to

marry, but had his three siblings to care for—Mary, eighteen. Elizabeth, sixteen, and Thomas, thirteen. All of them brown-eyed, curly-haired, pale, and as thin as rakes for want of proper feeding.

The four of them all slept in the same room, unable to keep fires burning in the rest of the house. They were all tired and hungry, but there was nothing they could do about it, other than for Hardy to keep trying to find work...but scraping together coins and scraps only went so far.

Mary wheezed again, and this time tears sprung into her eyes as she descended into a fit of heaving coughs.

Hardy gestured for Elizabeth, who scurried away from the fire to fetch some water for her sister. He helped Mary sit as he took a cup from Lizzy and pressed it to her lips.

Hardy couldn't bear seeing her suffer like this. She was choking; the sickness was wringing what little breath she had right out of her lungs, and the coughing sapped her strength.

Consumption.

She'd started bringing up spots of blood two days ago, and Hardy didn't know what to do. He was the eldest, it was his responsibility. *He should know what to do.*

"She's getting sicker," Elizabeth whispered, turning her large brown eyes onto her older brother.

"We have to send for the doctor," Tom said from the shadows by the fire.

Hardy shook his head and helped Mary back into bed. He knew the doctor wouldn't come. Not at this hour, and certainly not for their kind. They had no money or status, and their worth as people were only comparable to those two things.

Mary coughed again, and he leaned over and dipped a cloth into the basin of stale water by his feet. Wringing out the material, he pressed it against his sister's fevered forehead.

He didn't know what to do. Their parents had died some years ago, and with no family to care for them, the role had fallen upon Hardy's shoulders. He was a full grown man, and that was the way things were. *If he couldn't find a way...*

"Lizzy," he said, gesturing to the girl, "sit with your sister."

"Why? Where are you going?" Her eyes widened, and he flinched as he saw hope in them.

He said nothing and went into the next room, closing the door quickly so the heat from the fire wouldn't escape.

Reaching up into the cold chimney stack, his fingers found the ledge and the small leather pouch hidden there. He took it out and emptied the contents into his hand. The coins glinted in the candlelight and he counted, even though he knew how much there was.

There wasn't enough. There was *never* enough.

The sound of Mary's heavy coughs echoed through the thin walls, and he closed his hand around the coins.

"Freddy?"

Hardy looked up as Tom edged into the room. "I have to go out for a while," he told him. "You're head of the family until I get back. Understand?"

He nodded, his gaze falling to the pouch. A boy of thirteen, and he already understood the hand they'd been dealt. That meant there was a good chance he knew what his older brother was about to do.

Hardy smiled down at the boy and pressed the pouch into his small hands. "You should know where I keep the money."

"I be beggin' your pardon, brother," Tom replied, "but I already know."

"Of course, you do." He chuckled and roughed up his brother's hair.

"Do you have to go?"

His smile faded. "I have to do something."

Tom said nothing for a moment, his pale fingers clutching the money against his chest. "Is...is she going to die?"

Hardy glanced at the door, his heart twisting. "I'm going to get her some medicine to make her all better. You'll see."

"Are you going to steal it?"

"Ask no questions and you'll get no lies." He

grimaced and pulled the boy into his arms. "Man of the house, remember?"

Tom nodded and Hardy let him go.

Reaching for his coat, he said, "I'll be back before sunup."

Hardy paused by the door and gave Tom one last look. Mary coughed in the other room, the sound piercing his already battered heart.

"Be strong," he murmured before he left.

***

Hardy pulled his flea-bitten coat closer, sinking into the threadbare material, trying his best to take comfort in the little warmth it provided.

He watched the road, but the hour was late and there was little movement. Mist clung to the shadows, covering everything in a ghostly haze. The gas lamps had dimmed, their light doing little to cut through the haze.

The apothecary was dark, the windows covered with blinds for the evening.

Satisfied that no one was lingering, Hardy crossed the road and ducked under the eave. He assessed the door, looking at the lock and window. He waited a moment longer, then cracked the small window above the lock with his elbow.

Hardy listened, but nothing stirred. Satisfied the sound of shattering glass hadn't woken the apothecary, he reached inside and rattled the latch. The door clicked open, and he slipped into the darkness.

The shop smelled like oils and herbs. A long counter ran the length of the room, on which sat an enormous till made of metal and gold. Rows of shelving sat behind, each laden with bottles, boxes, cloth, and other assorted packages. Other goods were stacked in a glass-fronted display case at the far end, as well as little pyramids of colourful tins full of miracle ointments along the bench. Another door sat at the rear of the store, where a darkened staircase sat beyond.

Hardy ducked behind the counter and ran his fingers over the contents of the shelves, reading labels and turning over packages.

The words meant nothing to him but when he saw the small vials of laudanum, he shoved as many as he could into his pockets. The glass clinked together as he looked over his shoulder into the darkness. Moving down the row, he found some cod liver oil, and he took that, too.

Something here had to help Mary. *It had to.* If not, then something to ease her suffering.

The thought of helping her slip away terrified him, but she wasn't getting any better, and mercy seemed better than allowing her to suffer. He wiped his eyes, knowing the laudanum ought to do it and do it gently.

His heart stopped at sound of footsteps creaking on the staircase beyond, and he turned to see a man in a white nightshirt fly towards him, brandishing a wooden bat.

"Thief!" the man shouted. "*Thief!*"

Hardy stubbled backwards and collided with the shelves. They rattled, the force dislodging several boxes and bottles that crashed to the floor.

He looked frantically towards the door and tried to leap over the counter, but the man swung the bat at him. Unfortunately, the apothecary was a big man, so his blow landed with enough force to knock Hardy onto his back.

He crashed onto the floorboards with a cry and tried to scramble away, but he was caught behind the counter with nowhere to go.

The man's shadow loomed over him. "Dirty scoundrel!" The bat hit Hardy in the head again. "Vagrant!"

A commotion sounded outside, and Hardy lifted his arms to protect himself, but it did him no good. The next blow knocked him clean out.

He'd been caught.

The courtroom was freezing, and Hardy's fingers numbed as he stood on the dock. The apothecary was describing the circumstances of the charges he was bringing against him in great detail, recounting every detail of the night's escapades with grand embellishments that made Hardy out to be a hardened criminal.

There was nothing he could do but lower his gaze and take whatever punishment was handed down. He was caught red-handed. Would the judge be sympathetic to his sister's plight? So far, the man hadn't bothered to hear his testimony.

And why should he? One look at him and they all knew what kind of future he had. He was dirty, his clothes threadbare, and his shoes were coming apart at the seams. Society wouldn't miss him if he were given the rope...but his family would. They'd starve without him, and Mary would suffer.

"Look at me when I am speaking to you, *boy*," the judge demanded.

Hardy looked up, his heart sinking.

The judge was staring down at him with cold, unsympathetic eyes. His white curled wig sat askew atop his bald, fat head, giving away that he'd already sat through a long day of hearings. It wasn't even mid-morning, but this was London. Crime and punishment was a fine-tuned instrument.

"Frederick Marmaduke Hardy," the judge bellowed, his cheeks red, "for the crime of burglary—"

Hardy pulled against his chains. "But my sister—"

"Pardon me, *sir*," the judge boomed, "but this is not up for discussion. The court has ruled, and the sentence will be carried out forthwith." He picked up the gavel. "For the crime of burglary and damage of property, I sentence you to seven years transportation."

"Seven years?" Hardy shouted, panicking. Seven years? *His sister...* Without him, they'd suffer, and Tom... Tom was only thirteen.

"You stole seven bottles of laudanum," the apothecary said, glaring at him.

"It's a first offence," he argued. "Surely—"

"*Seven* bottles of a highly valuable and addictive drug," the judge snapped. "A year will be served for each one. You will be sent on the next available ship to the colony at Van Diemen's Land to serve the duration of your sentence."

Before Hardy could fully understand the gravity of his situation, the gavel slammed down with a *bang* and a policeman grabbed his arms, dragging his stunned body from the dock.

Outside, a carriage was waiting to take him away.

Two large, brown draft horses were harnessed to the front, tended to by two uniformed policemen. The carriage was large and black, made from iron and steel. It had no windows, save for the grate in the back door, which swung open as Hardy was dragged towards the rear.

"It's your lucky day, *boy*," the policeman holding him said in a thick cockney accent. "There's a putrid shite stain of a ship leaving at midday."

The door opened and dirty faces looked out at him from within. How many were in there? Five? Six? It didn't matter. He was being sent to the other side of the world without a chance of seeing his brother and sisters before he left.

When he didn't move, the policeman shoved Hardy into the back of the carriage with the other men. He landed face-first on the floor and splayed out across what felt like a dozen pairs of tattered boots.

"*Bon voyage*," the policeman called. The door slammed closed, plunging the inside of the carriage into shadow, and metal clanked on metal as the lock was secured.

Hardy looked up into the dirty faces of his new 'friends' and swallowed hard.

"On yer feet, lad," one man with rotten teeth rasped, his chains clattering.

Hands grasped Hardy's arms and hauled him up as the carriage began to rattle away from the courthouse.

"What'd you do?" one of the men asked their new arrival. Perhaps they'd been taking stock as the carriage filled up.

Hardy said nothing, still in shock over his situation.

"Don't worry," another man said. "Young Walter there got himself transported for nicking a loaf of day-old bread."

"Don't worry?" the rotten teeth man scoffed. "It's a long way to the colonies. You want to know what I got done for?" He licked his teeth, the murky light doing nothing to improve his ugliness. "I killed a chap. Bloodied him good."

"Why?" Hardy rasped.

"Cos I wanted to." His grin widened. "Transportation's better'n hangin'. Maybe I'll stick you on the way." He bit his teeth together, laughing as Hardy flinched.

The carriage rattled down the road, bumping over cobblestones and inching closer to the port on the Thames where Hardy knew they'd be loaded onto one of the tall ships bound for Australia and the island to the south known as Van Diemen's Land.

In that moment he knew two things. He was going to the penal colony at Port Arthur where nothing but filth and misery awaited him, and he would never see his family again.

Forgive me, Mary, he thought, closing his eyes. *Forgive me.*

CHAPTER 8

The sounds of AC/DC's hit song, *Dirty Deeds Done Dirt Cheap,* blasted through the pub as Blue wiped down the bar. There hadn't been much through trade today, so he'd decided to take some of the stick off the top of all the surfaces in the place.

He picked up one of the bar mats and shook it out, singing along with the music. *"Dirty deeds, done dirt cheap."*

The Exiles would come in around teatime, but until then he had the run of the place. Unless a customer stopped by on the way through to Lightning Ridge or Longreach if they were going north. Blue never understood why people came up this way from the Ridge when Bourke was closer and on the highway. There weren't that many corners to turn out here and all the roads were long. Anyway, the term 'close' was relative to need.

He picked up the next bar mat. *"Dirty deeds, done dirt cheap."*

It seemed like the perfect song after what Kyne had told him earlier. *EarthBore* was on the move with their drills and shovels, looking to dig up that patch of iron up on Walawala Station. There'd been way too much excitement in the last six months, and it looked like things were only going to keep getting busier. If it kept up like this, it'd affect his trade.

Blue snorted and shook out the bar mat. He'd have to get a sign made for the door that said *'Closed - Out saving the world'* or something like it.

Just as he was chuckling to himself, the door opened and a customer breezed in. By the way they crossed the room and slipped onto a barstool in the span of a millisecond, he knew it was Hardy.

"Beer?" he asked the vampire.

Hardy shook his head. The bloke looked miserable. "Have you got anything stronger?"

Blue knew a troubled soul when he saw one, so he knew what would help soothe his ailment in the short-term.

"Sure have," he replied. "Whisky, bourbon, scotch. Even got a bottle of vodka." The standard drink out this way was beer, but not everyone liked it. Some people liked bourbon and Coke, or the scotch variant. Jim Beam and Johny Walker were popular blokes. "Got all the basics covered."

"Besides gin."

Blue chuckled. "Besides gin and a couple of others. Don't get many blokes asking for cognac."

"What about the women?"

"There isn't any difference." Blue turned and took down the whisky and scotch off the shelf. "People like it all the same, no matter who they are."

"What a diplomatic answer." Hardy chose the whisky and poured a few fingers into the glass Blue offered him.

The publican watched with a raised eyebrow as the vampire downed the entire lot in one gulp. He didn't even cough as the liquor went down.

"In all the years I've known you, I've never seen you drink like this," he said as the vampire topped up the glass for a second round.

"Did Kyne come and see you today?"

Blue nodded. "He did."

"So you know about *EarthBore*."

"The basics, I'm assuming. I gathered we'd talk about it more tonight when we're all here." Blue sighed. "But that's not why you're here now, is it? I know things are tough with the seal and all the folks trying to crack it open like an egg, but I know a troubled bloke when I see one."

Hardy didn't say anything; instead, he just drank some more.

"Maybe I'll never understand because I'm human, but I can try," Blue went on. "In the very least, I can listen. Bartenders are good at that." He leaned against the bar, his old bones creaking, and patted the wooden surface. "I've been behind one of these most of my life. Most people are all right with getting on the grog—know their limits and stick to 'em. Then there're others who can't control themselves." Blue snorted. "Happy drunks, sad drunks, angry drunks, violent drunks… Seen some blokes who were so tied to the bottle, they could never give it up. Some had sad stories that drove 'em there, others just seemed to be predisposed to it."

"It's not like that for a vampire," Hardy murmured. "Not at all."

"Then what's it like?"

"Alcohol helps soothe our hunger." He waved at his throat.

"*Ahh*," Blue said, not taking his eyes off Hardy. "Blood is a vampire's alcohol. I can see where there'd be conflict in that. You need it to survive, yet…"

"It drives everything we do with disastrous consequences."

"Bloody oath."

Hardy snorted. "Ain't that the truth."

Blue looked him over and knew something was bothering the man. It didn't matter if he was vampire or human, he'd turned to alcohol to calm the angry beast inside him. Either there was something he wanted to forget, or something he was at odds with.

Hardy looked up at him. "Why are you looking at me like that?"

"Just because you're the only thing in this town

older than I am, doesn't mean you know more than I do."

"I know age is relative, old man."

"Stuff age. Blokes need to talk about their problems a little more," Blue said. "Just because you're strong on the outside, it has nothing to do with what's on the inside. It ain't going to shrivel your balls to talk through shit." He nodded at Hardy. "That's a general 'you' and 'your,' just so you know."

Hardy was quiet. Blue knew better than to prod a conflicted man, especially not a vampire, so he let the man be. He'd talk when he was ready and he'd say what he wanted. No more, no less.

"I have a bad feeling about what's coming," Hardy muttered.

"With *EarthBore*?"

"*EarthBore*, and if we can protect the seal, beyond that." He sighed the most mournful sigh Blue had ever heard come out of a man. "My mind is filled with memories of the past. Memories I'd rather forget."

This time Blue topped up the vampire's glass. "What kind?"

"People I left behind." Hardy grimaced and lifted the glass to his lips. "People who are long dead." He drank.

"Strewth, well the dead are gone and they're done talking." He snorted. "Well, not unless you know a witch or a young woman who can bend the stuff the so-called universe is made of."

"I don't think I can talk to them."

Blue hesitated, then sighed. 'They' meant several people, and from the look on the vampire's face, he assumed 'they' were his family. His *human* family. "They weren't supernatural?"

Hardy shook his head. "I don't know what happens to humans when they die, but I do know it isn't the same as supernaturals. There's a different place for us."

"Vampires, you mean?"

"Yeah."

Blue was beginning to see what had Hardy so mixed up. He didn't like being a vampire and was still tied to the things that'd happened in his human past. Perhaps it was his own anniversary, just like it'd been Vera's.

"Have you looked them up on Ancestry dot com?" he wondered.

Hardy tensed. "Ancestry dot com?"

"You've never heard of it?" Blue was surprised. He was an old fella and even he knew what it was. Being a boomer and computer literate weren't mutually exclusive concepts.

"I know what Ancestry dot com is," Hardy drawled. "I'm a vampire, not an idiot."

"Then why don't you look on that computer of yours and see if there're any records?"

"Of whom?"

"You don't have to play with me," the publican told him. "I know you can do that mind trick on me, but you don't have to. I won't talk if you don't want me to. Have a little faith in this old bugger, eh?"

The vampire hesitated, his eyes glassy. "No, I..." His fingers tightened around the glass. "I don't think it'd do any good to know."

"Closure is a damned thing," Blue told him. "Good or bad, maybe the door needs to be closed either way. It might hurt, but it'll be put to rest." He nodded to the bottle of whisky. "Might save you some *soothing*."

Hardy took the whisky and topped up his glass again. "Can I hang out here?"

He looked at the bottle. The vampire was avoiding his troubles, but Blue'd said his piece. The next bit was up to Hardy.

"I won't bother you or put a dent in the roaring trade," the vampire added, waving at the empty pub.

"Sure," the publican said. "Stay as long as you like. But that whisky's goin' on your tab."

Kyne stood with Eloise at the bottom of the newly dug shaft out at Black Hole Mine and placed his hands on her shoulders.

"You want to press the tip into the wall at an angle," he said. "Then push your weight into it...but not too hard."

She giggled and almost lost her grip on the jack. "That sounds dirty."

He rapped his knuckles on her hardhat. "Dirty when you ricochet the end off the wall and put it through your foot."

Her laughter faded. "Maybe you should be doing this part."

"Nah, you've got it." He placed his hand over hers and felt the reverberation of the earth flow through her into him. "You can already sense the opal, all you've gotta do is focus."

Bloody oath, it felt good to be underground again, especially after the other night at the pub. Hardy's bad news about *EarthBore* had all the Exiles long in the tooth. Even after a whole night discussing it, no one had any answers.

Then the following day, when Kyne and Wally had gone into Lightning Ridge to return the Caldweld drill, it was like they were off to a funeral. In all the years he'd known the old werewolf, Kyne had never seen him so silent.

Everyone was strung out, including Kyne. The only thing that was in his power was to head back out to Black Hole Mine and work on the drive in his newly sunk shaft. Life had to go on, and maybe old-fashioned hard work would grease the cogs in his brain into action.

Bringing Eloise was just an added bonus. It gave her the perfect opportunity to practice using her powers on something other than cutting and polishing opal, and they got to spend some alone time together.

Solace was a small town, but sometimes it felt more crowded than the city.

"I've got spaghetti arms," Eloise complained. "You really want me to jackhammer my way into you new mine after what I did to the last one?"

"This is nothing like last time," he told her. "You're not going to collapse the drive over our heads." He braced his body behind hers. "Use my strength to prop yourself up, then use your power to guide the jack."

"Won't this take a million years to dig out? Look at this thing. It's like bringing a butter knife to a sword fight."

It was Kyne's turn to laugh. "We're elementals, Eloise. Once we're underground, the rock just melts away."

"Really? Are you sure?"

"*Of course, I'm sure.* Make sure your safety gear is in place." He tapped her hardhat, then her safety glasses. "Earphones on, too." He fixed them in place over her ears. "Good?"

"What?" she shouted. "I can't hear you!"

Kyne shook his head and tapped her hand, signalling for her to start up the jack.

She pulled trigger and the machine burst to life, the recoil pushing her lithe frame back into his chest. He held her in place, helping her steady the jack, and then her power flared as she guided it into the wall.

"Holy moly!" Eloise shouted as the hard rock began to fall away like soft butter. "Is it supposed to do that?"

"Not usually, but it does for us."

"This is so easy!" He felt her excitement as she shouted over the noise of the jack as it bit into the wall.

Easy as it was monotonous, he thought with a grin. But the back-breaking work was all worth it when the first trace of opal flashed in the wall. Shiny potch was a sign from the gods themselves—a trail of ancient silica that eventually led to the good stuff.

The noise of the jack died as Eloise let go of the trigger. "How much longer do we have to do this?"

"Until we get to the opal," he replied.

"How far is that?"

He chuckled. "You tell me."

Eloise frowned and pressed her hand against the wall. "Shit," she muttered. "Longer than I've got any patience for."

"Luckily rocks are my thing," Kyne said. "Is it still worth ten percent?" That was the amount he'd offered for the work the first time he'd brought her out to his claim. The trip hadn't quite worked out the way he'd hoped when the mine had collapsed on their heads, but that was another story.

She laughed and wiped the back of her arm over her sweaty forehead, smearing dirt along the way. "Well, I was desperate for the cash."

"Not so much anymore, huh?"

"No," she said, picking up the jackhammer. "Not anymore."

"You want to keep going?"

"Sure. How far do I go?"

"I want to get about a metre in so I can hook up the hoist and get a bucket down here. We're gunna need a bit of room to move."

Eloise glanced over her shoulder at him. "That's that big metal conveyor belt thing?"

"The one and the same. It'll get all this rubble out."

"Okay, boss," she declared and lifted the jack, "your wish is my command."

***

That night, Kyne and Eloise set up a campfire in a clearing not far from the drive. The horizon glowed with bands of greyish blue, muddy yellow, and burnt orange as the last sliver of sun dipped out of sight. The heat of the day still lingered in the earth, the red dirt warm to the touch.

Eloise sat in one of their camp chairs as Kyne set the billy on the fire. Nestling it into the coals, he tipped some water in and sat back on his heels.

"You did good today," he told her.

"You reckon?"

"Sure. Your powers are growing fast." Faster than he'd anticipated, which he wasn't sure was entirely a good thing. As far as elementals went, she was the strongest he'd ever met by a long shot—though there weren't that many of them out there.

"That's good, I suppose." Eloise picked up the small

plastic container of tea he'd sat on the ground and took off the lid. Sniffing the contents, she asked, "What's this?"

"Jilungin tea," he replied. Whatever was happening with her power was irrelevant. He trusted her ability one hundred percent. "Have you had it before?"

"No."

"Vera orders it in from a business in the Kimberly. It's a traditional indigenous tea used to aid sleep."

"So only drink it before bed?"

"I reckon that's wise." Kyne chuckled and sat in his camp chair.

"It's earthy. A little tangy..." Eloise sniffed the tea again. "It reminds me of the paperbark tree that grew in the playground of the primary school I went to as a kid."

"A paperbark tree?"

She nodded. "Hot summer days, peeling the layers off the trunk and getting into trouble. I wanted to see if it was really paper and tried to draw on it."

Kyne smiled, trying to picture Eloise as an eight-year-old. "How'd that work out for you?"

"Terrible." She set the container of tea back down. "It was all soft, and the pen went straight through. Turns out, paperbark isn't a very literal description."

He laughed and leaned his head back. The sky was ablaze with the tail of the Milky Way, the dusting of stars beautiful to look at. Sometimes, he couldn't help being drawn into the infinite spaces between the light and feeling insignificant compared to it all.

Coen had told him that the stars were important, but it was actually the dark places where memory lived. The Dreaming was a complex and mysterious place to Kyne, and he didn't dare try to understand all of it. He doubted any one man could...except maybe Coen. He'd be a fool to disregard anything the Indigenous man had to say.

"I like it out here," Eloise murmured, breaking through his reverie. "It's quiet. I can almost believe we're the only two people in the entire world."

Kyne glanced at her and felt an overwhelming pang in his heart. "I know what you mean."

"I'm worried," she whispered.

"About?"

"*EarthBore*." She shrugged. "I know we discussed it all last night, but we didn't get anywhere. Not knowing what to do...it frightens me."

Kyne knew it took a lot for Eloise to open up, let alone admit her feelings, so he edged his chair closer to hers. "The answer will come to us. It'll just take some time."

"I know, but..." she trailed off, her brow creasing.

"You have doubts?"

She nodded.

"About what?"

"We don't know that *EarthBore* has anything to do

with the seal," she told him. "For all we know, they just want to mine."

"It doesn't matter," Kyne said. "All that activity would screw with the seal, and we'd have to go back to hiding ourselves. Most of us can pass as humans easy enough, but the fae would have a hell of a time."

Her expression fell. "And Wally wouldn't be able to turn without raising suspicion."

"I don't think it's coincidence that a massive iron ore deposit is so close to the seal," he went on. "All of it's connected, even if we can't see or understand it yet."

Kyne looked up at the sky and focused on the points of light scattered across the darkness. Everything was bound by the same stuff that lived in the dark places between the stars. The iron ore, the seal, the black mountain, it was all connected. Maybe even the opal he mined was a part of it.

Now that he'd seen Eloise's vision for himself, he was beginning to believe another power slept underneath the volcanic rock, just like the one that was trapped under Solace. It had a *presence,* and those tentacles looked like roots to him. Roots that fed the mountain with the energy of the universe.

That would make them...*gods.* Was there another word for it that wouldn't make him sound like a small-minded idiot? Thinking about all that'd happened to them, it didn't seem like such a farfetched notion.

Exiles and gods.

Who created all of this and why? Or was it just all

some miracle chemical reaction? What did the seal and the iron ore have in common?

Kyne looked at Eloise, who was staring into the fire. Maybe they were mining in the wrong spot.

"Maybe we should go mine that land ourselves," he said, drawing her attention away from the flames.

"Huh?"

"That iron ore. Maybe we should go check it out before *EarthBore* get here. We've got the geological surveys and the reports. And your powers are growing every day. I reckon we'd be able to find out something together."

Eloise blinked. "Find out what? Isn't it just a giant lump of metal down there?"

"I don't think so." He shook his head. "There's something we're missing. A link between the seal, the ore, and the mountain. There might be something supernatural about it that we haven't sensed. Something new."

Eloise's eyes widened and she pulled a face. "Can we not talk about the mountain?"

"We have to. It's a part of this. There's a reason you're the only one who's seeing it. I think it wants you for something."

"It wants me?" She looked bewildered, as if it hadn't occurred to her before now.

"Andante told you it was the heart of the ocean," he said. "She alluded that it was sentient. She gave us no proof, and I still haven't had the pleasure of meeting her, but maybe we ought to believe it."

"You think the mountain is alive? Like a *person* alive?"

"You can't tell me that the thought hasn't crossed your mind," he said.

Eloise sighed. "What on earth could it want me for? I'm a nobody."

She was definitely a somebody, but he didn't want to frighten her with more talk about unknown entities stalking her dreams.

"I hope it isn't one of those light versus dark clichés," he muttered instead.

"It would make things easier," she told him. "Knowing who was good and who was evil."

"Yeah, but life isn't like that. There's a helluva lot of grey out there. Maybe they're both as bad as each other where we're concerned. Maybe humans and us supernaturals are just the equivalent of ants."

"Has the billy boiled yet?" she asked. "All this talk of doom and gloom and conspiracy theories has exhausted me. I'm going to have an emotional hangover tomorrow if I don't get a good night's sleep."

"Let me check." Kyne got up and knelt by the fire. The water was beginning to bubble inside the billy, and he picked up the enamel cups.

"I don't think I can handle all the existentialism," Eloise went on. "Right now, all I can handle is *EarthBore*, and even that's a stretch."

Kyne nodded as he tipped some tea leaves into each cup. "It's a lot, I get it. We're all stressed in our own ways. It hasn't been that long since all that business with the Nightshade."

Kyne busied himself by the fire, retrieving the hot billy from the coals and tipping the bubbling water into each cup. As the tea began to steep, it released a rich earthy scent that now reminded him of paperbark trees on a hot summer's day.

"Kyne?"

He handed Eloise a cup. "Hmm?"

"I'm worried about Hardy."

"Still?"

"Yes, *still.*" She rolled her eyes and blew on the hot tea. "He's different. It's like...he's sad but..."

"But?"

"But..." She pressed her palm against her heart and frowned. "It's like he's sad all the way through."

"Maybe it's his turn," Kyne said, breathing in the steam rising from his cup of tea.

"Turn for what?"

He stared into the fire and thought about everything that'd happened since Eloise had arrived. All they'd faced, from her discovery of her power, the return of his own, Vera's past with the Nightshade, Drew's reckoning with the Dust Dogs...all of it. It seemed to him that they would all have a turn at facing what haunted them at their core. Maybe the seal was testing them...or the mountain was.

"Kyne?" Eloise prodded. "Turn for what?"

"His reckoning," he murmured.

"Reckoning?"

"He's lived a long time. There's got to be a few skeletons in his closet."

She lowered her gaze, her brow knitting as if she knew something he didn't. If Hardy had confided something to her, then it wasn't Kyne's place to ask...as long as whatever it was didn't screw with the seal.

"Don't worry about Hardy," he told her. "He's the strongest man I know."

"That's the problem..." she said. "I have a feeling he carries more than the rest of us combined."

Kyne sipped at his tea to avoid replying. Hardy wasn't the most forthcoming bloke. His past was a mystery—as was how he'd become a vampire in the first place—but he'd never once given the Exiles reason to doubt or fear him.

"I think I ought to go back tomorrow," Eloise said.

Her voice had taken on a dreamy tone, and Kyne reached out and took her hand. His touch startled her and she almost spilled her tea.

"Sorry," he said.

She blinked and smiled at him. "I feel stretched out and oversensitive."

He squeezed her hand. "I can feel it."

"Is that normal? I reckon I over did it with the powers today."

"Sure," he replied. "Good thing I brought the tea along."

Eloise watched him for a moment, her eyes glowing dimly in the evening light. She was right about her powers, and that meant he should probably listen to her about Hardy. Her talents lay with spirit and if she felt the vampire's was changing, then he supposed the opal could wait another day. It wasn't like it was going anywhere—they'd barely scratched the surface with their digging—and Hardy's wellbeing was more important.

"We'll head back into town in the morning," Kyne said, letting Eloise's hand go.

"Thanks," she murmured. "I know I'm being dramatic..."

"No," he said. "You care. It's one of the many things I love about you."

CHAPTER 9

Eloise and Kyne returned to Solace at first light the following morning.

The golden sun shone into their eyes as they bumped down the track, the ute dipping in and out of the potholes that'd sunk into the baked earth by way of wind, rain, and drying heat.

Eloise dipped the brim of her hat over her eyes, thankful that Kyne had taken the wheel. She hated to drag him away from Black Hole Mine, but she was worried about Hardy. She just couldn't shake the feeling that something was wrong. The vampire said he was prone to bouts of melancholy from time to time, but it didn't feel like it to her.

"Hey," she said as she spotted the rusty windmill through the gumtrees, "last night you said that you thought we'd all get a turn at facing our pasts."

"Yeah," Kyne said, glancing at her.

"Do you think Hardy will try to open the seal like Vera did?"

He was silent for a moment as they bumped over a deep rut in the track. "Honestly, I don't know. Maybe it's not related."

She wrapped her hand around the edge of the seat. "I just wish I paid more attention to it before we went out to the lease."

"Yeah, nah, it's cool," Kyne told her. "Elemental magic works in mysterious ways."

He turned the ute onto the highway and crossed to the opposite side, pulling up outside Hardy's opal shop. The handbrake made a crunching sound as he wrenched it up, and he turned to Eloise. "What are you going to tell him?"

"The truth," she replied, unbuckling her seatbelt. "I overused my powers and got all existential."

"Maybe, but he's not known to be a talker."

"Under all that vampire, he's still a man."

The elemental shook his head and leaned towards her. "Eloise, Hardy is one of my best mates and I would do anything for the bloke, but if he ever lost control, he wouldn't hesitate..." He lifted his hand and ran a finger across her neck, his touch sending shivers down her spine. "He knows it just as much as I do."

"He wouldn't," she argued. "I trust him."

"It's not about you. Hardy doesn't trust himself." Kyne unclipped his seatbelt and opened the door.

"There was a reason he gave you the day off...and wanting to talk to Finn was only part of it."

Eloise bit her bottom lip as Kyne climbed out of the ute. The vampire had wanted to get out of the workshop because he was on edge. He wasn't anxious; he was *hungry*...or at least, that's the vibe Kyne got from him.

The realisation startled her, but she shook her head and got out of the ute. Slamming the door, she slipped into the shade of the verandah, her concern only deepening.

She liked Hardy a lot and couldn't bare knowing he was suffering. If there was something she could do for him, she would do it in an instant. But it wasn't just him, it was the same for all the Exiles. They'd helped her when she was nothing more than a stranger, knowing she could have been there to open the seal and destroy them all. Hardy wasn't just her boss; he was her *family*.

Kyne stared down the highway to the south, his shoulders tense.

"What is it?" she asked, following his gaze.

A truck was approaching in the distance, the metal exterior shimmering through the mirage wavering above the already hot asphalt. Lifting Kyne's arm, she checked the time on his watch. 8:47.

"It's a bit early for a road train," she mused as the sound of the rumbling engine reached their ears.

"I don't think it's a road train..."

They waited in the shade, watching the approaching truck that she now saw was leading an entire convoy of vehicles. When the lead truck hit the town limits and slowed from the 110kph highway speed limit to 80, Eloise's expression fell as she caught sight of the blue and black logo on the door of the white cabin.

EarthBore.

She heard Kyne swear, but she was too busy watching the approaching convoy. A large block of machinery was mounted on the back of the first truck, and thanks to Kyne, she knew it was a Caldweld drill. The second truck was transporting a yellow and black excavator, and behind it was a white ute and another small flatbed truck with more equipment.

"That's not a core drill," Kyne murmured. "They're not sampling. They're drilling."

As they filed past, Eloise's eyes narrowed at the sight of the *EarthBore* logo, but there was one final car that didn't seem to fit with the others. A large black luxury Land Rover with tinted windows brought up the rear, coasting along the highway like a heat-seeking missile. As it passed, Eloise felt a pang of ice shudder through her body.

Her breath caught as her gaze followed the 4WD, her sensitive power latching onto something dark and cold...and it wasn't the air-conditioned interior.

"Kyne," she said, reaching out blindly for his hand.

"What?" He wound his fingers through hers and

warmth returned, seeping through him and into her. "Eloise? Your fingers are like ice."

"I think we should go inside," she whispered, backing towards the door.

The sound of a key rattling in the workshop door forced Hardy's gaze to rise.

He'd been staring at a new piece of opal for the past twenty minutes, his focus so broken he couldn't see the best place to begin cutting. *He always knew.*

Eloise appeared in the door and hurried inside, followed by Kyne and a gust of hot morning air.

"You're back early," he said. "Tired of mining already?"

"*EarthBore* is here," she blurted. "A whole bunch of them just drove by."

Hardy stilled. "What?" He hadn't heard anything. *Damnit.*

"A whole convoy," Kyne said. "A couple of trucks and a 4WD."

"There was something supernatural in that car," Eloise muttered, shivering.

"How can you tell?" Hardy asked.

"I overused my powers and now I'm all..." She shivered again and shook out her arms. "*Over-stimulated.*"

Hardy's eyebrows rose.

"There was a black 4WD and..." Her brow furrowed.

"Your hands turned to ice," Kyne said. "Like all the warmth had bled out of you."

Hardy's jaw tensed and he dropped the piece of opal back into the plastic Ziplock bag with the rest of the rough. All this anguish he'd been feeling...what if it was his turn? *Someone* was riding in that car and his bets were on the supernatural.

"Tell me," he said as Kyne sat Eloise in her usual chair. "No matter how silly it sounds."

"It felt cold. Like..." Her gaze rose to meet his.

Vampire.

She didn't say it out loud, but he knew. Eloise had felt the cold darkness of the living dead inside that 4WD. Her over-stimulated power felt it in him now, so she understood.

"Well," he said, "I think I better go out there and have a look around."

"They're not drilling core samples," Kyne warned him. "They're sinking a shaft."

"Then we were right to be worried."

Eloise pushed Kyne's hands away. "I'm coming with you."

"You better go home and get some rest," Hardy told her with a shake of his head. "Vera will have something to help with your elemental overload."

"I'm fine," she argued. "I'm worried about you, Hardy."

"Me?" He glanced at Kyne, who nodded. "Don't worry about me. If a vampire is riding with *EarthBore*, it'll only be a matter of time before they figure out that I'm here, then the seal will be next. Vampires can be devious creatures...all spite and bloodlust."

Eloise stared at him. "Hardy—"

"No." He shook his head. "I'll be back as soon as I can." He turned towards the door and looked over his shoulder at the elementals. "Stay inside and don't go outside if you can help it. Best not stay here, either."

Leaving his shop behind, Hardy ran. Solace was gone in a flash, his vampire speed hurtling him through the scrub and across the outback faster than any human eye could follow.

What could vampires want with the seal, if the seal was what they were after?

He'd met many vampires over his long life who had developed tastes for more than blood. Power and wealth walked hand-in-hand, and it was far easier to remain undetected by doing things the old-fashioned way—meaning they complied with human law—than compelling humans to hand over what they needed to survive. It was necessary in this modern world where every step of a human life was recorded not only by some government agency, but surveillance cameras and satellites, too.

That's why Hardy wasn't surprised that a vampire had their fingers in the pie that was called *EarthBore*. His kind could pass as human, but it also meant they had to act like it if they wanted to become more than nomads skulking on the edges of society.

Hardy came to a halt on top of a rise overlooking the remote edges of Walawala Station, the property line barely discernible from the rough scrub. The lack of fencing wasn't that much of an issue this far out from the main homestead as livestock rarely raged this far. If they did, they were closely monitored by the station hands, or stockmen as they were once called.

Out here, his problems usually disappeared with the rush of wind as he ran. The vast sky and unforgiving landscape made his immortal life seem fleeting in comparison, but not today. Both seemed to be closing in on him and forcing one to reconcile with the other.

His brow creased as he looked down on the assortment of trucks and cars. They were unloading a great deal of equipment, but it was for small-scale mining. Kyne was right about them not drilling for cores, but what did they expect to find with that Caldweld?

Standing as still as he possibly could, he focused his vampire eyes on the movement below. A dozen men dressed in high visibility vests and hardhats wandered around as the excavator was driven off the back of a flatbed truck, the tracks kicking up clouds of red dust as they churned up the earth below.

The black 4WD Eloise had seen sat back towards the highway and a group of three men in suits lingered in front of it. Two had left their suit jackets behind and had rolled their shirtsleeves up but had forgotten to bring hats. Their ties flapped in the wind as they referred to a map they'd rolled out across the bonnet of the 4WD.

The third man looked at the excavator and seemed uninterested in what the other suits were discussing. Not only did he still have his black jacket on, but all the buttons were done up tight.

He stood out amongst the human workers, not only for his unreasonably dark clothing, but for his presence. Hardy only had to look once to know he was a vampire, and an old one at that.

As Hardy watched the scene below, trying to figure out what they were up to, the vampire turned, and he saw a face he'd hoped he would never see again.

Darius.

The name pierced a long-hidden memory in his mind—one full of blood and suffering—and he ducked low, his breath catching.

"You see."

Hardy jumped, his cold heart lurching in his chest, and he turned to see Coen lingering in the shade of a gum that's been twisted by the wind.

"Coen," he hissed, wiping the back of his arm across his clammy brow. "*Bloody hell*."

The Indigenous man chuckled, clearly pleased with himself. "I managed to frighten a vampire."

"I wouldn't be proud of it. I could've torn you to pieces."

Coen grinned at him unperturbed and looked down at the *EarthBore* trucks. "It's testing you."

Hardy screwed up his face. "What?"

"The seal."

"The seal is testing me?" The vampire snorted. "Whatever for?"

"It tests you all in its own way," Coen went on. "Why is not for us to know."

"Why am I not surprised?" Hardy didn't want to believe in cosmic forces—they never spoke plainly. "I'm here to watch *EarthBore*." He looked for the *marlu*, but the kangaroo wasn't anywhere to be seen. "What are you doing out here?"

"Watching the paths in the Dreaming," he replied. "This land is scared by many things. The wars with the white fellas and more things... Older things."

Hardy grunted and rose to his feet. Turning his gaze back to the trucks below, he felt slightly reassured to see Darius still down there and not up here with them.

"Are you prepared to face the ancestor's paths?" Coen asked.

He turned, his brow creasing. "What?"

"Together we'll watch the vampire," Coen went on. "I'm teaching Drew how to see with his dingo eyes." He waved Hardy away as the vampire took a step towards him. "The lightning will watch and wait for the moment to strike."

"I—" Hardy bit his tongue, not sure if he should reveal he knew the vampire with *EarthBore* or not.

"You haven't opened all your eyes yet." Coen poked Hardy between his eyes, making him cross-eyed for a moment. "*Go.*"

"Go?" He pointed to the trucks. "I can't go."

"You're not ready."

Annoyance flared and he felt his blood quicken. "Not ready?"

Coen either didn't understand or care that Hardy's vampire side was rising. He grabbed Hardy's shoulders and turned him to face the way back to Solace. "*Go.*"

Hardy's mind filled with thoughts of darkness and blood, and he knew Coen was right. He hadn't come to terms with what he'd become, even after all this time.

Casting one last glance at Darius, he turned to Coen. He knew what the vampire was capable of and felt uneasy leaving.

"Go," the Indigenous man said, more firmly this time.

So he went.

CHAPTER 10

P*ort Arthur, Van Diemen's Land, Australia, 1835*

Humid darkness wrapped around Hardy as he gripped the heavy pick in his blistered hands.

The dull light of his lantern barely cast enough light for him to see the rock face before him and the coal he was forced to mine. The sounds of men working in the dark reaches echoed down the tunnel —*tink, tink, tink* as their hand tools slammed against stone—and the rattle of a laden cart rolling along the steel tracks towards the main shaft made his ears ring.

Hardy breathed deeply, desperate for the fresh air that awaited above ground. Sweat rolled down his back as the humidity wrung what little moisture was left in his worn body.

Lifting the pick again, he heaved it towards the

wall. When the end of the pick hit coal, the force of the blow vibrated up his exhausted arms.

In the darkness, gasping for breath, he almost gave in to the memories he'd been running from for four long years. Just over half of his sentence had passed and every single day of it was misery.

Hardy hadn't made a particularly good thief, but he learned fast. With nothing left to lose, he'd made a name for himself amongst the other convicts at the Port Arthur penitentiary, his antics drawing the ire of his gaolers. His name had even made it to the desk of the governor, a British man by the name of George Arthur. Hardy's back bore the permanent memory of *that* encounter.

His lamp flickered beside him, the pitiful flame struggling to stay alight. He looked down as the dull shadows danced across the rock face.

Seeing how low the flame had burned, he dropped his pick as the light faded. "No, no, *no*."

He lunged for the lantern, but it was too late. The pitiful flame faded to blue, gave one last gasp, then snuffed out, plunging the tunnel into pitch-black darkness.

Hardy landed on his knees and rock cut through his trousers and bit into his flesh, but a few scratches were the least of his problems. With no light, he wouldn't be able to see any coal, let alone find his way out of the awful pit. If he didn't make his quota...

Still, he tried. He swung his pick at the wall,

missing more than he struck, and flung anything he could into the cart behind him.

When the whistle blew down the shaft to signal the end of shift, he fumbled his way to the end of the cart and began pushing, knowing it was full of useless rubbish and not enough of it to escape what was coming.

Hardy's heart sank at the thought of escape. The only way out of Port Arthur was by the grace of the governor and he had none of that.

He saw light ahead as he pushed the cart along the tracks. His spirits rose even as they sank as the first taste of sweet, cool air filled his lungs. He kept moving.

"Where is that filthy shite Hardy?"

The voice boomed down the tunnel and he quickened his steps, pushing the cart out into the sunlight.

Hardy blinked as the clearing came into view and his heart sank as he saw the men waiting for him. He was the last out and there was an *un*welcoming party assembled.

The overseer was a sadistic man by the name of Henry Davis, who had a mean pinched face, little beady eyes, and a thick moustache that was too big for his face. Hardy always through he looked like he'd strained too hard on the privy and the wind had changed, locking his face in a perpetual shitting motion. But at that moment, there was nothing comical about it.

Davis looked into the cart and turned his glare onto Hardy. "Explain yourself."

"My light went out."

"Your light went out?" The overseer's face turned red, his eyes bulging. He tightened his grip on the truncheon on his belt—the same truncheon that saw a great deal of use both when it was warranted and not.

Hardy was a little grateful he wasn't going for the rifle slung over his shoulder but knew both would sting from firsthand experience.

"You're under quota."

He jutted his chin out in defiance. "And?"

The other convicts began to mutter, their hard gazes turning on him.

"You know the punishment," the overseer said. "One under quota, the whole shift is punished."

The convicts began shout and pressed forwards, their angry faces smeared with coal dust.

Hardy knew if he didn't do something, he'd cop it from both sides—and both would be as bad as the next. Losing the respect of his fellow inmates would be the death of him, and up until now he'd managed to absolve all but himself from the bite of the overseer's whip. It was the only way to survive Port Arthur, and he wasn't about to let Davis stop the tradition.

Hardy flung himself at the overseer with a roar. He moved faster than he ought, considering the exhaustion weighing him down. The blow jarred up his arm as his fist slammed into Davis' nose.

The overseer shouted as blood poured down his face, and the convicts hollered. As the soldiers stared in shock, they took the opportunity to push back against their captors.

Fists began flying in all directions and Hardy was jerked backwards. He fell and felt several boots collide with his back and sides.

"Grab him!" Davis shouted, hurrying into the fray. "Get back, you scum!"

Whistles blew shrilly as soldiers hurried into the clearing and began pulling men away. A scuffle broke out between a few of the rowdier men, and they suffered nasty blows courtesy of several rifle butts.

The soldiers quickly got the scuffle under control, driving the convicts back and pulling them away from Hardy.

Davis wiped the back of his hand across his bloodied nose, smearing the red stuff through his moustache. "You just got yourself ten lashes for that, Hardy," he said with a sneer, "and a stay in solitary."

Hardy scrambled backwards but was caught by two soldiers. They grasped his shoulders and hauled him up, dragging him across the yard.

"Chain him to the pole," Davis commanded, "and get me my whip."

"I'll take it all," Hardy cried as he was dragged through the dirt. "I'll take for all of them."

The overseer scoffed and looked back at the coal-stained convicts, who'd all fallen silent at Hardy's cries.

"You want to take the cat-o-nine-tails for this sorry lot?" Davis asked as a solider handed him his favourite weapon. "So be it, *boy*. Fifty lashes...and I'll count every one."

If it were any other occasion, Hardy would've laughed at the overseer calling him a boy. He was a grown man at twenty-five and aged beyond his years thanks to life at Port Arthur.

He grit his teeth as the solders chained him to the pole at the head of the clearing. They tore off his threadbare shirt and hoisted his arms above his head, fixing him in place. The soldier to his right had the grace to give him a look filled with shame, knowing the sorry state Hardy would be in after...if he survived. The man seemed regretful for his part but did nothing to stop it.

Hardy pressed his forehead against the pole, waiting for the sting of leather to open his already scarred back. Many men would have taken that moment to think about their loved ones, but he thought of nothing at all.

As the first lash landed, the whole bush seemed to fall silent as the whip crack echoed.

"One," Davis declared.

The leather bit into his back again.

"*Two*."

Warm stone pressed against Hardy's cheek, his eyes wide and unseeing in the pitch-black of the solitary cell that lay deep within the coal mine.

His breath came in shallow gasps, the only motion that didn't send fire coursing through his body. The air seemed thin and thick at the same time, but he barely cared.

Death seemed like it was calling, and he was glad. He never dared to take his own life for fear of damning his soul, so Davis had done him a favour.

His back had been seen to and bandaged, but his care had only been rudimentary. Why waste precious medical supplies on a troublesome convict when the well-to-do families back in Port Arthur needed it more.

"What a sorry sight," a voice murmured from the darkness. "A truly pitiful soul left to die in a wretched hole."

He didn't move. There was no one here. He was down in the mine alone, and his fevered mind was playing tricks on him. It wasn't the first he'd heard unknown voices in the dark and it wouldn't be the last...if he survived his latest sojourn in solitary confinement.

"Your wounds are festering," the voice said. "I can smell the sickly rot of infection in the air." The unknown man sighed. "Not that there's much of *that* in this God forsaken hole."

Hardy ran his tongue over his cracked bottom lip and tasted sweat, blood, and charcoal.

The sound of metal squeaking echoed through the cell—an oil lantern—and warmth permeated the darkness. The sudden light, meagre as it was, blinded him, and Hardy blinked furiously as his vision adjusted.

Hardy now saw his visitor clearly. He'd crouched beside the convict and looked down upon him with cold eyes. His hair was dark and close-cropped, and his face was clean shaven, which was a stark contrast to the long, full beards the men of the colonies preferred. His eyes were big and round, the irises so dark they appeared black, and his clothing... The unknown man was the cleanest, most presentable man Hardy had ever seen outside of the officers themselves.

What was a man like that doing in his cell, two hundred metres underground in a stinking coal mine?

The man smiled, revealing the whitest teeth Hardy had ever seen. "I've been watching you, Frederick Hardy."

"W-who..." The words barely made it out of him.

The man didn't seem to hear. "What did you do to warrant transportation?"

"I stole."

"*What?*"

Hardy coughed and the rough stone cut into his cheek.

The stranger snarled and grasped the convict's threadbare shirt, hauling him up off the ground. "What did you steal, convict?"

Hardy cried out as pain seared through his back. His heartbeat began to quicken as he found the words tumbling from his mouth unbidden. "Medicine for my sister."

"Medicine for your *sister*." The man's lip curled as if he was disappointed. "Well, at least your spirit is broken. I would have preferred a little murder and mayhem in you, but it's been a long time since I've shaped a clean slate."

Hardy barely understood what the man was saying. His head spun with pain, and his ears buzzed from the lack of oxygen in his cell. There were many questions he should have asked the stranger, but he lacked the sensibilities.

"The wretched make the best vampires," the man murmured, gazing upon him with unfeeling eyes. "When I save them from their misery, they become so thankful that they would follow me to the ends of the Earth if I command it. Will you be grateful?" The man smirked and trailed a finger over Hardy's charcoal-smeared forehead. Holding up his finger, he peered at the blackened grime. "I think you will be." He shoved the convict away.

Hardy landed on his back, bellowing in agony as his ruined flesh tore. The man poured hot liquid into his mouth and he gagged as a sickening copper taste hit his tongue. *Blood.*

Hardy spat, gagging and gasping, desperate to rid himself of the foul stuff, but the man had other ideas.

"Swallow, you fool," he hissed, forcing Hardy's mouth closed. "Swallow and *live*."

He couldn't help it. He swallowed and his stomach rolled, but the man grinned triumphantly, letting him go.

"What have you given me?" Hardy managed to ask through ragged gasps.

"Blood," the man replied. "It takes some getting used to, I'm afraid, but tell me...do you feel better?"

Hardy wiped his sticky face and hesitated. His back... *It didn't hurt anymore.* He sat up and grasped at the bandages.

"Oh no, don't take them off just yet. We'll need those for a little while longer. Just until that charming overseer comes back to fetch you."

Hardy didn't understand what was happening to him. "Who are you?"

"Me?" The man smiled, his lips pulling back to reveal a row of pointed teeth, with two elongated fangs. "I am Darius."

Hardy didn't have time to recoil as the man struck. The last sound he heard was the snap of his neck breaking.

CHAPTER 11

The pub was silent that night—a rather odd thing considering Blue always blasted his Aussie pub rock mixed CDs.

The Exiles sat around their usual table, but in place of their usual rowdy conversations was a hell of a lot of nothing. No one spoke. He reckoned not one of them knew what to say after the day they'd had.

Maybe Eloise had tapped into something a little more prophetic when she asked to come back to town. She was worried about Hardy, but their timing had been impeccable to the minute. It felt a little creepy, if he was being honest. Her dreams, even her arrival, were starting to become *bigger* than all of Solace's supernatural powers combined.

He glanced at her, hoping the potion Vera had given her had helped calm her hyped-up powers.

Kyne sighed and rubbed his eyes. He'd rather be out at his claim going after that black opal.

Finn lounged beside him, playing with a single blue dreadlock. "I think I'm going to get a new snake," he stated, breaking the heavy silence. "I think I'm ready." Everyone turned to glare at him, and he screwed up his nose. "*What?* You don't think I can handle it?"

"If you want a snake, then go charm yourself one," Drew told him. "We don't care."

"Drew," Vera scolded.

"Just trying to make some conversation," the fae drawled. "You lot look like you've just been to a funeral. Look around." He spread his arms wide. "We aren't dead yet... Oh, *wait.*"

"Speaking of..." Vera said. "Where *is* Hardy?"

"I don't think he's coming," Blue murmured, looking at the beaten-up black digital watch around his wrist. "Hardy's never late."

"Do you think something happened to him?" Eloise asked. "He did go out to spy on *EarthBore*."

"Nah." Drew shook his head. "Coen has been watching the land to the north. If something was up with Hardy, he would've seen it."

Kyne's gaze dropped to the book sitting on the table in front of the shifter. It was a hefty tome on mineral exploration and the spine had been cracked in several places. Either Drew had gotten it secondhand, or he'd read that thing cover to cover.

"What?" the shifter asked. "Ain't seen a dog with a book before?"

"No need to get testy," Kyne fired back. "I'm impressed. Learn anything?"

Drew faltered for a second, then replied, "I know what auriferous means."

"Congratulations!" Finn clapped, drawing more glares for his efforts.

"Stop antagonising each other," Kyne warned. "We've got enough going on without you two reigniting old feuds."

Finn snorted and picked up his wine glass. Drew said nothing, he just leaned back in his chair and nursed his beer.

"Where is *EarthBore*?" Vera wondered. "They haven't come into town, only driven through. They have to be somewhere."

Kyne frowned. She was right. Wherever they were staying, it wasn't in Solace.

"They're probably camping out there," Wally said. "Crazy buggers."

"No one in their right mind would camp in this weather," Blue told him. "It hit forty today and won't dip below thirty tonight."

Eloise squirmed beside Kyne. She'd been uncharacteristically silent, even for her.

"What?" he asked, sliding his hand onto her leg.

"That 4WD..." she murmured. "I know who was in it...and so did Hardy."

Silence fell in the pub as all eyes turned to Eloise.

"Who was it, then?" Finn drawled. "Don't leave us in suspense."

"It was cold," Eloise began with a shiver, "like death. Then, when I went into the workshop and saw Hardy... I, uh...I felt the same thing."

"A vampire?" Blue jerked upright. "Working with *EarthBore*?"

Vera pursed her lips and glanced at Drew.

"Do you think...?" the dingo asked.

"Think what?" Kyne butted in.

"That guy," the witch replied. "The one who bought the party poppers."

"You think he has something to do with them?" Wally asked.

"He did buy a hi-vis vest," Drew said with a shrug. "Maybe he was the scouting party."

Kyne screwed up his face. "Big mining doesn't have scouting parties. This isn't a hunt. An army isn't on the march."

The dingo narrowed his eyes. "Aren't they?"

The elemental sighed, wondering what exactly Coen had been teaching the shifter out there. They'd been going into the outback together a lot lately.

"Hardy can look after himself," Kyne said. "We can't wait for him."

"And what are we supposed to do, fearless leader?" Finn asked, swirling red wine around in his glass.

"I don't know," he admitted.

"Well, that's helpful," the fae stated.

"At least he's got the balls to admit it," Vera snapped. "I don't see you coming up with any ideas."

"That's because he's always day-drunk," Drew said.

"Shut your face! You have no idea what I went through in that tank!" Finn cried.

"Of course, we do," the shifter retorted. "You haven't stopped moaning about it since Eloise dragged you out."

"Stop it!" Eloise shouted, jerking to her feet. "Just...*stop it*." She balled her hands into tight fists. "Arguing won't help any of us. Something's happening with Hardy and he needs our help. He can't always handle himself...none of us can." Her glare intensified. "We're a family. A dysfunctional one, but that's what we are. *Family*."

Vera coughed and lifted her hand, her silver rings clacking together. "If Hardy's not back by morning, I can cast a locator spell."

Eloise blinked, the tension easing in her shoulders. "You can do that?"

"Yeah. It's been a while, but I can give it a go."

"I'll go check his dugout," Kyne said. "But we should give him some time to come back on his own."

"Maybe he just wants to be alone," Finn declared, his nonchalant tone raising Kyne's ire. "Did you ever stop to think that? No everyone needs therapy, especially the kind that's forced on them."

"*Finn*," Kyne warned. "If you know something, now's the time to spit it out."

The fae rolled his eyes. "And why would I do that?"

"Finn, please," Eloise murmured, sitting back down.

He sighed. "I know he's going through something, desert pea, but he's a musty, old undead man. He's been around the bush a couple more times than all of you combined, and he won't talk until he's ready. The sooner you get it through your pretty little skull, the sooner we can all focus on the real villain here."

"And who's that?" Drew prodded.

The fae grinned and held up his glass. "Blue, because I'm out of wine."

The publican sighed and got up to get another bottle.

"*EarthBore*," Kyne said, slouching. "They can't dig or the vibrations will crack open the seal or worse."

"Sounds like doomsday to me," Finn said. "I reckon it calls for more wine, don't you?"

A lone dingo padded along a remote ridge in the lonely desert north of Solace, the stars guiding his meandering path northwards.

Drew sniffed, studying the currents in the air and all the scents that came with them. Warm eucalyptus and earthy baked dirt that hadn't been disturbed in a long time. Wild, untouched land that was now being eyed by *EarthBore*.

He followed his nose and focused his eyes, the night welcoming him as he passed through the outback.

Drew's sight changed while he was in his dingo state and the world opened up in more ways than were obvious. Thanks to Coen and his bizarre way of teaching, his eyes were opening to his true abilities as a shapeshifter. Changing his shape was only the beginning of what he was capable of, and the Indigenous man was determined to guide him towards the path he should have been walking from birth— from before his pack was massacred by the Dust Dogs.

Drew snorted, his nostrils flaring. Sometimes it still angered him, knowing what could have been *if only*... He couldn't change it now, but at least he had someone to learn from.

Ahead, the night sky blurred with the glow of floodlights. The dig site lay hidden beyond the rise, so he approached, setting his feet as lightly as he could manage.

Drew wasn't sure what he would find, let alone what he was looking for, so he moved carefully, using all his senses to lay out the path before him.

He thought about what Eloise said at the pub earlier. Cold death, the same she felt when she looked at Hardy. *Vampire.*

Through Coen's teaching, he'd managed to work out the difference between the supernaturals living in Solace. The coldness of Hardy, the warmth of Kyne, the metallic tang of Wally's werewolf curse, and Eloise's… Well, she felt like the sun, which was just another star in one of the great arms of the Milky Way. He could see why Coen liked her; he was always prattling on about the stars.

And then there was Vera, who was just as precious to him. Her magic reminded him of static electricity—all prickly and volatile like her personality—but after she'd severed her contact with the Nightshade, he felt what he suspected was the manifestation of the raging ocean in her. Whatever magic she wielded, Vera Walsh would always be a little wild.

Drew's inner human sighed. Wherever their future took them with the seal, he knew her magic would be needed. Apparently, they lived on top of the heart of the ocean itself.

Finally, he topped the rise and looked down on the scene below.

The *EarthBore* workers had set up a camp consisting of three massive khaki canvas tents pitched in a horseshoe formation. Floodlights burned impossibly bright, shining white light on the clearing and machinery, which was still positioned around the hole they'd been digging with the Caldweld drill. A campfire sat in the middle of the tents, and he saw several men sitting around it, drinking and laughing.

It wasn't the full industrial set up Drew had been picturing, but they seemed keen to break ground. He'd learned a bit from the books he'd been reading, and from Kyne's prattling at the pub, and nothing he saw looked like they were core sampling.

What were they doing, then?

He kept to the trees, even though he knew they couldn't see much beyond the ring of artificial light. If something supernatural was down there, there was a chance he could be spotted, not just by sight, but by scent, too.

The men around the campfire were human, their presence bland compared to the Exiles. They reminded him of the way Blue looked through his dingo eyes, though the publican's spirit had taken on a little of the company he kept without him knowing. It was a roundabout way of saying their magic had rubbed off on the bloke.

As Drew studied at the workers, he saw a little of the same taint, but it wasn't the rich earthy warmth he saw in his friend. It was something else and it didn't feel friendly to him.

Suddenly, he wished Coen was here to help explain it.

The flap on the centre tent flung open and the movement drew his gaze away from the workers. His hackles rose as he watched a newcomer emerge and stride across the clearing towards the fire.

Narrowing his eyes, Drew sunk back into the cover of the tree, a clump of spinifex grass pricking his backside.

Eloise was right. There was a vampire down there...

and it wasn't Hardy. Wherever the opal buyer had gone to, it wasn't here. *Probably a good thing.*

Strangely, the man below didn't look anything like Hardy did through his dingo eyes. This bloke carried a power that'd stained his soul blacker than the finality of death itself.

He was the beginning, but he wasn't the first.

The strange thought bounced around in Drew's mind, and he shook his head as his ears buzzed. *The hell...* The only thing he understood about what he was seeing, was that there was a vampire working with *EarthBore* and that meant trouble for the seal.

Coen had asked him to watch, so that's what he was going to do.

Drew nestled into place along the ridge and peered down at the camp. It was going to be a long night.

The next morning, Eloise hurried down the hill with Kyne hot on her heels.

"Slow down," Kyne complained. "You'll trip and break your arm if you're not careful."

"I won't," she called over her shoulder.

When the miner had gone over to Hardy's dugout after dinner, his door had gone unanswered, and now Eloise was one big knot of worry.

"You will, and the nearest hospital is hundreds of kilometres away." He failed to mention that vampire blood could heal broken bones, but it would only wound her up more.

"You go see Vera," she said, ignoring him. "I'll check the workshop."

"I'm starting to get jealous."

Eloise turned and pressed her hand to his chest. "Oh, don't pout. It doesn't suit you."

Kyne smirked and planted a kiss on her lips. "Go on." He nodded towards the opal shop. "I'll be at Vera's."

"Thanks."

Eloise jogged across the road and fished her key out of her pocket. She hoped she'd see Hardy sitting at his bench as he always did, sorting through a Ziplock bag of rough opal, and all this worry would have been for nothing.

Darting into the shade, she shoved the key into the workshop lock and jiggled the handle. Her overtaxed power was just playing tricks, right?

Wrenching open the door, relief washed over her as she saw the vampire sitting right where she hoped he'd be...but he wasn't working on his usual bag of opal.

At her abrupt appearance, he'd looked up from the pile of paperwork on the bench. "Now that's an entrance." It was a lame joke and one that she didn't appreciate.

"Bloody hell," Eloise said, slamming the door behind her. "Where have you been?"

"Not far," he told her, his brow creasing. "You were that worried about me?"

"Kyne went to see Vera about a locator spell," she told him with a roll of her eyes. "I better let her know not to worry."

"Leave it," he replied. "She needs the practice. I have a feeling her magic is going to be useful before long."

"Why?"

The vampire said nothing for a moment. He picked up a stack of papers from the bench in front him and paused, his brow furrowed. "Eloise... I need to ask you a favour, but you have to promise that you won't ask questions."

Her uneasiness grew. "What kind of favour...?"

"Nothing bad," he reassured. "I just need your signature on something."

Eloise curled her nose. Signatures could get people into a whole lot of trouble, so to her, it wasn't just a little thing. Legally binding contracts could be more deadly than a knife in the dark.

"A signature for what?"

"These are papers for the shop," Hardy explained. "They say I sold it to you for the sum of one dollar. I had them drawn up after all that business with Vera and the Nightshade. All you have to do is sign and the deed will be in your name."

"Why?" She stared at the papers and the little

yellow tags that showed where she was supposed to sign her life away.

He thrust the contracts at her. "You promised."

She took them and shook her head. "Hardy... I... What could you possibly get out of this?"

He held out a pen and clicked the end. "*Please.*"

There was a moment where a sharp ball of turmoil bounced around in her chest, but the look in his eyes forced her to crumble.

Eloise plucked the pen from his fingers. "Okay...but know I'm not entirely convinced."

Hardy nodded and nudged the papers.

Eloise bent over the desk and signed on the line where the first yellow tab pointed. Flipping the page, she found the second. The pen scratched over the paper and her worry grew. She'd get a stomach ulcer if she wasn't careful. Honestly, she probably already had one.

"That's the last one," she said, clicking the pen and folding the papers back over.

"Invite me in," Hardy said, grimacing.

Her gaze rose and her breath caught. He looked like he was in pain—the frozen kind of rigidness people got when they were trying to hold themselves together.

"*Hardy.*" She jerked to her feet and the pen fell to the floor.

"Eloise, *invite me in.*"

"Uh... Come in?"

He visibly relaxed and drew in a deep breath. There was even a thin sheen of sweat across his brow. Whatever had just happened to him, it'd been bad.

"What in the bloody hell was that?"

"I hoped it would work," he murmured. "You're still mostly human, despite your elemental powers."

Eloise scowled. "Uh, thanks?"

"Vampires can't enter a dwelling occupied by a human," he explained. "They have to be invited, otherwise they cannot cross the threshold."

"That's crazy. Why?"

Hardy shrugged. "It's probably something to do with how the first vampires were created. I don't really know."

Eloise looked down at the contract. "And a little signature did all that?"

"Contracts exist in many forms...even on paper."

This was getting stranger by the second. He'd forced her to promise not to ask, but she had a whole lot of questions she was dying to know the answers to. Whatever he'd seen out there, it'd spooked him into action, and if a guy like Hardy was wigged out, then she ought to be terrified.

"What did you see out there?" she demanded. "Who was—"

"A bunch of blokes preparing to drill a hole."

"*Hardy*. You were gone all day and night." She didn't like his silence, so she continued to argue, "Hardy, if you know something, y—"

"There's nothing you should know," the vampire interrupted.

"Of course, there is!" she cried. "You just signed your shop over to me! Who the hell does that?"

"Semantics of being immortal."

"You're a terrible liar."

"More fool me trying to trick a spirit elemental," he murmured. He pinched the bridge of his nose and leaned back in his seat.

He looked exhausted. Eloise didn't know vampires could tire, but she was staring to see that even the undead had limits to their strength.

"You're scaring me," she whispered, her throat tightening.

"*Eloise*..." Hardy leaned forwards and took her hands in his, knowing what it meant for him to touch her. "I know you're worried, but I need you to trust me. There's something I need to do, and it needs to be done in my own time."

His skin felt cold to the touch, and her elemental powers stirred. She sensed his emotional turmoil and the threads of her magic reached out in order to change him, but she pulled away. She wasn't ready to let go, and he didn't want her help. This was his journey. He had to walk the path alone.

"I'll be waiting," she murmured, curling her fingers into tight fists. "If you need me..."

"I'll let you know."

CHAPTER 12

Vera sat behind the counter inside the *Outpost*, tapping away on her laptop.

Spreadsheets full of numbers scrolled across the screen and a tired sigh escaped her lips. On days like these, she almost wished she'd opened in the Ridge where business was a year-round affair.

Summer was a bad time for a general store in the outback, but at least the weather was starting to turn. Her first customers of the day had been a group of rumpled backpackers who smelled worse than they looked, but it was a sign the season was turning.

They'd pulled up in one of those campers spray painted with tacky slogans most people would feel were in poor taste. The vans were affordable, so backpackers could deal with the stares. Australia was an expensive country to travel around—the fuel prices were unbelievable going by the chalkboard out the front of Wally's.

One guy was German, another Estonian, the Dutch girl was 'hanging out' with the German guy, and the fourth was a girl from Finland who seemed bewildered by the vast, and awfully dry, flatness of the outback. Vera supposed she was used to mountains, snow, and reindeer, though she didn't know much about that part of the world.

The second time the bell rang, it heralded an unexpected visitor. Her heart leapt as it always did when she saw the uniformed man walk through the door, and her sigh turned into a goofy, lovesick grin.

Andrew Clarke was the local police sergeant in Lightning Ridge. Due to the immense size of Outback, New South Wales, his jurisdiction also took in Solace, even though it was over two hundred kilometres away. And that's how they'd first met.

He'd been investigating the disappearance of Craig Roth, the previous alpha of the Dust Dogs, and had become embroiled in all that nonsense with the Nightshade. There was a bit where she'd gone crazy and imprisoned him inside an abandoned opal mine —the same one Wally used as his monthly werewolf den—but he didn't remember that. Hardy had used his vampire abilities to wipe away the memories.

He'd forgotten all about the supernaturals of Solace, and that she was a witch. In fact, he'd forgotten about her entirely until she'd 'bumped' into him during a visit to Lightning Ridge.

He probably shouldn't be here, but she didn't have

the heart to send him away. It took almost two hours to drive here from the Ridge, after all.

"Doing some social media scrolling?" Clarke asked, tapping the edge of her laptop.

"Just going over the books," she told him with a wave of her hand. "Crunching numbers. Totally boring." She snapped the lid shut and rounded the counter. "What are you doing so far out?"

"What?" He pressed a quick kiss on her lips. "Can't I drive 224 kilometres to see my girlfriend?"

Vera's eyebrows rose. "Girlfriend?"

Clarke's smile faded a little around the edges. "Yeah? Aren't you? Unless you're..." He coughed nervously. "Which is fine. I mean, we didn't expressly say..."

Vera laughed and pressed a kiss in his lips. "Who else do you think I'm dating around here?"

"That opal buyer?"

"Hardy?" Her laughter intensified. Hardy was the last person to have ever crossed her mind in *that* way.

"Well, I couldn't see you and Drew hitting it off romantically."

Vera snorted. The dingo had thought about it, but he was more like her little brother than a potential boyfriend.

"Wally's a good bloke, but he's a bit old for you."

She screwed up her nose. "Stop, or I'll have to give you a shovel to finish that hole you're digging yourself."

Clarke grinned and wrapped his arms around her. "Maybe I'll find you some opal."

"Wouldn't that be a miracle?" She poked him in the chest. "Now, tell me why you're really out here."

"I'm trying to be an attentive boyfriend here, Vera," he groaned.

She raised her eyebrows. "*Spill.*"

"Word is, a big mining company is doing some work out this way."

Vera's skin prickled. She didn't want him going anywhere near that mine site. If Eloise was right, a vampire was heading up the exploration. "Yeah, I heard they blew through town."

"*EarthBore*," Clarke told her. "They have a multi-billion-dollar iron ore operation in Western Australia and are looking to move it out here."

"What do the police want with them?"

"Nothing, but it's my job to go out there and see what's what." He sighed, his brow creasing.

"What?" Vera loosened her hold and leaned back.

"It's strange," he murmured. "There was no forewarning. No community notices, no due diligence. The local elders had no idea a mining corp was moving in."

She pursed her lips and lowered her gaze. It had compulsion written all over it, of course, but she couldn't tell Clarke that, could she? Her feelings had only deepened the longer they were together, and one day she'd have to tell him the truth. Why not bring him into the fold?

The Nightshade was gone, but the danger wasn't. Clarke couldn't go to that mine site, but she couldn't see a way to dissuade him without revealing it.

"Vera?" He cupped her cheek. "What is it?"

She met his gaze and her heart twisted. "Andy, I—"

The bell above the door rang and a hot burst of air wafted into the *Outpost*, cutting her off in the nick of time. Clarke let her go and she plastered on her best customer service smile.

As she faced the newcomer, her expression faded as cold fingers of death reached inside her chest and twisted.

The man standing on the welcome mat smirked, his black eyes gleaming. He was average height, but his stature made him appear like a giant. Strong shoulders enhanced by the clean-cut lines of an expensive dress shirt held a hidden power and betrayed the coldness of his skin. It was over forty outside—the kind of heat that could cook an egg on the highway—and there wasn't an ounce of sweat on him.

His close-cropped black hair had a tight curl to it, and his eyes were round and wide-set. Was he Italian? Greek? She wasn't sure. The only thing she knew was that he was a vampire...and an old one.

"I thought I smelt witch," the man purred.

Clarke tensed and angled his body in front of her. "Hang on there, mate. I think that's a bit disrespectful."

"What's disrespectful is a weak mortal challenging me. Your uniform means nothing…" he leaned closer and peered at the badge pinned on Clarke's shirt, "*sergeant*."

Vera tugged on his arm. "Andy…"

He wasn't listening. "I don't know where you've come from, but no one is above the law."

The vampire spread his arms wide. "And I have broken none." His eyes moved to Vera. "Is this how you treat all your customers?"

"What do you want?" she demanded.

"You can deny this bloke service, Vera," Clarke told her. "You don't have to take this. In fact," he turned to the vampire, "I think you ought to leave, mate."

The man's smirk faded. "I'm not your mate."

He shot forwards and grabbed Clarke around the neck, hauling him up onto the counter. The sergeant's back slammed down with a bang, rattling the shelves of confectionary at the front and dislodging the display of Chupa Chups. The lollipops fell to the floor and scattered across the linoleum.

Clarke made an awful choking sound and clawed at the hand around his neck, but the man didn't seem bothered by his squirming.

"Leave him alone!" Vera cried.

"Or you'll what?" the vampire asked, his smile widening. "You'll make a vein pop in my head? I know all about you Irish witches. You're not the same as—"

Vera twisted her hand in the air, her magic flaring.

Briny sparks filled her palm and burst into life around the vampire.

He grunted, the only sign he felt any pain at all, and let go of Clarke. "There it is. The little witch has some spark in her after all."

Clarke jerked upright, coughing and pressing his hand on his bruised neck.

Vera rushed to his side, glaring at the vampire. "After all? What do you mean?"

He didn't reply. Instead, he strolled around the front of the shop, his gaze taking everything in.

"What a picturesque little place this is," he remarked.

Vera pressed her hand on Clarke's chest. "*Explain yourself.*"

***

Kyne knocked on the door leading down to Vera's dugout, his shoulders heavy.

Eloise was acting a bit clingy towards Hardy, and it had his hackles up. There was caring about the bloke, and then there was *caring*. If Kyne was an insecure guy, he would've thought there was something else going on there, but he wasn't that kind of guy...was he?

The elemental shook his head and snorted, knocking on Vera's door again. Nah, he didn't need to be worried about Hardy nicking Eloise from him. Not at all.

Kyne knocked once more, but there was no answer. He'd check the *Outpost*. Maybe Vera had opened early.

He strode down the road and hopped up onto the verandah. A crash echoed from inside the shop and he didn't think much of it at first, not until he saw the now familiar police 4WD parked on the side of the highway...and the black Land Rover beside it.

His pace quickened and he shoved the door open, the bell ringing as he entered. Clarke and Vera stood in front of the counter while an unknown man loitered in front of the display of bottled water at the head of aisle two.

Vera turned at his arrival, and she held out her hand, her magic flaring. "Kyne, he's a vampire. Stay back."

The miner jerked to a halt as steely blue magic crackled across the floor, placing a barrier between him and the man. Kyne's gaze darted around the shop, taking in the red marks around Clarke's neck and the anger in Vera's eyes. Whatever this guy was playing at, it wasn't amicable.

"There you are," the man said, gesturing for Kyne to come in. "This is starting to look like one of those jokes. A vampire, a witch, and an elemental walk into a bar..." He smirked and angled his gaze towards Clarke. "And what did the bartender say?"

"What's he on about?" Clarke demanded.

The man looked at the sergeant and laughed. "He

doesn't know? Oh, this is starting to get good. And who said small towns were boring?"

"Enough," Vera snapped. "I asked you to explain yourself, *vampire*."

"Me?" he replied with a smirk. "I just came to see the sights. There are so few of them out here."

"Who are you?" Kyne demanded.

"I am Darius," the vampire said, fixing his black gaze on the elemental.

He said it like it was meant to cast fear into their hearts, but Kyne had no idea who this bloke was supposed to be, other than the vampire at the helm of *EarthBore's* operation.

Vera snorted. "*Never heard of you.*"

The vampire's eyes darkened, but Kyne stepped forwards. "A vampire in a suit," he murmured. "All the way out here? What does a guy like you want with the largest iron ore despot in the Southern Hemisphere?"

Darius smirked. "Finally, someone has the brains to ask the right question. Unfortunately for you, I'm not willing to answer you just yet. Perhaps I came to cut you a deal, or to see who I needed to kill first, but from the reception I received, I see I'm not welcome here."

Before Kyne could reply, the door crashed open, and Hardy appeared in a gust of hot wind. He came to a halt in front of Darius, his fangs bared.

It was the first time Kyne had seen him like this,

and he found himself taking a step back, but Darius didn't move an inch. In fact, he hadn't even blinked.

"And there he is…" Darius snarled. "*The turncloak.* This is how you greet me? After all I've done for you?"

Kyne's brow creased just as Eloise stumbled into the *Outpost*. She let out a yelp and he grabbed her arm, jerking her behind him.

"What are you doing here?" Hardy demanded, his gaze never leaving Darius. "I know you've got your fingers in *EarthBore*. What do you want with them?"

"What I want is none of your business, Frederick," the vampire replied. "You lost the right to that privilege decades ago."

"Frederick?" Eloise whispered, looking at Kyne.

Darius's gaze fell onto the elemental. "I see he's left out a lot of details. Shall I fill you in, or will I keep it to myself and watch you all implode as you try to drag it out of him? It all depends on how sadistic I'm feeling." He turned and pointed at Vera. "And thanks to your little witch, I'm feeling particularly *devious* this morning."

"You deserved it," she spat.

"Perhaps," his grin widened, "but your boyfriend fired first."

Vera scoffed. "He did not! All he did was ask you to leave!"

"Words hurt, love." His grin disappeared. "They cut right to the bone."

"You're not welcome here," Hardy snarled.

"I can see that," Darius declared. "Well, now that we all know where we stand, the battle lines can be drawn in the sand. Interfere with my little project and I'll consider it a declaration of war." He turned to Kyne. "I assume from your authoritative tone, that you're the leader of this ragtag group of outsiders. So know this. Things could have gone differently, but you chose to back a traitor. So when he inevitably stabs you in the back and forces you to cross the line, remember you brought my retaliation upon yourselves." He took a step towards the door, but Hardy placed a hand on his chest.

"This isn't over," he snarled.

Darius looked down at Hardy's hand with disdain. "Of course, it isn't."

Then he disappeared, speeding through the door faster than Kyne's eye could follow. A moment later, the Land Rover peeled away from the *Outpost* and zoomed up the highway.

No one said anything for a long time.

Hardy cast his gaze onto the floor, which only served to turn Kyne's annoyance into anger. The vampire was keeping secrets—they all had them, of course—but now they'd come knocking, threatening them all. It wasn't just about Hardy anymore.

"Where's Drew?" the miner asked.

"Out with Coen, I assume," Vera replied.

"If there's a way to contact him, do it." He turned

his glare onto Hardy. "Someone has some explaining to do."

"*Kyne...*" Eloise tugged on his sleeve, but he ignored her.

Clarke cleared his throat. "At the risk of turning into cannon fodder, what about me?"

Kyne had to give the sergeant points for his balls. This was his second go at learning about the supernatural, but at least it wasn't turning out to be as horrific as the last time...*yet*.

"That's up to Vera," he said after glaring thoughtfully at the cop for a moment.

The witch's eyebrows rose. "Really?"

"It's obvious he's going to become a fixture around here regardless of what anyone else says," he told her, exasperated.

"Kyne," Hardy said, taking a step towards him but pulled up short when he saw the look on the miner's face.

"Pub. *Now*."

CHAPTER 13

Port Arthur, Van Diemen's Land, Australia, *1835*

Hardy gasped, his eyes flying open.

The scent of pungent grime and dirt filled his senses, and he sat upright, pinching his nose. The darkness of his cell had been absolute when he'd been thrown in, and it still was, but somehow, he could sense where the door was. A humid breeze filtered in through the cracks in the hinges and it tickled his dirty face, coaxing a sensitivity that was new to him.

He pressed his hands against his back and found the pain was gone. The bandages were stiff with dried blood and putrid ointment, but he could move again. His torn flesh didn't feel so torn anymore.

How was that possible?

Letting go of his nose, Hardy breathed deeply. He

instantly regretted it and gagged as his lungs filled with new and unusual scents, all pungent in the worst way. Coal, sweat, *blood*...

He swallowed as his throat burned. He was thirsty...and hungry. He'd felt extreme hunger before and had found a way to live on the scant scraps that were fed to the convicts, but this was different. His stomach wasn't churning, but his veins felt as if they were running dry and filling with sand.

Hardy stood, his head swimming. He stumbled towards the door and pressed against it.

Barely aware of what he was doing, he struck his shoulder against the metal. It gave way with a snap, flinging open with a screeching groan of metal on stone. The momentum almost sent him flying out into the tunnel beyond, but he managed to hold his ground.

Dumbfounded, Hardy stared into the darkness. The door had just given way...*just like that*. The least amount of pressure had sent the metal careening outwards, the lock sheering clean off.

This was a dream.

Davis would never let him out or allow the solitary cells to become so poorly maintained that the lock broke with such a paltry push. Not even if Hardy couldn't stand to save himself. Not even if he was already dead.

So, it had to be a dream, or at best, a hallucination. If his mind wanted him to taste the fresh air of freedom before he took his last breath inside his prison, then that's what he'd do. Why not?

Leaving the cell, he hesitated. He heard nothing but the ragged sound of his own breathing.

If this was a dream, then no one would stop him. Deciding to keep walking, he made his way to the surface.

When he finally stepped into the cool night, he gasped. The humidity of the mine pulsed out of the opening behind him, but he barely felt it. He looked to the sky, his heart clenching in wonder.

The stars were brighter than he'd ever seen them. The silver points had turned into a dusting of precious jewels—diamonds, rubies, sapphires—and the dark places in-between were darker. It was as if he could see the road to Heaven itself.

This was a dream.

He thought of Mary, who he assumed was long dead by now. Maybe she'd be waiting for him at the end of the road. She'd take his hand and welcome him, then lead him through the gates. She'd forgive him for getting caught at the apothecary, and together, they'd watch over Tom and Elizabeth as they grew and had families of their own.

Hardy choked, his hand moving to his throat. It burned like he'd swallowed molten steel, but his hunger was worse.

Davis.

The lure of tearing him apart was stronger than the

longing he felt for his sister. He felt the ghostly bite of the whip as it tore into his flesh and the lick of leather as it hit bone. Pain, it seemed, was stronger than love.

So that's why, when revenge held out its clammy hand, Hardy took it.

The overseer's cottage sat some distance away from the coal mine, flanked by bush and overlooking the ocean.

The convicts were all locked up for the night; the usual evening shift had been given a reprieve after the circus Davis and Hardy had performed. All slept soundly, except for the soldiers on lookout, of course.

Hardy stole through the trees, moving silently around the guard postings along the path. His feet moved faster than he'd thought possible, closing the distance in mere moments. He'd gone by the men in a blur, and they hadn't even lifted their heads at his passing.

Who was he?

What had he become?

A window was ajar at the rear of the cottage and an intoxicating sound floated through the gap, luring him to it like a siren called to sailors out on the open ocean. Hardy approached, listening to the *thump-thump, thump-thump,* transfixed.

He eased open the shutters and stole through the opening, landing lithely in the room where Henry Davis lay in his bed, fast asleep.

The overseer wore a white linen nightshirt—the

fabric finer than anything Hardy had ever owned—and slept between fine cream-coloured sheets, with a feather pillow beneath his head. The candle on the bedside dresser had burned down to the wick, but Hardy still saw the loaded revolver beside it, the moon bathing it in brilliant silver light.

He looked down at Davis and listened to the rhythmic thump that'd called him inside. *His heartbeat*, Hardy thought. *I can hear his heartbeat.*

Hardy leaned over him and sniffed. *Yes, this ought to do.* Revenge and…something else he seemed to need.

The overseer stirred and opened his eyes. It took a few long seconds before the man realised that he wasn't alone, but when he did, he burst into life.

"*What in the bloody hell*," Davis cursed, jerking upright. He reached for the revolver on the nightstand, but his fingers slipped over the butt and he knocked it to the floor.

Hardy started at the overseer for a moment, his expression blank. He felt pressure in his mouth as his teeth ached, but he was too disoriented to care.

He lunged at Davis and pushed him back down onto the bed. The overseer opened his mouth to scream, but Hardy stifled his cries with his filthy hand and wrenched the man's head to the side.

The vein in the overseer's neck pulsed, and Hardy knew it was what he was looking for. He bit down hard, his teeth tearing through warm flesh, and blood poured into his mouth, flooding the mattress and smearing across his face.

He swallowed, and the metallic liquid soothed the burn in his throat. It hit his stomach and fed into his veins, washing away the sand and bringing life to him once more.

He was dying and now he was alive. It was an odd thought to have, but it seemed fitting, nonetheless. Why, he didn't know, just that it was.

Hardy drank, swallowing mouthful after mouthful until there was no more. He growled in disappointment and pushed himself off the corpse. The patter of Davis's heart had stopped, and the room was silent.

Warmth had returned to Hardy's body and with it, his senses started to clear. As he stared down at the bloodied corpse, his horror grew as his understanding returned, and he realised two things.

He was well and truly awake...and he'd just murdered a man for his blood.

Davis was a sadistic bastard who revelled in causing the inmates harm that bordered on barbarism, but did that give Hardy the right to kill him? Did he deserve it? Maybe, but murder was the worst crime of them all.

Hardy would hang for this. If they caught him, he'd be strung up at first light. He'd get no trial—not that his first one had been a fair one—and his suffering would be over with a snap of his neck...which he rubbed like he'd already felt it break once before.

Suddenly, Frederick Marmaduke Hardy realised he didn't want to die.

So he did the only thing he could.

He ran.

Eaglehawk Neck was a thin strip of land that connected the small peninsula where Port Arthur was located to the mainland of Van Diemen's Land.

It was little more than a sandbar, less than thirty metres wide. Rough, rocky shark-infested ocean lay on either side, ruling out swimming...unless he wanted to drown.

The Neck was the only safe crossing, though that only meant it was well guarded. A specially trained pack of dogs lay in wait for escapees and would bark at any movement, alerting the guards stationed at either end. There was no cover, so he'd be shot without warning.

Davis's body had likely been discovered by now and a search party would be marshalled, headed by the best trackers Port Arthur had to offer. His only saving grace was the few hours he'd gain from them trying to work out the circumstances of his murder... and linking it to the escaped convict who'd received fifty lashes the day before.

But it didn't matter how or why. It was only a matter of time before they found him.

Hardy's window for escape was rapidly closing, and the only way out of here was across that narrow strip of land.

Which way do you want to die? he thought. *Getting shot, eaten by sharks, drowning, or hanging?*

Either way, he'd be seeing Mary soon enough. He just hoped he hadn't disappointed her too much.

He sat on the hill overlooking the Neck and took off his shirt. Unravelling the bandages around his chest and middle, he threw them aside and reached to feel his puckered flesh. The ribboned wounds had healed, but the scars beneath remained untouched.

How was it possible? What miracle had taken away the torn remains of fifty lashes and left him with an unbearable hunger for blood? Was it an act of God...or a trick of the Devil? He'd endured four years of torment at Port Arthur and now *this*.

What was he thinking? Where would he even go? It wasn't like he could get on a ship and go back to England. He had no money and he'd be caught the moment he tried to board.

Maybe he could find a captain who'd take pity on him and offer passage for work. It was a long shot... providing he could get off the peninsula.

God help you, Hardy, he thought. *How could I go back? I just killed a man and escaped from prison.*

He'd killed a man.

An unbearable wave of guilt slammed into him, and he fell to his knees.

He'd killed a man...*and felt nothing.*

Foggy memory returned to him, and he rubbed his grimy hands over his blooded face as he recalled the sharp sting of the whip biting into his back and the searing pain that'd numbed him into a stupor in the darkness of solitary confinement.

A man had come. Hadn't he? The image of him was a dull blur in Hardy's mind, but he was there. *Not a dream...*

He raised his fingers to his lips. When he'd latched onto Davis's neck, it wasn't the first time he'd tasted blood.

That man must be the Devil. He'd possessed his soul and turned him into a beast.

Hardy almost clasped his hands together and prayed, but the first rays of light had turned the horizon a washed-out bluish-yellow.

The light almost heralded a glimmer of hope, as if God was calling to him, but as the rays danced over his chilled skin, something unexpected happened...he began to burn.

Crying out, he rubbed his reddening flesh and clapped his hands onto his cheeks. The sun... He looked at the sliver of yellow peeking above the horizon and didn't understand. *How?* When his exposed skin started to smoke, the mechanics didn't seem to matter anymore.

He scrambled back down the hill, darting into pockets of shade. The moment he did, the burning stopped, but it wouldn't for long. The sun would eventually rise and then there'd be nowhere to hide.

He tripped and rolled into the creek, sending water and sludge flying.

That's it...*the mud!*

Lunging into the shallows, he scooped up mud in heaped handfuls and slathered it over his body.

The day continued to brighten and still, his skin seared.

He desperately heaped more mud over himself, fighting a losing battle until he plunged into the creek bed headfirst. Cool relief soothed his burning flesh, and he buried deeper into the boggy mess. *It was working!*

Hardy lay there for hours, submerged in dirt and slime, waiting for the sun to set. His worn boots filled with mud and he felt insects crawl against his skin, but he didn't dare move.

How I burned. If he'd stood on that hill a moment longer, he was sure he would've burst into flames and then would have died on the spot.

Maybe it wasn't such a bad idea, though there was one flaw. He was afraid of dying.

As the day went along, Hardy had a great deal of things to ponder. His family back in England, the voyage out to Port Arthur, his interment at the penal colony, the first time he'd been lashed, the long hours in the coal mine, and his last stand. Fifty lashes, solitary confinement, and now...*this.*

If what he was now had a name, he didn't know. All that mattered was that he'd killed the overseer. *How* was a thought too difficult for him to handle.

When the sun finally lowered enough to cast the creek in long shadow, Hardy crawled out of his hiding place and washed the mud from his face. He was coated with sludge, but he didn't care—the dogs wouldn't catch his scent. Honestly, there was scant left for him to care about after the turn his pathetic life had taken. All he could focus on now was escape.

Running from your problems, Hardy? a small voice asked.

He ignored it.

Making his way back up the hill, Hardy looked down over Eaglehawk Neck. This was his last chance. If he couldn't escape, then he'd let the sun take him in the morning. It seemed like a fitting end, and the best he could hope for. Death on his own terms, rather than on the end of a rope.

All was quiet below. There was no sign of reinforcements, or any sign of the usual guard postings. Hardy didn't know where they were, only that they were here someplace. Stories had passed between the convicts of those who attempted escape, along with the warnings given by the warden. *Escapees will be shot on sight.*

He kept to the trees for as long as he was able,

watching for signs of the soldiers he knew lingered in the shadows. He was fast now, and rifles took time to reload. He could be across and on the mainland in a blink of an eye. If he made it, then he'd worry about the part that came afterwards.

Lingering in the trees, he scanned the small patch of grassy sand. A small stone hut sat at the midway point of the neck, a faint glow pulsing from the small south-facing window.

Now or never.

He was about to run when two soldiers emerged from the shadows, rifles in hand. He'd been so intent on the neck, he hadn't heard them, and he gritted his teeth.

Frozen, he watched them approach his hiding spot, the men oblivious.

If he moved, they'd spot him. If he did nothing, they'd spot him.

God, help me, he thought.

Hardy leapt out of the shadows like a bolt of lightning and tackled the first soldier to the ground. The sickly scent of blood filled his nose and he struck, barely aware of what he was doing. It was as if a demon had taken control of his body, telling his limbs what to do.

Hardy tore the first man's neck open, and when he gurgled his last breath, he turned on the next. Then the reenforcement, and the one who ran after him.

They never got one shot off between the four of

them, and the dogs... The short skirmish had come to a standstill and the animals had ceased their howling.

Hardy stood in the middle of the corpses, covered in blood and shit, listening. Even the native animals had scurried away, carrying the last of the bush sounds with them.

Some of who he'd once been returned to him in the calmness, and as he looked down at the chaos he'd wrought, he fell to his knees.

Monster.

"What. A. *Mess.*"

Hardy spun at the sound of a voice. He fell on his behind as the man he'd seen in his cell wandered silently out of the trees, a spectre in the dark.

"Look at you," the man drawled. "How disappointing."

Hardy scrambled backwards and his hands fumbled over something soft. Seeing it was a severed arm, he jerked away in horror.

"You're wondering if you're too far gone," the man said in a bored tone. "Well, I'm here to tell you that you haven't gone far enough." He looked down at the dead soldier and sighed. "It's something, but I wish you had waited for me. It would have saved you from burying yourself in shit."

"Who are you?" Hardy rasped. "What have you done to me?"

The man stared at him, unblinking. "I am Darius,

and this..." he gestured to the bloody carnage, "this is my gift to you. The corpses of your captors."

Hardy buried his face in his hands, but the smell of blood filled his nose once more, stirring the beast inside him. This wasn't a gift, but a curse. A terrible curse brought by the Devil himself.

"I killed them. I..." He choked. "I-I'll hang for this."

"I doubt it," Darius drawled.

"I don't want to die," he sobbed.

"That's rather ironic," the man told him. "Considering you're already dead."

His hands fell away from his face as he felt a stab of fear pierce his heart.

"I'm a vampire," the man said. "And I made you one."

Hardy stared at him, dumbfounded.

"I fed you my blood and I broke your neck," Darius continued. "Now, you are like me. Strong, beautiful—well, once I have you scrubbed clean—and *immortal*. It's also why you can see more than you ever have before, and why you can move so fast. All your senses are amplified... They're all advantages of becoming the ultimate predator."

"Advantages?"

"Yes, though as with all things, there are some drawbacks."

The sun. Hardy rubbed his filthy arms and cringed.

Darius smirked knowingly. "That's not all."

"It's not?"

"If you are hungry enough, you will do *anything* for blood."

"Anything?"

"There is always a price." The vampire looked down at the remains of the soldiers and sighed. "You've already tasted it. I'm here to make sure you don't do it again."

"Why?"

"I will help you, Frederick," he said, not offering an explanation. "I will take you from this place and give you a new life...one where you aren't a prisoner. One where you have all the power. One where you will never be hungry again." He knelt beside Hardy and grasped his face, his fingers biting into his stubbled jaw. "But I have one condition..."

Hardy knew he didn't have any choice, but he asked anyway. "What is it?"

"Your unconditional loyalty."

Hardy nodded, knowing he'd made yet another deal he didn't understand.

"Now... Let's get off this accursed island and find some civilisation."

Hardy stumbled to his feet. "Where can we go? They'll be looking for me."

"Hobart," Darius replied. "And I wouldn't worry about the law finding you." He waved a dismissive hand at the bodies. "I know a witch who will help you with the sun and you need a bath...*among other things.*

Then, we will return to the mainland where I will teach you what it means to be a vampire."

Darius looked at him like he was a stray dog he'd just picked up out of the gutter, but Hardy was too stunned to be offended. "A witch?" he asked.

"Yes, Frederick. *A witch*." Darius's smile widened. "Welcome to the *real world*. I think we're going to have fun, you and I."

CHAPTER 14

For the first time in his long life, Frederick Marmaduke Hardy told his entire sordid tale to the Exiles of Solace...and in the presence of one human police sergeant. He wasn't a superhero with an origin story; he was just a pitiful man who'd had his mortality stolen from him.

"Little did I know that fun to a man like Darius was more akin to mindless slaughter. He inflicted worse than I'd seen or received at Port Arthur. Ten times worse..."

"He said you'd betrayed him," Kyne said.

"I did." He raised his gaze to the elemental. "I'd agreed to give him my unwavering loyalty, but in the end...I left him. It seemed I still had remnants of humanity lingering inside me after all."

"Now I understand why you signed the shop over to me," Eloise murmured. "When you went out there, you saw him."

Kyne narrowed his eyes and turned his glare onto the vampire. "You signed the shop over to Eloise?"

Hardy nodded. "It needs to be a safe place. Darius won't be able to enter."

"He seemed to know you were here," Kyne went on. "He wasn't even a little surprised to see you."

"I would've said something if I had known Darius had his fingers in this," Hardy told him.

Would he have, though? His history with Darius was troubled to say the least. The vampire's idea of teaching was to bring out all his worst qualities. Torture, blood, and pain—that's what Darius was...and it was why he'd left.

"Who is he exactly?" Vera asked. "What's his deal?"

"Darius is the oldest vampire to have ever walked *this* Earth," Hardy replied.

"*This* Earth?" Eloise frowned.

"He claims he comes from another Earth, just like this one," the vampire went on, knowing there were multiple realities existing alongside theirs. "He was the first of our kind in this world and the origin of all vampires here. He was made by another, almost two thousand years ago, by a man who was said to be the first created."

"Created," Vera mused, "not made. What kind of magic could create a vampire?"

"It doesn't matter if he was made or created," Hardy said. "He's still the oldest vampire in the world, and that makes him the most powerful. His meddling in human affairs goes back a thousand years, making him beyond influential amongst the elite of our world, and that's without using compulsion. Darius is all the bad things about being a vampire. He's ruthless and unfeeling, a hunter who relishes each kill."

"That's how he got *EarthBore* to follow him so easily," Kyne said as if he hadn't heard the last part of Hardy's explanation.

"They're compelled," Drew said. "That's what I sensed."

Kyne turned. "Who?"

"The human workers," the shifter replied. "Their auras had this strange taint... I reckon he's mind controlling them all."

"Since when can you see auras?" Finn asked with a pout.

"Since Coen has been teaching me," Drew fired back. "When I shift, I can see more than you'll ever know."

"Give it a rest," Vera scolded. "Trust you two to make this about yourselves."

"What's he doing here?" Finn asked, leaning down to peer at Clarke. He narrowed his eyes at the sergeant. "You finally seal the deal, Vera?"

"Rack off, Finn," Kyne snapped.

"Rack off where?" the fae asked with a sneer. "We've got vampires up to our eyeballs, and now a cop is sitting here listening in on all our secrets. You may as well give him the password to your Bitcoin wallet, Kyne."

"Hell," Blue muttered. "I don't even want to know how a fae trapped in the outback knows about Bitcoin."

Hardy was only half-listening to the Exiles as they descended into their usual bickering.

"Now that's all cleared up, the question still remains..." Finn said. "What are we going to do about the vampire and his massive drill?"

Vera choked and grasped Clarke's hand. The sergeant tensed, his brow creasing.

Hardy peered at him but caught the shake of Kyne's head out the corner of his eye. The miner had decided Clarke was Vera's problem to deal with...if it was a problem.

"It's a cover," Hardy murmured, disregarding them. "He's after the seal, but I don't think he knows where it is."

"I want to say we need to go on the offence," Vera began, "but he could come back at any moment."

"He won't come back straight away," Hardy said. "He'll give me a chance to go to him first."

"That's out of the question," Kyne said.

"If you go there, he'll rip you to bits," Wally said. "I know alpha behaviour when I see it. He made you, Hardy. In his mind, the bloke owns your entire existence."

"The way I see it, we're screwed," Blue said with a

heavy sigh. "The Nightshade was a hell of a fight, but a thousand-year-old vampire...? How can we defend against that? He could sweep in here and mind control me."

"Vampires can't enter human dwellings," Wally told him.

"The pub's not a dwelling," Blue declared, his cheeks turning red, "it's a *business*."

"I might be able to help with the mind control," Vera told the publican, wincing at the mention of the Nightshade. "Vampires aren't of this Earth, but there has to be a way to combat their abilities. There's a balance to everything, and nature corrects itself constantly...even in different realities." She glanced at Clarke. "I need a little time to experiment, though."

Kyne snorted and turned to the sergeant. "You've been silent as the grave. What would you do, *Sergeant Clarke?*"

The Exiles all turned to stare at the newcomer, who didn't yet understand he wasn't so new to the supernatural shenanigans of Solace.

"Make him wait," the sergeant murmured. "You need time to strategise, and the longer an arrogant man like that waits, the angrier he'll get. Angry men make mistakes."

Hardy stared at Clarke, his unblinking gaze making the man squirm.

"You want us to face an angry vampire?" Kyne asked. "I know this is a stretch for you, Clarke, but—"

"He's right," Hardy interrupted, rising to his feet. "We need time."

Vera needed to figure out a way to protect Blue, and they needed to create as many safe zones in Solace as they could. Darius would rain hell on them the moment they attempted to challenge him, and the more thresholds they had, the better.

Eloise stood, her expression full of worry, but he shook his head.

"I, uh..." He swallowed hard.

Before anyone could reply, he'd flown out the door.

Eloise followed Hardy outside, leaving the other Exiles behind. Kyne had wanted to come with her, but she'd pushed him back in his chair, forcing his arse to stick in it with a little elemental magic.

The proverbial crap was about to hit the fan in there—what with Clarke now one hundred percent aware of Solace's little secret—but she was more concerned about Hardy. He'd unloaded some pretty heavy stuff, tearing open old wounds in the process.

It wasn't because he was a vampire and everyone was worried he'd snap and go on a bloodthirsty rampage. It was because he was her friend.

She found Hardy standing outside the opal shop, holding his hands out in the sunlight. He turned them over a few times, and as she approached, she saw they were shaking ever so slightly.

"Eloise," he murmured.

She stepped into the shade of the verandah. "Are you all right?"

He lowered his hands. "You've been asking me that a lot lately."

"I know." She shrugged. "So, are you?"

"As well as I could be." He turned his gaze on her. "You have questions."

A sigh escaped her lips. "About a million of them."

"Have at it, then."

She hesitated at first but took her chance. "You didn't say how you ended up at Port Arthur. I can't reconcile a convict with the man I see now."

"In those days, they needed people to build up the colonies," Hardy told her. "Not enough were going voluntarily, and they needed numbers. Convicts were the solution. It was slave labour without it actually being classified as slavery. People would get sentenced to transportation for stealing a potato." He said it bitterly, as if his sentence had been for something just as paltry.

"Hardy?"

The vampire scowled and lowered his gaze. "Theft," he said. "I'd never broken any laws before, but my sister was sick and..."

Eloise felt his anguish and she placed a hand on

his arm. Her touch startled him and he blinked away tears, turning his head so she wouldn't see.

Too late, she thought.

"She was sick and you needed medicine," she murmured. "*Oh, Hardy…*"

There was so much more he wasn't telling them, but Eloise knew enough about Australia's convict past to know what kind of treatment he would've received at Port Arthur. Conditions were as bleak as the weather at the southernmost point of Tasmania. The next stop south was Antarctica.

"They sent me away the next morning," Hardy said, startling her. "I was caught, sent before a judge, and put on a tall ship leaving London that morning. One hundred and fifty-five days at sea…"

She felt the burn of her tears. "You never got to say goodbye?"

He shook his head.

"What was her name?"

"Mary," he whispered.

"*Mary*. That's a beautiful name. Regal."

"Mary, Elizabeth, and Tom," he went on. "Our parents were dead, and it was up to me…"

Eloise didn't know what to say. He'd had a whole family and some judge had sent him to Port Arthur for trying to save his sister's life. It was easy to look back and be outraged on his behalf, but times were different. They were harder, and the gap between rich and poor was a gaping divide.

"What was wrong with her?" she wondered.

"Consumption," he replied. "Known as tuberculosis these days. No cure, no treatment, only mercy."

"God, *Hardy*. I'm—"

"I know," he interrupted. "Just don't say it."

"Okay."

She looked across the road where Wally was rolling up the door of the garage. The metal rattled, the sound echoing through the stillness of Solace. He spotted them standing in the shade of the opal shop and raised his hand.

Eloise waved back, but Hardy simply sighed. They were all worried about Darius and *EarthBore*, but they also worried about their friend. His story was *a lot*.

"Can I show you something?" the vampire asked once Wally had gone inside.

"Sure." Eloise nodded. He unbuttoned his shirt, and she let out a nervous cough. "*Uh...*"

He grimaced and turned around. "My back," he said, shucking off his shirt. "This is what almost killed me."

The khaki material fell away, revealing a twisted mess of scars. She gasped and her hand flew to her mouth to stifle the sound, but it was far too late. Whatever she'd thought he was about to show her, it hadn't been *this*.

Some scars were thin and long, while others were clumped knots. His flesh had healed poorly, a sign they'd barely been treated at all. Her eyes narrowed as she realised what had caused them—*a whip.*

"The night Darius came to me, it wasn't the first time I'd been lashed," Hardy told her. "Those wounds healed the moment he gave me his blood, but the ones that came before...they became permanent."

"How many?" she whispered.

"Fifty."

She reached up and traced her fingers over his scars, making him flinch. He turned and put his shirt back on, fastening the buttons with lightning speed.

"The first time, it was ten," he told her. "The second, it was twenty, but third time's a charm."

They said nothing for a long time after that. There wasn't anything Eloise *could* say now that she knew some of the things Hardy had been through. His scars were a mark of the brutal punishment he'd faced, and a constant reminder of what he'd been forced to leave behind.

He'd shown her simply because he had to tell *someone,* and he trusted her the most. More than Kyne, who'd lived with him for years before she'd arrived, and more than the old guard—Blue and Wally.

Eloise didn't know what she'd done to earn it, but she'd never betray him. *Never.*

"Did you ever find out what happened to your brother and sisters?" she asked.

"No. Blue said something about using one of those websites. Ancestry."

Well, fancy that. "Blue figured it out? Or did you tell him?"

Hardy smirked. "Blue's a perceptive bloke."

"He is a publican," she said. "Their prowess at diagnosing what ails someone's heart and mind is only second to *actual* therapists."

The vampire chuckled and leaned back against the wall. "Thanks."

"What for?"

He looked at her and narrowed his eyes. "*You know.*"

She fancied she felt his spirits lift despite the threat of Darius hanging over them all, and smiled. "Frederick?"

"Not so many Freds around these days."

"It's not so bad. A little old-fashioned, but still totally fancy pants. Do you have a middle name?"

"No," he said with a faint smile. "Of course, I don't."

He was deflecting, which meant it was more embarrassing than Frederick.

"You'll tell me what it is one day," she told him, shouldering open the door. "*Just you wait.*"

***

Vera walked along the highway, her sandals filling with dust. Girt rubbed between her toes, chafing her skin, but she didn't care.

Clarke followed, his expression unreadable. Hardy

had just dropped one hell of a story on them, but as far as he remembered, the standoff with Darius was his first encounter with the supernatural. Things, that to him, didn't exist.

Vampires, witches, werewolves, shapeshifters, fae, and elementals were the stuff of stories. They didn't live in little outback towns. They didn't run businesses or mine opal. They...

Vera sighed as they approached the boab. The tree was ancient, the trunk so bloated it'd become a landmark in its own right. It was impressive, but also harboured its own latent magic that protected the entrance to the mine that led down to the seal.

The seal. The creepy bluestone that started this whole mess.

Vera stood underneath the twisted branches of the boab and looked up at the stars. She wanted to ask Hardy about the witch he'd met in Hobart all those years ago, but it wasn't appropriate. The covens rarely left Ireland in modern times, let alone in the nineteenth century. Who was she and what magic had led her to Tasmania in such a turbulent time? It was a story for another time.

Now she had to explain things to Clarke and hope... *Bloody hell.* She wanted to burst into tears but trying to explain witchcraft while bawling her eyes out would be the least crazy way of breaking the news to him. Not that anything she was about to say would be classified as 'sane' to a human police officer.

"You didn't say much in there," she said, finally looking at him.

"I don't seem to be qualified," Clarke told her. "There were a lot of things I didn't understand. Compulsion, shapeshifting dingoes, elementals, and a thousand other bloody things I thought were Halloween stories." He ran a hand over his face. "Christ, Vera. What am I supposed to say?"

"I don't know," she admitted, scuffing the toe of her sandal in the dirt. She wanted him to be okay with it. She wanted him to take her in his arms and say it didn't matter, that he loved her anyway, but the look on his face dashed her hopes.

"So, I either accept it or have my memory wiped...*again*," he said. "Hell of a choice, Vera."

"I won't let them. I'll get Hardy to return your memory."

Clarke ran his hand over his face. "I don't know if I want to know what happened to me last time."

Vera didn't either, considering what she'd done to him as the Nightshade. Locking him in a mine frequented by a werewolf during a full moon wasn't something easily forgiven.

"I guess I should be grateful I'm still alive to have a second go."

"*No*," she cried. "It wasn't like that."

"And I suppose that day we met outside the bank in the Ridge was all a setup?"

Vera's cheeks heated and she bit her lip.

"I knew it." He scoffed. "Is this real?" He pointed back and forth between them. "Or is this all a convenient play for police backup?"

"No!" She took a step towards him. "It's real. *It's all real.*"

"Are you sure? Because I'm having a hell of a time trying to figure it out."

"You deserve the truth, Andy," she said. "All of it, no matter how painful." She took a deep breath. "If you love me, if there's a future for us...then I want it to be without secrets. I want you to understand what Solace is. What I am."

"What Solace is?" He frowned, his brow creasing so deep, she was worried he'd have permanent lines.

"We have a responsibility," she began. "Uh... We protect it from others like us and sometimes from ourselves."

"*Christ.*" Clarke sighed, the sharpness of his breath piercing the night air. "Damn right you owe me an explanation, but am I going to understand it?"

"Yes," she murmured, "you will."

"Then you better get on with it." His stare was cool, and she almost let go of her tears.

It was a fifty-fifty chance, right?

Vera took a deep breath and centred her magic. This was going to be one hell of a story, and she wanted to tell it right.

"I think you better sit down," she said, picking a comfortable root beside the boab.

Clarke sat beside her, which she hoped was a good sign. He wasn't running away screaming or trying to put her in handcuffs, though when she told him about Roth and the Dust Dogs, maybe it'd be Drew and Eloise in her place. Or maybe he'd call in a paddy wagon for the whole lot of them. Darius would be the least of their problems, then.

Vera placed her palm on the boab and called on its latent power. "It all began when we discovered the seal..."

CHAPTER 15

Eloise stood outside Hardy's opal shop, enjoying the peace and quiet of the morning.

When she'd passed Vera's, she saw Clarke's police 4WD was still parked by her dugout. She could still see the corner of it now, glowing bright white in the brilliant sunshine. She hoped it bode well for them—Vera deserved some happiness—but she was also concerned for the sergeant.

She was supernatural herself, so she'd easily accepted all the crazy things she'd seen in Solace. Shapeshifting dingoes, witches, magical tornadoes, transporting people to other dimensions, shaping rock with mysterious elemental powers...it was all pretty exciting to her.

Clarke, on the other hand... He was human. A man of the law. He was the kind of guy who believed in what he saw right in front of him, which was tangible stuff he could control—the exact opposite of every Exile in Solace.

She sighed and glanced down the highway as the sun glinted off the windscreen of an approaching car. Vera knew what she was doing. She was formidable at the best of times, but she was also one of the most caring people Eloise had ever met.

The car reached the limits of Solace, slowing to the recommended eighty kilometres per hour. Though instead of sailing through, the shiny silver sedan eased even farther, coasting to a stop on the opposite side of the road.

Now she saw a man behind the wheel, his outline just discernible through the tinted windows.

At first, Eloise almost went back inside, but decided to stay put to see what he'd do. Just because Darius was going about poking holes in the ground, didn't mean that everyone who drove past was under his creepy vampire mind control. She couldn't be skittish, especially since it was her duty to protect the seal. Wary, yes. *Afraid*, no.

The man got out of the car, unfolding himself gracefully, and closed the door. It *thunked* shut, the sound echoing dully in the still air.

He wore a short-sleeved khaki shirt—the kind that looked like he should be exploring a jungle someplace, not traipsing around the Outback—and a brown fedora more suited for a hipster Sydney suburb. Dark-coloured jeans and heavy black boots with ochre-stained toes finished up his ensemble.

Eloise raised an eyebrow as he approached. Her powers had returned to normal by now, but it didn't stop her from feeling a little gust of cool air on the back of her neck.

"Hello," the man said, plastering a cheesy grin on his face.

"Can I help you?" She looked him over. He was easy enough on the eyes, though a little on the short side. *Like that lowered the threat indicator.*

"Full disclosure," he said, taking off his aviator sunglasses. "I'm a—"

She took a step back towards the door. "Vampire."

The man grimaced. "I thought you'd be clever. You look clever."

"Okay…?"

"I'm not here to start anything," he went on. "I just want to have a chat. Just say, G'day." He rubbed his hand on the back of his neck. "Do people say that round here? G'day? Or is it like that 'shrimp on the barbie' thing?"

"Uh, yeah…they do." Eloise nodded, a little stunned. *What in the world was going on here?*

The vampire seemed to be nervous talking now and continued to babble. "I swung by a little while ago and visited that charming little shop." He pointed to the *Outpost*. "Spent some tourist dollars and sniffed out a few supernaturals along the way."

Eloise blinked as she put two and two together. *The tourist with the party poppers...*

"I thought you'd be the nicest of the lot," he went on. "I get a good feeling from you. You're...like a warm hug."

Eloise stifled a laugh. She wanted to be on her guard, but the vampire exuded his own warmth that she found infectiously hilarious. He wasn't a threat, though he could be if he decided it was lunchtime.

"Words ain't my strong suit," he added with a shrug. "Sometimes I forget to apply a filter and put my foot in it, so to speak."

"Well, if talking is all you want to do, then you ought to start with your name," Eloise told him.

"Oh shite, where are my manners?" He dusted his palms over his jeans and slapped on his best smile. "Joseph Cheapside, at your service."

"Cheapside?"

"Yeah. Back in the olden days, the powers-that-be gave street kids the names of the filth-encrusted cobblestones they slept and begged on. Nice buggers, eh? Everyone had to have a family name for their fancy record books, I guess."

"Cheapside, as in London?"

"Born and bred, love." Joseph flashed her a wink. "And you are?"

"Eloise Hart."

"Ah... *Hart*. I like it."

"What did you want to talk about?" she asked,

raising her eyebrows. "I'm smart enough to know that something's going on here. A vampire doesn't just come out here for no reason."

"I bet no one does," he replied. "It isn't exactly easy to get here."

"So?"

"I've been tracking *EarthBore* for a while now," he told her. "I've been looking for a certain someone who likes sticking his fingers in all sorts of pies. Looks like a bug-eyed Roman." He held up his hands and circled his fingers around his eyes like glasses.

"Bug-eyed?"

"Yeah. Romans have these beady little eyeballs. Makes them look like they're constantly high." He turned thoughtful. "Maybe that's why they put coins over them with they die… They don't need to pay the ferryman, it's just the only thing round enough to cover 'em up."

Eloise blinked. "If you say so."

"Think about it, sweetheart."

"*Oh.*" She finally got it. Darius began his human life in Ancient Rome.

"I take it you've seen him, then?"

She nodded. "So, whose side are you on?"

"We're already to that bit, eh?" Joseph whistled. "Bastard works fast. He's barely stuck his drill into the ground."

"I know you're playing coy. You've already paid us a visit, so what's your conclusion?"

His cheeky smile faded, and some of the vampire began to emerge. "My conclusion is that you're either a bunch of outcasts nobody wants, so you set up a little supernatural commune out in the desert...or you're hiding something."

She stared him down, refusing to let him see she was intimidated by his sudden change. There was nothing she could do about her heartbeat, though. From the look on his face, he'd definitely heard a shift in tempo.

"Either Darius came along and stuck his nose where it didn't belong, messing up your little secret," he went on. "Or you just don't like him." It was the first time Joseph had said his name. Pretences were over then.

"What do you want, Joseph?" she asked, loosening her grip on her powers. She had little experience fighting—except for the time when she'd punched Vera's witch friend Rosheen in the face—but she'd give it a go. *Who was she kidding?* If Joseph decided to strike, she'd leg it towards the door.

"I'm here for Darius, but I'd also love to have chat with the fellow in there." He pointed to the opal shop. "Frederick Marmaduke Hardy. I reckon you know him."

"So *that's* his middle name," she murmured.

"Sure is," Joseph went on. "It's been a while since I've seen old Hardy, and I'd love a squishy elemental barrier between us."

Eloise snorted. "You're worried he's going to tear your head off?"

"Yeah, *and* I need an invitation." His grin widened.

"I see you've been watching us more than you've let on." She looked him over, not sure if she should be freaked out or not. Not one of them had sensed it, and that worried her.

"I like to do my research."

Eloise regarded him for a moment, but the vampire didn't make a move to retreat or advance. He was waiting for her, and it was that decision that made her nod.

"I think you ought to wait here," she said, giving him the once over. "I'll invite you when I'm sure you're not full of it."

Joseph smirked. "'It' being shite, right?"

Eloise chuckled, despite herself. "Can I ask you one thing?"

"I guess so."

"What were the party poppers for?"

His smile widened. "Why, the afterparty, of course."

***

Hardy looked up from the sliver of black opal he was polishing as Eloise came into the workshop.

"There's someone here to see you," she said, cutting right to the chase.

He cut off power to the machine and the whirring

wound down, whizzing to a stop. "A customer?" He hadn't heard the showroom door and he should have, even over the buzz of the polisher.

"No," she said. "A visitor. *Outside.*"

His frown morphed into a glare. *A vampire.*

"He said his name was Joseph Cheapside," Eloise went on.

The name conjured a flurry of memories, and Hardy sighed. He put the opal he was working on back into its little plastic Ziplock bag and stashed it in the drawer.

"So you *do* know him," the elemental said.

Hardy nodded. "We go back some. Darius is far from the only vampire I've known these past centuries."

"And he's outside..." She was fishing, but if Joseph was here, then the Exiles would know the whole story, eventually. That man had a mouth on him.

"Did you invite him in?"

She shook her head.

"Good." He stood and took a step towards the door.

"Hardy?"

He turned.

"I think he's here to kill Darius," she told him. "I'm not sure his motives are..."

"Pure?" he finished for her.

Eloise nodded.

"If he's here to murder someone, then I'm fairly sure they're not."

She scowled. "You're not concerned?"

"Oh, I'm concerned," he replied. "Just not about Joseph."

Hardy moved through the shop and opened the showroom door. He stepped out onto the verandah as Eloise hurried to keep up, crossing the threshold.

When he laid eyes on his old friend, he smiled for the first time in weeks. Joseph Cheapside hadn't changed one bit, despite the clothes.

"There he is!" the older vampire declared, opening his arms. "Come here!"

They embraced, thumping each other on the back.

"The little elemental looks stunned," Joseph said, pulling back. "I think she thought I was here to rip your noggin' off, old fella."

"Can you blame her?" Hardy replied. "She just met the worst of us."

The vampire snorted and looked him over. "How long has it been? Thirty, forty years…and you're still in this out of the way place?"

"I hate boats."

"You do know they have these amazing things called aeroplanes these days, right?" Joseph waved his hand through the air, imitating a 747. "Tin cans with wings? Any of that ring a bell?"

"Smart arse," Hardy drawled.

The vampire glanced at the elemental. "Be a sweetheart and invite me in."

"Only if Hardy say's it's okay," she said, narrowing her eyes.

"It's fine," he told her. "He's a pain in the arse, but I trust him."

"If you say so." She sighed as if his antics had already exhausted her. "Come in."

Joseph grinned and crossed the threshold. Once inside, his gaze flew around the little showroom, taking in the display of raw and polished stones. "Wow. Look at all this. Opals?"

"It's big money," Hardy replied. "I'm good at it."

Joseph smirked. "Look at you going all honest and upstanding. A sight better than scratching around in the mud for that yellow stuff, eh?"

Eloise raised her eyebrows. Another piece of his past was being revealed and he could tell she was itching to ask for more details, but as far as he was concerned, there'd been more than enough sharing as of late. There'd be time for campfire stories after they dealt with Darius...*if* there was an after.

"It helps having an earth elemental as my chief supplier," Hardy said, nodding towards the workshop. "We can talk in the back." He looked at Eloise, who was still lingering by the door. "You coming?"

Her gaze shifted to Joseph, then back to him. "I'm invited?"

"Of course, you are." He led the way into the back, sensing a silent exchange moving between his old friend and the elemental.

"What's with all the glum faces around here?" Joseph asked as they left the showroom. "It's like someone died." When no one replied, he snorted. "What? Is one hundred and ninety years too soon to start cracking jokes?" More silence. "Ah, I see. You just got the miserable backstory." He clapped a hand on Hardy's shoulder. "Well, it happened a long time ago, and despite our penchant for wallowing in past miseries, it's time to buck up and be the bad arse I know you are, old fella."

Hardy narrowed his eyes. Eloise was right; Joseph was here to kill Darius. *Finally*.

"So, you're finally ready to act," he said with a shake of his head. "After all this time..."

"All talk, is he?" Eloise wondered.

"You don't just wake up one day and decide to murder the oldest living vampire in the world, love," Joseph drawled, wandering along the row of grinders. "I've been looking for our illustrious daddy for the better part of a century. This is the closest I've been to the bugger, and who do I find? *Frederick Hardy*." He poked at the bag of rough-cut opal on the vampire's workbench. "Polishing rocks of all things."

"And here I am," Hardy said. It was a coincidence, but the seal had a way of binding multiple threads of fate—as they'd discovered with Vera. Why was anyone's guess. "What's changed, Joseph? Why now?"

The vampire smirked. "Darius is trying to find a way back to his own world, and by the way he's ramped up his operations, I suspect he thinks he's on the money. This might be my last chance to give the bastard what's coming to him."

Of all the things Hardy could take away from Joseph's statement, his first thought was Eloise. Her elemental powers allowed her to manipulate ether. Ether was spirit, but it was also the stuff that bound their world to the greater universe. It was how she was able to send the Dust Dogs to...well, wherever she'd managed to send them.

His thoughts then turned to the mysterious Andante, the old woman who'd saved Eloise when she'd become lost in the outback. If she even existed, he still didn't know for sure, but he wasn't about to discount it. Anything was possible in the supernatural world.

Then he thought about Finn and the fae. They had a connection to the portal in Ireland, but Darius wasn't fae. He wouldn't want to go to the fae homeland.

What about the seal? To open a portal, he'd need a vast amount of magic. The seal certainly provided enough, but why was he drilling into the iron ore?

Something just wasn't adding up.

"I can see those cogs turning in that brain of yours," Joseph said. "You need to stop internalising and start *vocalising*."

Hardy looked at Eloise. He couldn't say anything without revealing all of Solace's secrets to Joseph, and

Kyne wouldn't be happy. In any other situation, he wouldn't be, either.

Eloise shrugged. "Do you trust him?"

"I wasn't thinking about that," he told her. "I was thinking about you and the..." He coughed.

"Oh, *shit*," she murmured, her eyes widening. "He wants to go back to his own world."

"What are we shitting about?" Joseph asked. "Can I shit along with you?"

"Can we reverse a little here?" Eloise asked, trying to deflect. "If Darius isn't from here, where is he from? Then when, why, and how?"

Joseph leaned towards Hardy and muttered, "She asks a lot of questions."

"I know." He smirked at the elemental. He'd been on the receiving end of a handful shy of a million of them.

"And why do you want to kill him?" the elemental added. "And why should we care?"

"I think you ought to start writing these down," the vampire replied. "I've got a good memory, but even I'm having trouble keeping up with you, love. Besides, who says I'm going to answer?"

Hardy snorted. "If you want my help, you will."

"Who says I want your help?"

"Why else are you here, then?"

The vampire chuckled, his eyes glinting with mischief.

Hardy shook his head. "I'd like to help you, Joseph—"

"I can sense a but coming," he declared. "One thing I haven't missed about you, by the way." He then turned to Eloise. "This guy is always poking holes in my plans with all his buts."

"Because they're always horrible plans," Hardy told him.

"*Are not.*"

"This time, it isn't about you or me," he went on, ignoring Joseph. "There are more things at stake than our own survival."

"I see." Joseph's gaze flickered to Eloise. "Your little supernatural outcast club."

Hardy watched their exchange. Maybe Joseph was the catalyst they needed to take on Darius and *EarthBore*...if their interests aligned, that was.

"Darius has already been here causing trouble," Eloise said. "We have our own reasons why we want to move him on, but it's not for Hardy or me to tell you. In Solace, we decide together."

Hardy nodded once at the elemental, his lips quirking. Knowing how skittish and shy she was when she'd first arrived in Solace, he was proud of her resolve. Eloise Hart was a formidable creature.

Joseph seemed to think so, too. "I knew I was right to approach you first." He opened his arms wide and grinned. "Like a warm hug."

"Don't push your luck," she drawled. "You haven't met the others yet."

"Oh, they're going to love me. Just you wait and see."

Hardy raised his eyebrows. Joseph hadn't met Finn yet—that was an experience he didn't want to miss. Lock them in a room together for five minutes, and they'd either come out best mates or in bloodied pieces.

"So, how do we do this?" the vampire asked. "Do we activate the phone tree? Where's the BatPhone?"

"Is he always like this?" Eloise asked as Joseph began opening and closing drawers like a restless toddler.

"Unfortunately," Hardy drawled. "But don't worry… He'll wear himself out eventually."

CHAPTER 16

Blue's pub was lit up like a Christmas tree. Music and voices echoed from inside, and across the way, Hardy and Joseph lingered outside the opal shop.

Eloise and Kyne watched from underneath the gum tree as the sun set, both anxious to hear what the newest arrival had to say for himself. Dappled light played across the ground as a hot breeze buffeted the eucalyptus leaves overhead and the squawking of parrots echoed across the outback as a flock passed on their way to their own local watering hole.

After witnessing Hardy and Joseph reunite, Eloise pondered the few things she'd learned about Solace's newest vampire. He'd been turned by Darius, he'd also escaped his maker's clutches, and he was plotting revenge—she assumed for the vampiric gaslighting part. He was also another London expat, and judging by his last name, Joseph Cheapside was at least several hundred years older than Hardy. She guessed sixteenth or seventeenth century, though it was still up in the air.

"I feel uneasy about all these vampires," Kyne admitted in a low voice. "Compared to us, they're overpowered."

"Joseph seems decent enough," Eloise said, looking towards the pub. "A little on the smartarse side, but Hardy trusted him enough to have me invite him into the shop."

"I seem to be deferring a lot lately. So much for being a leader."

"As I remember it, it was *reluctant* leader." She kissed him on the cheek. "At least we can't be mind-controlled."

Kyne chuckled. "Oh well, after the super strength, speed, and the fangs, there's always free will. We'll all have the option to scream as our heads are torn off."

"Don't get ahead of yourself," Eloise said, then dissolved into fits of giggles. "*Ahead... Get it?*"

He groaned and wound his arm around her waist. "Don't quit your day job."

Eloise pressed against him. "Are we going to tell him about the...you-know-what?"

"I reckon we hold off for now. Keep it need-to-know. See what he says about Darius."

She nodded as she caught sight of the two vampires approaching.

Kyne followed her gaze and narrowed his eyes,

studying the approaching vampire. Joseph did the same, then flashed her a cheeky wink.

"This is Kyne," Hardy said.

The miner held out his hand, which Joseph took, and they shook firmly.

"Mate," Kyne said gruffly. He didn't appreciate the wink.

It was so full of macho bravado, Eloise sighed.

"The earth elemental," the vampire declared, "otherwise known as the rock supplier."

Kyne glanced at Eloise, his eyebrow rising.

"I warned you," she reminded him.

"Shall we go inside?" Hardy asked. "The others are waiting."

"Yeah, I reckon." Kyne took Eloise's hand and glared at the new vampire. "We have a lot to discuss."

"I'll say," Joseph declared, sweeping his arm towards the pub. "After you."

When they went in, the core Exiles were already seated round their usual table, drinking and discussing theories about the man Drew and Vera had already labelled as 'the tourist'. When they saw the vampire, they stopped abruptly, falling into complete silence.

"Welcome to Solace!" Joseph cried. "Where normal people are weirdos!"

Eloise rolled her eyes and sat beside Vera.

"You weren't wrong," the witch whispered in her ear.

Blue fussed behind the bar, bringing out another jug of beer and a cider for Eloise.

Hardy began the introductions as Kyne pulled up a chair beside Eloise. "This is Blue, the publican, and Wally runs the garage."

"Werewolf, right?" Joseph asked the old mechanic.

"We're the old dogs around here," Wally said with a nod. "We sit back, relax, and let the young ones do all the work."

"We're retired," Blue told him. "Keeping the supernatural peace is hard on my back."

Joseph laughed and shook his head. "Would that I had the same excuse. It gets tiring, always fighting something."

"You wouldn't know what to do with yourself if you were idle," Hardy said. "And that would be terrible thing for everyone involved." He gestured to Vera. "This is Vera. She owns the *Outpost* and is our resident witch."

"How many vampires are there?" Vera wondered. "I never met one until I left Ireland."

"There's more than enough of us," Hardy muttered.

"We stay out of Ireland," Joseph explained. "That's old witch territory. There's certainly more of you all over the world these days, but it's best us vampires don't go there."

"Why?" Eloise wondered.

"We like to keep a low profile," Hardy explained. "By keeping our existence secret from humans *and* supernaturals, we retain a certain power that can work to our advantage."

"Something that was drilled into all of us by a certain maniacal mastermind," Joseph quipped. "Started from day one, then just became the thing that was done. Apparently, vampires are more flashy in Darius's home world. Probably thought he could do better this time around."

Hardy gestured to Finn, who was cradling a bowl of hot chips in his lap. "This is—"

"Finn Oreah'anza," the fae said, smirking.

Joseph looked him over. "And what are you?"

"Fae." He stared at the vampire and shoved a slice of potato into his mouth, chewing slowly.

"With eyes and a getup like that, I don't doubt it."

Eloise watched their exchange closely, but neither man fired up at each other, which was a good start, but the night was still young.

Joseph's gaze moved to Drew. "And I've already met you. The shifter."

"Drew," the dingo-shifter said, narrowing his eyes. "What were the party poppers for?"

"Like I told your pretty elemental, they're for the afterparty."

"For?"

Joseph grinned. "Why the death of Darius, of course. I'm going to pop them over his withered corpse and dance a little jig."

"I think I like this bloke," Finn said.

"You would," Vera muttered.

"We're missing one fellow," Joseph added. "The curious little man I met up a tree."

Eloise laughed, covering her mouth with her hand as the Exiles all turned to look at her.

"That'd be Coen," Hardy told him. "He's on a walkabout."

"A walka-what?"

"Walkabout," Kyne explained. "It's a spiritual journey. An ancient rite of passage for Indigenous Australians."

"*Hmm...*" Joseph mulled over this new bit of information. "You don't say?"

Wally leaned forwards. "What did he tell you?"

"Oh, not much. It was hard to follow, but..." He shrugged. "I don't think he is what you think he is."

"*Sure.*" Vera screwed up her nose. "Then what do you think he is?"

"You do know he's supernatural, right?" When the Exiles nodded, he went on, "I've been around a lot of 'places' in my time and met a lot of 'our folk'—the magically inclined as you'd say—and I've never met anyone quite like him, but I *have*. If you know what I mean."

"No," Kyne drawled, "we don't."

"I do," Finn quipped.

"Oh yeah?" Drew asked the fae. "Then tell us."

"He's talking about the magic that's in all of us," the fae stated. "Coen *is* magic."

"Coen is magic?" Vera asked incredulously. "You're worse than he is!"

Eloise reached for her cider and sipped the sweet liquid. This conversation was going sideways, and fast. "So, how exactly do you know one another?"

"Joseph was the first vampire I met after I left Darius," Hardy explained. "When was it?"

"1850-something," Joseph reminded him. "In the gold rush days at that little tent city. What was it called?"

"Ballarat."

Joseph clicked his fingers. "That's the one!"

"You escaped a raving psychopath to go scratching for gold with a thousand other blokes?" Finn asked with a snort. "You really know how to live it up."

"That's what I said to him!" the vampire declared.

"All this reminiscing is fascinating and all," Kyne said, "but I'm more interested in what we're going to do about Darius."

"We go up to that dig site and descend en-masse," Joseph said. "Kill the bugger and be done with it by dinnertime."

"And what about the *EarthBore* team?" Eloise asked with a shake of her head. "He's compelled them all. If we go up there guns blazing, he'll use them as a human shield. I, for one, would like to avoid collateral damage."

"Make that two of us," Kyne said.

Vera slapped her hand on the table. "Three."

"It won't be that simple," Hardy said. "According to Joseph, Darius wants to go back to his world."

"Hang on a second," Finn declared. "We've got *another* parallel world to worry about?"

Joseph explained it to the Exiles, outlining the few things he knew about the origins of vampires in their world—how they were created by witches from a group of Ancient Romans, *allegedly*—and about Darius's origins. "He's single-minded in his pursuit. He will stop at nothing to see this done."

"If he finds out Eloise can manipulate ether, then he'll try to take her," Kyne said.

"Oh, that's a new bit of information," Joseph stated. "A little portal-opening elemental."

Eloise squirmed. "I can't control it. I can only manipulate what's there. I can't make a wormhole out of thin air, let alone know where I'm sending someone."

"That won't matter to Darius, love," the vampire murmured. "He'll try *anything* once."

Hardy nodded. "I thought the same thing, but I also wondered if it's past time we sought out this mysterious Andante."

"Who's Andante?" Joseph asked, looking between them. "I'm guessing you're not talking about sheet music."

"Huh?" Drew asked, wrinkling his nose.

"Andante is a tempo," the vampire explained. "It's an easy pace. Moderately slow."

"Andante is an old woman I met when I was lost in the outback," Eloise told him. "She knew things."

"Ooh, *things*..." the vampire mocked. "This place just keeps getting wilder and wilder."

Hardy kicked his friend under the table, making the beer glasses rattle.

"Coen's been teaching me how to see when I'm in my dingo shape," Drew told them. "I can keep an eye on *EarthBore* and try to figure out what they're digging up."

Kyne nodded. "Good idea."

"This is all fascinating," Blue said, "but I'm human. Last thing I want is to end up a liability."

"He's right," Joseph said. "He can be compelled."

"I'm working on that," Vera said. "I've found some herbs that I think I can use to counteract the magic you use to do all that, but I need to test it."

"Unless you want to go on a holiday until this is all over," Joseph added, looking at Blue. "Spend a little time by the beach and get a massage for that bad back of yours."

"I'm not the holidaying type," the publican snarled. "I'm staying right here."

"Ah, another fighter, I see," the vampire mused.

"For now, we bide our time," Kyne said, his voice taking a commanding tone. "We watch, learn, and don't take any unnecessary risks. We need to understand what Darius is trying to dig up out there. No one goes on the offensive until we can make sure our homes are secure and Blue is protected from compulsion, got it?"

It seemed like a sensible plan to Eloise, so she nodded her agreement.

"What about me?" Joseph asked. "Do I get membership into the club?"

"Hardy trusts you," Kyne said, narrowing his eyes, "but we don't know you from squat. 'Membership' is earned around here."

The vampire chuckled. "It was worth a shot."

"I know you like to think you're charming," Hardy said, "but you can't expect to come in here with your revenge plot and one-liners and expect us all to jump on board and tell you all our deepest, darkest secrets."

"Of course not," Joseph told him. "I *have* learned a thing or two after four hundred years of throwing stuff at the wall and hoping it sticks. The definition of insanity is trying the same thing over and over again and expecting different results...but sometimes people *are* that insane." He craned his neck towards the bar. "So, since we're on the down-low with daddy dearest, how about a good old piss up, eh? Got any hard stuff, Blue? Why do they call you Blue, anyway? Is that your *actual* name?"

"Before I went grey, I had flaming red hair," the publican replied as he got up. "That's why they call me Blue."

"Makes total sense," the vampire drawled. "I'm guessing it's an Australian thing."

As the man laughed and got down to their drinking, Eloise leaned back and shook her head. Joseph had slotted himself in with little effort; his personality, though harsh at times, was infectious to everyone around him. It wasn't just her who'd sensed it —even Kyne was beginning to ease up on the guy.

She was thankful for the small distraction the night was providing, though Darius and the seal weren't far from her mind. He was trying to get back to his own world and would need something, *or someone*, to open a portal.

If there was a way to send him back without involving the seal, then why didn't they just do that? Flick him off someplace else, like she'd done to the Dust Dogs.

Even as she mulled over it, Eloise knew it wouldn't be that simple. She could only manipulate what was there and had no control over the destination. If she couldn't sense the currents when they needed it, then Darius wasn't going anywhere, and they'd wind up on his lunch menu.

But she'd decided where to send the Dust Dogs and they'd gone. *No*, she thought. *A vision brought me here, and it probably made me think I'd had control when the path was already laid out before me.* Fate and destiny had led her and the current to entwine at the right moment, nothing more.

Then there were the things Joseph was telling them about Darius and his intentions. The Exiles were keeping information back, but so was he. Eloise didn't doubt his intentions—he really did want to end Darius—but his explanation was a little lacking, which left the puzzle with more than a few gaping holes.

Vera tugged on her sleeve. "Hey, you okay?"

Eloise blinked, startled out of her reverie. "Yeah, just puzzling it all out."

"It's certainly a bind we've got ourselves into this time," the witch replied. "You'd think fighting a vampire would be easier than a possessed witch, but here we are."

"Here we are..." She picked up her cider and drank. "Speaking of... How's Clarke?"

"Taking some time out," Vera replied, frowning. "Just until this vampire business clears up."

"Probably a good thing," Eloise told her. "All of this...it's a lot."

The witch nodded. "I'll go see him once I perfect my potion. I don't want to go empty-handed and..."

Eloise placed a reassuring hand on her shoulder. "He'll come around. He did the last time. He wanted to stay and fight for you until Hardy sent him away. This time will be no different."

"I hope so," Vera murmured. "I really do."

Joseph Cheapside was 435 years old. Born in a London that was a great deal more putrid than the polluted

Victorian cityscape Hardy had been pushed out in, he'd seen more cities—and the people in them—rise and fall than he could count.

Solace, though tiny, was no different. These 'Exiles' had only lived a blink in the long span of his lifetime.

He lingered in the shadows outside the ramshackle pub, his mind working overtime. He hadn't revealed everything, not just yet, but neither had they.

Hardy stood beside him, all high and mighty. He was just that kind of guy—all moral and upstanding. Vampirism was a curse to a man like Frederick Hardy —he would struggle with it his entire immortal existence.

"Are you my babysitter now?" he asked, straightening his shirt collar.

"The moment I leave, you'll go straight up to that site looking for Darius," Hardy told him. "I wasn't born yesterday."

"You're keeping things from me, Hardy," he said. "Important things."

"For good reason."

"Oh, I'm sure your reasons are noble, but they sure are inconvenient like that perpetual stick up your arse."

"It goes both ways, Joseph."

His eyebrows rose. "The stick? I hope not."

"You know what I mean."

The vampire smirked. "You were always a smart cookie."

"Still am."

Joseph kept quiet. Hardy was always a tough nut to crack, but he wasn't a threat. There was no way in hell he'd be working for Darius, not after the number the guy did on him. There was twisted manipulation, and then there was Darius.

No, Hardy was his friend and always had been.

"There are things here that need to be protected at all costs," Hardy said with a sigh. "Darius and his operation threaten them."

"Hmm," Joseph murmured. "You have something he needs." Hardy said nothing, which meant he was on the money. "Does it have something to do with that funny feeling I get when I stand in the middle of the highway? Or is it just the anticipation of knowing a truck might be coming along at any moment to squash me?" He laughed. "Which is complete and utter nonsense, because there won't be a truck on that road for another million years."

"You never know."

Knowing he hadn't earned an explanation yet, Joseph glared at the highway. "As long as Darius is dead at the end of this, I don't care what else happens."

"Those are bold words."

"They're *deserved* words." He turned to leave, but Hardy grasped his arm.

"What did he do to you?"

Joseph sighed and clenched his jaw. "He prayed on your vulnerabilities and spent the better part of two decades turning you into a literal monster. Isn't that enough reason?"

"Perhaps, but after all this time, I'd like to hear about you, Joseph."

"I got in his way," he muttered. "That's what happened to me."

"How?"

"You really like to torture a bloke, don't you?"

"Joseph... Have you ever talked about it?"

The vampire snorted. Of course, he hadn't. Who would care about his sob story? Everyone had one and his wasn't any different, and telling it wouldn't change his mind about killing Darius.

"Until recently, I rarely thought about the things that led me here," Hardy admitted. "I didn't want to relive it, but ever since I told the Exiles, I feel lighter. More at peace."

"That's you," Joseph argued. "It's not me."

"It might help." He shrugged. "I'm not about to tell anyone else about it. You know the kind of man I am."

"You're not going to let it go, are you?"

"Probably not."

Joseph scowled, his head filling with long lost memories he'd done his darnedest to push aside. Four centuries was a long time to dwell on all he'd lost, especially since he'd spent the better part of it hunting the vampire responsible.

He was a happy-go-lucky kind of guy, but that was just his mask. Underneath, he was a pit of darkness and anger. Revenge was the only thing that had helped him cling to his afterlife for as long as he had. He didn't fear death...he'd welcome it.

"I was human," Joseph said sharply. "Darius was trying to infiltrate the English court and I caught him. He was outed, his plans destroyed, and I paid the price." Joseph hissed and looked away. "He slaughtered my family. My wife, my son, and my baby girl. *A baby*. After he was done, he turned me into a vampire. I spent decades under his thumb as punishment. Reliving what he did to them. Being tortured and healed over and over. It only stopped because I escaped." He turned back to Hardy, his eyes black. "So, if you try to stop me from tearing out his cold, dead, black heart, I will tear through you, *friend or not*."

Hardy's expression didn't waver. He lifted his hand and placed it on Joseph's shoulder. "I won't, but I need answers of my own." He glanced back at the pub. "And so do they."

Joseph let his anger subside, but it didn't fully recede. After all these years, it never really had.

"C'mon," his friend said, "let's go to my place. I live underground. I think you'll like it."

He felt the memory of his family fade into the background and his heart lightened. "Still scratching around in a hole?"

"Yeah, but this one's got plumbing."

CHAPTER 17

The night was clear as Drew prowled around the edges of the *EarthBore* camp, his dingo feet silent.

Coen had taught him enough so he could *see*, but he still didn't understand what he was looking at most of the time. Colours shimmered through the darkness, revealing the invisible auras and essences of the outback. The trees, the grass, the rock, the dust...he could tell it all apart with his dingo eyes.

Some things were the same hue, while others varied. Even the Exiles had their own unique colours, but they were more complex than plants and rocks, changing from day to day, hour to hour, minute to minute.

Drew had seen Wally tinkering in his garage before he left on his scouting mission, and the old wolf was a swirl of purple and red. Then, when he'd blinked, a flash of blue flared around the mechanic's head.

The *EarthBore* camp hadn't changed much in the last few days. It was still lit up with cold, white lights, but the hole they were drilling was deeper. They'd pulled out the Caldwell and had rolled in the excavator, extending the shaft into a wider pit, and had constructed a ramp out of the rubble to get the truck back down.

To Drew, it looked like they needed to go deeper than they originally planned. Whatever they were searching for was just out of reach, which bought the Exiles a little more time.

"Did you find what you were looking for?"

Drew jumped at the sound of Darius's voice and swung around to face the vampire who stood a handful of steps away. He hadn't heard him approach, let alone felt his presence, but Hardy had warned him before he came out here. Darius was old, and with age came strength.

"I could easily snap your neck, but I want to have a conversation with you, Drew," Darius said. "Which would go better if you were a man."

The dingo narrowed his eyes as he saw the muddy brownish-black aura float around the vampire. It didn't look healthy...for either of them.

"Come now," Darius added. "I can turn around if you'd like."

Drew growled, the sound rumbling deep in his throat, and began to shift.

Darius raised his eyebrows, watching the painful process with sick fascination.

When he was done, Drew stood, unfurling his naked human body. "You got your wish," he snarled. "Say what you want so we can get this over with."

Darius smirked and looked him over. "Those are some pretty scars, shifter. Have you seen Frederick's?"

He resisted the urge to cover his junk. "Stop being creepy and get to the point."

The vampire laughed and looked at the *EarthBore* site below. "Tell me, does your little town mean that much to you? Less than ten people live there, and it barely registers on the map. And Frederick Hardy... Does he deserve your friendship, knowing he is what I am? I did make him in my own image. I scraped him out of a hellhole and taught him how to cast aside his role as the prey and become the predator."

"Yes," Drew said with a roll of his eyes. "All of the above."

He was beginning to suspect Darius didn't know Joseph was in Solace, let alone that they knew about his plans. Best he kept his mouth shut...as much as his temper would allow him to. The vampire might reveal something new or contradict Hardy's new BFF.

"I am the beginning of my kind on this Earth, but I wasn't the first," Darius told him. "All I want to do is to return to my world, but I need magic in order to do so. What's so wrong with that?"

"If I could send you back, I'd open the door and

shove you through myself," Drew told him. "Then slam it in your face."

The vampire chuckled and shook his head. "Dingoes are spirited creatures. Pack animals, aren't they?" His eyes darkened. "Where is your pack, Drew?"

"Wouldn't you like to know." He wasn't about to take the bait or let on that it was Eloise's powers that sent the Dust Dogs to another place—it was what the vampire wanted. "With an attitude like that, how do you know they want you back?"

"Want and need are two different things," Darius replied. "But knowledge and power are the same. I know what lies beneath your little town, and I know what lies within this iron ore." He studied the shifter, searching for changes in his expression. When he smirked, Drew knew he'd found whatever it was he was looking for. "You don't know, do you?" He pondered this for a moment. "You suspect, but you don't know for sure. That's what it is, isn't it?"

Drew said nothing. He liked to think he was cleaver, but he wasn't exactly the sharpest tool in the shed. If he said something now, he'd just be putting his foot in his mouth.

"For all your amassed powers, you supernaturals don't know the first thing about what you're dealing with," Darius went on. "How do you know that what you're protecting deserves it? *Hmm?*" He narrowed his eyes. "How do you know if you're doing the right thing?"

"Of course, we're doing the right thing," Drew hissed. "If that power is released, then—"

"Then what?" Darius interrupted. "If you don't understand what's down there, how do you know what will happen? *You don't.*"

According to Eloise, who'd spoken to Andante, they had a good idea it was an entity tied to the ancient ocean that used to flow over the outback. The day she'd told them what she'd found out, Drew had learned a new word—*calamity*. That sounded bad to him.

Darius didn't care what happened to the people he left behind, only opening his stupid portal.

"And you do?" Drew challenged.

The vampire snorted. "Of course, I do."

"*Then tell me.*"

Darius grabbed his throat, moving so fast his hand was a blur. "No, I think not."

Drew gasped, grasping the vampire's wrist as he felt his eyes bulging.

"I see you people are obsessed with your little town, so I'm going to be crystal-clear, Drew." He jerked the shifter close as his eyes turned completely black. "I don't care about your seal, your town, or this world. I don't care about Frederick or the vampires I created. You are all a means to an end. After a thousand years of toil, I am *days* away from finally returning home. I won't let anyone stop me. Get in my way again and *I will kill you all.*" Loosening his grip, he wrenched the shifter's head to the side.

Drew managed to suck in a sharp breath before Darius struck. The vampire sank his fangs into his neck, tearing into his flesh with a painful rip that splintered through his entire body. Warm blood trickled over his chest and back, spilling onto the ochre dirt.

Darius jerked back, his mouth and chin smeared red. "I won't warn you again." He shoved Drew to the ground.

The shifter landed on his knees, his hand flying to his neck. His fingers slipped through his sticky blood and he hissed as his torn flesh stung.

Joseph was right. Darius deserved everything that was coming to him and more.

"Run dog," the vampire snarled. "Run back to your *pack* and spread the word. Tell them how easy it was for me best you."

Drew stumbled to his feet, backing away into the shadows. He shifted, his bones snapping with every hasty step until he was a dingo again. His neck stung and blood clung to his fur, but he chased the first hints of dawn all the way back to Solace.

Vera was dreaming about sun baking on a tropical beach—complete with white sands, clear blue water, and a hot police officer bringing her one of those fruity cocktails in a coconut shell—when loud banging startled her awake.

She sat up and rubbed her eyes, then checked the time. *Five forty-three a.m.* Who in their right mind would bother a witch before the sun had fully risen? Outside of the solstices, there was no time for sunrise in her world.

The banging continued as she slipped out of her comfy bed and pulled on her silky green dressing gown. Tying the belt around her waist, she hurried out of her bedroom and into the hall.

"Okay, okay!" She pushed through the beaded curtain, making the strands clack furiously. "I'm coming! Calm your farm!" She stormed up the stairs. "This better be good," she raged, wrenching the door open. "I was having the best dr—" The words died in her mouth when she saw Drew standing outside, his neck, shoulder, and chest covered in blood. "What happened?"

"I got chomped on by Darius," he said with a grimace.

Vera almost swore as she grabbed his arm and dragged him inside. Slamming the door closed behind him, she said, "What on earth were you doing to get yourself bitten?"

"Nothing!" Drew complained as they went into the kitchen. He pressed his palm over the bite. "Well, I was spying, but Kyne told me to. You were there, remember?"

Vera sighed and sat him on one of the mismatched chairs at her little dining table and handed him a clean tea towel. "Take that and clean some of that blood off yourself."

Drew leaned over and turned on the tap in the sink, dampening the tea towel. He cursed and carried on as he dabbed it on his bite.

Vera pulled ingredients out of the cupboards and picked sprigs of dried herbs out of the bunches hanging from the ceiling. Vampires didn't have venom on their fangs, so it should just be a simple healing salve she needed. Salt, paw paw seeds, lemongrass, hop bush leaves...

"Hardy could heal this in two seconds," she said, dumping leaves and bark into her mortar. "Why didn't you go see him?"

"Because I reckon it'd trigger that Joseph bloke. I know when a guy is on edge. It's a dingo thing."

"I'm sure it is." She began mixing the ingredients, the pestle releasing a pungent earthy scent.

"If I go marching over there with a vampire bite, it'll be on for young and old," Drew went on. "Kyne told us to lay low."

"Like you were?"

"I *was* laying low." He sighed. "At least, I thought I was. That guy is *creepy*. It's like he was *everywhere*."

Vera didn't say anything, focused on tipping some salt water into the salve to make it stickier. Once she was satisfied, she brought the whole mortar over to the table and scooped up the mixture with her fingers.

"He was fishing," Drew said, wincing as Vera slapped the salve on his neck. "Jesus Christ, what the hell is in that? *It stinks.*"

"Shut up and take it like a man," the witch told him.

He grimaced, his brow creasing. "Darius said the same thing Joseph did. He wants to go back to his own world, and he doesn't give two flying fruitcakes who and what he destroys along the way. We're collateral damage."

"The whole bloody planet is going to be collateral damage," Vera muttered. "For one lousy vampire."

"He knows about the seal, Vera."

She froze, her hand hovering by his neck. A dollop of salve plopped onto the floor and she blinked. "Of bloody course he does," she drawled. "And what does the iron ore have to do with it?"

"He wasn't in the mood to play twenty questions," the shifter retorted and pointed to his neck. "This was his last warning. Next time, it'll be a bloodbath."

Vera said nothing, she just bent over and cleaned up the salve.

"He said he knew what was under it," he added.

She stood and set down the mortar. "I don't think it matters at this point."

"Matter or not, he said he was days away from getting what he needed for his stupid portal."

"Days?" The colour drained from Vera's cheeks and she rubbed her sticky hands over her silky dressing gown. She'd better get a move on and rearrange her to-do list.

"You've got a plan," Drew said, straightening up. Some of the salve slipped away from his neck and fell onto his shoulder.

Vera nodded. "If I can connect to the elements, maybe my magic can guide me to whatever he's trying to dig out of that iron ore."

"Can you do that?"

"I think so." She slipped out of the kitchen and began fussing around in the living room, trying to figure out what she'd need for a spell of that magnitude. Crystals, iron, sage... Crap, Drew needed some bandages for his neck first. She did a U-turn and opened the cabinet under the television, taking out some cloth from her stash.

"Then why haven't you tried before?" Drew asked with a scowl.

"Because it's like a billion square kilometres of the stuff," she snapped, waving the cloth at him. "It's like searching for a needle in a haystack the size of the solar system. Now that they're digging, maybe I can narrow it down." They had days...*days!* "A spell like this is going to knock me out of play, Drew. I..." she looked at him, "I don't know if I should."

"First, I recon you should calm down a little."

Vera took a deep breath and began to unwind the

cloth. She fixed a small square over the bite and pressed Drew's fingers on it to hold it in place.

"The only thing I know, is that we need to stop Darius and free those *EarthBore* employees from his compulsion," the shifter added.

They knew what Darius wanted, but what did the iron ore have to do with it? It was the key to his plans, but why? *How?* Was it a natural amplifier? That much of it was an anomaly in itself, and considering it was this close to the seal, the two had to be linked. Maybe it was a back door of some sort... *That was it!*

Darius needed the entity, but not locked behind a slab of magicked bluestone, but *free*.

"All before he lets out the entity," she murmured, tucking the end of the bandage into the last wrap. "Because that's what he needs to do if he wants to go home."

Drew frowned. "How do you figure that?"

"I've felt what kind of power lies under there. I tapped into it as the Nightshade," she reminded him. "Its magic is dulled while it's trapped, but free... There'd be more than enough to punch a gaping hole through space and time." Whatever came next would be ten times bigger than the arcane tornado the Nightshade had conjured through her. "Darius doesn't strike me as the kind of guy who likes subtlety."

"We've got two vampires, two elementals, a werewolf, a shifter, and a fae," Drew murmured.

"That's got to be enough to stand against a thousand-year-old wanker like Darius."

"Let's hope so." Turning on the tap, she rinsed of her hands. "C'mon. Let's go find the others and tell them the bad news."

CHAPTER 18

E loise picked up the knife and fork and sawed a neat little triangle off the edge of her eggs and toast. The yolk was still runny, and she was careful to slice far enough away to stop it from bursting.

Blue made one hell of a good hot breakfast.

Kyne sat beside her with his own breakfast, eyeing her with a bemused smile. Wally sat to the side, with Blue opposite, and all of them were watching her.

"What?" she asked, raising her eyebrows. "Have I got something on my face?"

"Pick it up with your dukes," Blue told her with a chuckle. "You're not at a fancy restaurant out here. Shove it in your gob and enjoy it."

Kyne laughed and shook his head. "For someone who used to live in a van, you're the neatest person I've ever known."

Wally chuckled and picked up his bit of toast and

shoved it into his mouth. The yolk split and oozed out, dripping on his plate.

"See?" She pointed at the werewolf. "I was trying to avoid *that*."

The wolf chuckled and took another bite.

Eloise put down her knife and fork. "These eggs are the only thing I can control right now," she admitted. "All this business with Darius... We're waiting for the end of the world to come knocking, and there's nothing we can do about it."

"Don't say that," Kyne murmured. "We're working on it."

Her lips thinned. *Not fast enough.*

The door swung open, letting in a gust of warm air, followed by Drew and Vera.

Eloise's expression fell when she saw the bandage around Drew's neck. She didn't have to be a rocket scientist to know the jugular vein was a vampire's favourite target.

"Darius," the shifter said, looking at her. "He knew I was watching. It didn't matter how much distance I had on that camp...he still knew I was there."

"Strewth," Wally said, pulling out a chair for him. "Sit down."

"I'm not going to bleed out," the shifter grumbled.

"As long as you're all right, mate," Kyne told him.

Before they could get any more details, the pub door flew open again. This time it was Joseph who hurtled in.

He took one look at Drew and said, "I thought I smelled blood."

The shifter sighed and glanced at Vera as if he were asking for her permission.

"I want to do a spell to see what he's digging for," Vera said. "But it's going to take a lot out of me."

"How much is a lot?" Kyne asked.

"Almost all my magic...but at least we'll know what he's digging for."

"Are we just going to ignore the gaping wound in the dingo's neck?" Joseph declared. "Or is it personal?"

"We're not," Eloise told him. "Where's Hardy?"

"He went to get Finn."

"You two have the gift of foresight or something?" Drew asked, narrowing his eyes. "Because that's some coincidence."

"Blood in the air in a place like this almost always means bad news," the vampire drawled. "Especially with your newest neighbour hanging around."

Drew snorted. "I know you're looking for an excuse to fly up there and bash up Darius, but this isn't going to be your trigger."

Joseph stepped around the table and glared down at the shifter. "It might be if you don't start being truthful with me."

"*Hey*," Wally said, standing. "We don't go for that kind of behaviour around here."

"I've had enough of you people standing in my

way," the vampire hissed. "I came for Darius, and I'm going to rip his head off, *no matter what*."

"Calm down," Blue said. "Fighting ain't going to help anyone." He slammed a bottle of bourbon down on the table in front of Joseph. "I hear alcohol is just the thing vampires like when they get angry. Have a suck on that."

The vampire unscrewed the lid and downed a mouthful. "*Ah*," he said, licking his lips. "Breakfast of champions."

He was a third of the way into the bottle when Finn and Hardy arrived.

"Twice in as many days," Finn declared, spreading his arms wide. "How about we install some bunk beds out back? The walk here is hard on my feet." He sat at the table and kicked up his feet on a free chair. He saw the elemental's breakfast and reached for Eloise's plate. "*Ooh, eggs*."

"Help yourself," she said with a sigh.

As the fae began to polish off her breakfast, the two vampires shot each other knowing looks. They had a whole silent conversation going on until Wally asked, "Is that some vampire thing we should know about?"

"They're not telepathic, if that's what you mean," Vera said.

"Just as well," Blue muttered. "There's only so much an old human bloke can take."

Joseph glared at Hardy. "Don't you think it's past time?"

"For what?" Kyne demanded.

Hardy said nothing, he just narrowed his eyes. Eloise studied the two vampires, taking note of all the narrowed eyes. Maybe she should start a drinking game.

"Is someone going to tell me the big bad secret you're all keeping?" Joseph looked around at the Exiles. "I don't think we have the time to sit back and wait for me to prove my loyalty, do you?" He turned to Drew. "Darius took a big chunky bite out of you, dingo. Since you're here and not dead, I assume he had something to say?"

The shifter eyed him. "He might've said something..."

Joseph sighed. "Either you open the clubhouse door or I go rouge. *Your choice.*"

Finn sniggered, earning himself a warning glare from the Exiles. "What?" He shrugged. "If you can let me into the clubhouse, then you ought to let him. We all want the same thing and once he gets his revenge, where will he go? Out into the big bad world to tell all his vampire mates about this quaint little magical town he found on the arse cheek of the world. I'd rather slip him a membership form, a promotional T-shirt, and tell him about the seal before Darius pops the cork." The fae's smirk widened. "*Oops.*"

"God save us," Kyne muttered, shaking his head.

"That's one way of solving a disagreement," Wally added.

"Can we get on with it now?" Finn asked. "I'm tired of that vampire and his arrogance. He stinks."

Joseph had been watching with an amused smirk of his own. "What seal?"

"It's a magical rock imprisoning a powerful ancient entity," Eloise explained. "If it's opened, it might destroy the entire world."

"And there goes the cork," Finn said, smiling at Kyne. "*Pop.*"

Joseph's expression turned thoughtful as he mulled over this new information.

Eloise glanced at Hardy, who'd been uncharacteristically silent. The two vampires had become thick as thieves since the day before—they'd obviously spent their night bonding. Whatever plan the elder had been cooking, the younger had jumped on board. Both wanted their revenge, but when push came to shove, would either of them slow down and remember Solace?

Eloise's power tingled a little and she rubbed the back of her neck. She wasn't sure how this was going to go anymore...

"It must be that key," Joseph finally said.

"Key?" Eloise looked at Kyne. "Did he just say...?"

"Yep," the miner replied. "He said key."

Joseph sighed. "It's not the first time you've heard about it, I see."

"What do you know?" Kyne asked him.

"I know Darius made a big fuss over it," Joseph

went on. "Over the years, I've tracked down some of his operations hoping they'd lead to him. I assumed he was looking for magical artefacts to solidify his power, but ever since I realised he was trying to travel to a parallel world, things got a lot more interesting."

"What kind of artefacts?" Vera asked.

"Fae trinkets," Finn said. "There were a lot brought over when our people moved between our world and Ireland. It stands to reason some survived the closure of the portals and travelled to far shores."

Joseph nodded. "And a lot more besides. There are ancient civilisations that had their own supernatural comings and goings. Mesopotamia, Inca, Maya, Egypt, Babylon, the Celts, Norse...all throughout Asia, the Americas, and even Australia. Darius had interests in them all. He funded archeological digs, bought antiquities at auctions, even stole and slaughtered for them."

"So, what's different this time?" Eloise asked.

"This time, he's mobilised an entire company *and* government to dig up a small patch of iron ore in the middle of a remote desert. That's what's different."

"He's gone public," Hardy added. "Before now, he's likely worked in the shadows, keeping his name and presence out of all his dealings. If he's on the ground now, he believes he's found the key. *Literally*."

Eloise looked at Kyne.

"I didn't," he told her. "If I did, then I would've

known about the iron ore and we could've stopped this a long time ago."

"Didn't what?" Joseph asked.

"We already have a key. A coral key," Kyne said. "Whatever Darius thinks he's digging up—"

"*The mountain*," Eloise blurted.

"Bloody hell," the miner cursed, running his hand over his face. "It's *another* one?"

"What else could it be?" The black mass inside that mountain was terrifying. The writhing tentacles, the *nothingness* of it… Rosheen had heard it *speak*. If it was held back by its own seal and Darius found the key, there'd be more than calamity coming for them. If there was a choice between opening the two, she'd choose the one in Solace any day of the week and twice on Sundays, but she'd prefer not to open either.

"Where is your key now?" Joseph asked. "If you're right and this key is not the one he's after…"

"Kyne hid it somewhere only an elemental can retrieve it," Hardy said. "And only he knows its whereabouts."

"Smart," Joseph said.

"So he's got the wrong key," Drew said. "He's going to chuck a tantrum the moment he figures it out, then he's going to come for us."

"And if he can't get what he wants from us, he'll try to work out where the other key goes," Eloise said with a shiver. "Somehow, I think that'd be worse."

"Two seals," Joseph mused. "Two keys…"

"I think you're about to get your wish, vampire," Drew muttered. "Before he took a bite outta me, he said he was days away from getting what he wanted. If we try to stop him, he will kill us all."

Eloise was only half-listening. Her thoughts were fixed on Andante. She was sure the things the old woman had revealed were only a carefully handpicked selection. Kyne was right about her. It was past time they went to pay that secret cave a visit.

"Not just yet," Eloise said. "First, we need to see Coen and find Andante. I'm all for stopping Darius, but we need to understand what it is we're fighting. I'm over not knowing." She looked at the Exiles, then at Joseph and Hardy. "We need to buy a little time."

"If I'm not going to use my magic on that hole," Vera said, "I can cast a barrier spell around Solace. It'll keep Darius out, but I'll need more power."

"How can you get more?" Drew asked. "You're not going to tap into the seal, are you?"

"No, never," she replied.

"I'm out," Finn declared, backing away.

"Finn, I'd never ask you and I'd never use the seal," she went on. "But I *can* channel one of you. All supernatural creatures have magic. I can join it with mine to amplify the spell."

"I'll do it," Wally said. "I'm an old wolf. I'm not much of a fighter these days outside of a full moon. At least I'll be useful this way."

"What about that Coen fellow?" Joseph asked.

"Coen doesn't fight unless he has to," Kyne told him. "If we need his help, he'll come."

"And what about you, old friend?" Hardy asked.

"I think I can hold back my murderous revenge plot for a few hours," the vampire replied, his gaze shifting to Eloise, *"for a warm hug."*

"Don't push your luck," Kyne growled.

"I meant a *literal* hug," Joseph said with a roll of his eyes. "It wasn't a euphemism."

Eloise liked Joseph, but she could see his vampire traits emerging the more she got to know him. And now that she thought about it, she could spot the same in Hardy. The abrupt change in mood, the lingering haze of power, the reliance on their predatory senses, and the old-world thinking—the latter was the most infuriating of the lot.

"So, are we just taking his word for it?" Drew asked. "Cheapside says it's a key, so that's it?"

"No, it's not it," Kyne told him.

"Andante will know," Eloise said. "I've got a feeling she hasn't told me everything."

"And how is that any better?" the shifter asked. "I trust you, Eloise, but why should we put our faith in an old woman who lives in a cave?"

"An old woman who no one has ever seen, except when you were dying of exposure in the outback," Finn reminded her.

"She was real," she snapped. "Coen's seen her, and he wouldn't lie."

"He also likes to leave out most of the details," the fae quipped.

"I'll go with you," Kyne said, taking her hand. "That way, you'll have a witness...and some backup."

"And someone to turn the screws on her," Drew said sullenly.

Joseph snorted. "You're worried about believing what I said about the key and you're arguing over the existence of an old lady in a cave." Unfortunately, everyone had reached their peak Joseph Cheapside quota for the day and were ignoring him.

Hardy nodded his agreement with Kyne and Eloise. "Joseph and I will help you with your spell, Vera." He gestured at Drew. "And I'll sort out that bite. I don't doubt the miraculous magical qualities of that balm, but it's rather pungent."

"Told you so," the shifter said to Vera.

The witch punched him on the arm. "We better get to work. I've got to go home and get some things. The sooner the barrier is up, the sooner I'll feel better." She shivered. "The air feels heavy."

Hardy nodded. "I can feel it, too."

Eloise stood and brushed her palms over her shirt. "And the sooner we find Andante, the better I'll feel."

Joseph slammed the bottle of bourbon on the table. "If you're not back by tonight, I'm going to take matters into my own hands. I've waited long enough to give Darius a taste of his own medicine. I've cooperated with you long enough and old women in caves is where I draw the line." He tapped the face of the watch on his wrist. "Tick, tock, little elemental."

"And I was just about to offer you that warm hug," Eloise drawled.

Kyne took her hand and pulled her towards the door. "C'mon. We better get going before Darius figures out what we're up to."

"He won't give us any more warnings," Drew reminded them. "If he catches any one of us, it's over."

Eloise bit her bottom lip, her heart skipping a beat. Everything seemed straight forward enough within the safe walls of the pub, but she was out of her depth again. Vampires, keys, ancient entities, parallel worlds...it was all getting a bit much. Then there was the time crunch.

She just hoped Coen knew how to find Andante, because she didn't have a clue what to do next.

CHAPTER 19

Hardy lingered outside Vera's dugout, watching the surrounding outback for signs of movement. Other than the odd hawk wheeling overhead and the rustling of leaves in the ghost gums, nothing else stirred. Nothing that he could see, anyway.

He tried not to dwell on their impending doom, but it was difficult to say the least. He knew what Darius was capable of, and so far, they'd been lucky, especially Drew. His maker could've left the shifter's body on Vera's doorstep and it would've served the same purpose, so why didn't he? Why didn't Darius kill Drew?

The door opened, breaking through his thoughts, and Vera stepped out into the sunshine.

She carried a calico shopping bag over her shoulder—the outside printed with the words 'Wicca Happens'—and the fabric bulged with the various things she'd gathered for the barrier spell. A bit of paper flapped about in her hand as she fumbled with putting the key into the lock, and he hoped she hadn't had to write down the instructions. This spell had to go right if they wanted to protect Solace and the seal.

"I'm ready," Vera said, locking the door behind her. "Where's your sidekick?"

"Staying out of sight at the pub," Hardy replied.

"Probably a good thing to keep him on the sauce, but leaving him with Finn…?"

"They're fine," he told her. "They're both rash enough to keep each other in check."

She shook her head. "Two negatives make a positive?"

"Something like that," he said with a chuckle. "Besides, if Darius is watching us, I'd rather keep Joseph's presence a secret. What's the paper for?"

"I've made a map," she said. "To cover the whole town, I reckon we need at least twelve points. A dodecagon."

Hardy raised his eyebrows. "Who knew witchcraft was so technical?"

Vera chuckled and handed him a bit of paper. "I'll put a crystal on either side of the highway at the north and south ends, one behind Kyne's dugout, one behind Drew's, then one in the scrub here," she pointed, "then behind the pub, and mirror it on the other side."

"Then once the circle's complete?"

"Back to the pub to channel Wally."

Hardy looked over the map and nodded towards the highway. "Closest point is the road to the north."

They walked in silence. Hardy could hear Vera's heart thrumming a little faster than usual. Despite her brave face, she was worried—all the Exiles were. Standing up to a vampire as old as Darius was nothing short of a suicide mission. They needed some serious magic of their own if they wanted to best him. Luckily, they had Vera. Even without her Nightshade legacy, she was a formidable witch. Hardy had every confidence in her ability and then some.

Still, he kept an eye the road and the surrounding scrub. There was a chance Solace was being watched, whether by compelled *EarthBore* employees, an unknown magical artefact, or an unseen vampire, it didn't matter—Vera needed to make this quick.

They reached the northern limit of Solace in short order.

Vera knelt in the dirt, set the bag on the ground, and rummaged inside it. She took out a jagged piece of cloudy white quartz and held it up to the sun. When she was satisfied, she placed it on the ground, twisting it around until she found the perfect angle.

"I thought witches used salt," he said, watching her place the crystal.

"We do, and it would be preferable for this kind of spell, but we're a little short on table salt at the *Outpost*." She looked up at him and smiled. "In the absence of a metric tonne of the good stuff, we have to readjust our expectations a little. Besides, it's not good for the environment out here."

"And the crystal?"

"Quartz is a natural amplifier and battery pack," the witch explained. She stood and dusted the ochre dirt from her knees. "It can produce an electrical reaction given the right conditions. Put enough physical stress on it, and you have a little battery with a positive and negative end. That's not magic...it's science."

Hardy grinned. "Science and magic. Who would've thought, huh?"

"Oh, and clocks. Quartz has a precise frequency standard that helps regulate time."

"You're a wealth of knowledge." He nodded towards the crystal on the ground. "Where to next?"

She pointed across the highway. "The other side."

They crossed and the witch repeated the process, setting the crystal into position and angling it so it reflected the best light.

"How do you feel about it?" Vera asked as they hurried to the third point.

"About?"

"Everything," she replied. "Is revenge really what you want?"

Hardy shrugged and sidestepped a clump of vicious spinifex grass. "I never approached it like Joseph did. He had it a lot worse than I did, and I was never the kind of man who defaulted to violence."

"So, you don't want to kill him?"

He'd thought about it but had never tried to find Darius or plan any kind of punishment for what he'd been put through. He'd simply tried to move past it by going out into the world in an attempt to work out who he was as a vampire. Frederick Hardy wasn't the same person who'd tried to steal medicine for his dying sister—that man had died in Port Arthur.

"Darius saved me from certain death, but he also condemned me to suffer through his tutelage," he said. "Part of me will always want to honour the life he gave me, and the other part will always hate him for it. For me, revenge isn't as simple as it is for Joseph."

"Mercy isn't a strategy we can afford right now," Vera warned. "There's much more at stake here."

"Oh yes," Hardy said. "He certainly needs to be stopped, but it doesn't matter to me if I am the one who ends his life or not...if it has to be ended at all. Maybe it is as simple as helping him find another way back to his world."

"Even if we offered, do you really think he'd listen?"

Hardy grimaced and shook his head. "I don't think so."

The loss of any life was a damn shame, even the life of someone considered bad. Everyone was the hero in their own story, and no one was purely good or evil. Right and wrong was a constantly shifting barometer that moved wildly within the confines of society. He'd seen it change over the course of his long life as the world matured and modernised. What was acceptable a hundred years ago would never fly in the twenty-first century. What was evil now wasn't evil then.

And Darius…? A thousand years had twisted his soul until he saw neither good, evil, or the barometer of society. All he saw was his own self interests. Add in vampirism and his predatory nature, and the only person Darius was good for was Darius. He was his own hero, after all.

"There's nothing that ties him to this world," he said as Vera placed the last crystal. "There is nothing here he cares about. No family and no history other than his quest to return to where he came from."

"He has his own revenge planned," Vera mused. "I wonder what happened to him? Someone had to have been angry with him to send him all the way here."

"I don't doubt it."

They'd reached the next point and Vera took another crystal out of her bag. She knelt and positioned the milky white quartz, checking the alignment with the sun.

"Hardy?" Vera looked up at him. "There is a way out of this, isn't there?"

He didn't reply straight away. He didn't want to frighten her, but he wanted to be realistic. Every story didn't always have a happy ending. Some were tragic, some just faded, and some never came to a close. He wasn't sure which of those this mess with Darius fell under.

"There's always a way out," he finally told her. "We just have to have the courage to find it."

They returned to the pub once all the crystals had been placed.

Vera knew Hardy was just trying to be realistic yet optimistic about things, but she'd faced her own fair share of trouble to know the magnitude of what was coming for them.

Finn sat at the bar, snacking on some hot chips, while Blue loaded some shells into his shotgun. Joseph lingered, eyeing the gun with exasperation.

Wally stood as Vera and Hardy came in. "All set?"

"All set," she confirmed with a nod.

"Where do you want me?"

"Here." She sat on the floor and gestured for Wally to sit beside her. The old wolf managed it, with some grumbling about his old bones, and took her proffered hand.

"So, what do I do?"

"Nothing," she replied. "Just sit still and don't say anything."

"Any trouble out there?" Joseph asked.

"All quiet," Hardy told him. "Hopefully, it was the good kind of quiet."

"*Shh*," Vera hissed. It'd been a long time since she'd done this kind of magic—being possessed by the Nightshade didn't count—and she needed to concentrate.

The pub fell silent, and she closed her eyes. Calling on her power, and searching out Wally's werewolf magic, she opened her mouth to begin the spell...but the words died in her throat.

The door flew open and Darius stormed in, his eyes black and fangs bared.

He smashed a piece of quartz against Drew's temple, sending the shifter flying across the pub. The dingo slammed against the wall with a bang and blood poured out of his torn flesh.

Blue reached for his shotgun, but he had no hope. Luckily, Darius thought the same thing and let him be. The vampire picked up a chair and smashed it against the wall and picked up the broken leg.

Joseph launched himself at the vampire with a roar, but his flight was met with the shard of splintered wood. Darius rammed it into his chest, staking Joseph in one fluid motion.

Then, as Finn's magic began to rise, the vampire grabbed the fae around the scruff of the neck and threw him over the bar. Shattering glass echoed through the pub as Darius turned, grabbed Hardy's head, and twisted.

Hardy went limp and crumpled to the floor, and Vera stood, her magic flaring. Before she could unleash it, Darius scooped up Hardy's prone body and disappeared.

It was over in seconds.

Vera let her magic wane and Wally scrambled across the floor to Joseph.

"*Bloody hell*," the werewolf cursed, leaning over the vampire. "He's turning grey."

"The..." Joseph coughed, spitting blood. He swatted uselessly at the chair leg protruding from his chest. "*The wood...*"

"It's next to his heart," Vera said, pushing Wally aside. "It's killing him."

"*Pull it out*," Joseph gurgled.

Vera didn't think twice—she would've chickened out if she did. She straddled the vampire, wrapped her hands around the splintered chair leg, and heaved.

The wood came free with a sickening slurping sound, followed by a strangled cry of agony from Joseph, and she tossed it aside.

"Did it work?" Wally asked, his eyes wide.

Joseph gasped and sat up, almost knocking Vera flat. His skin was regaining its colour and his lips quirked. "Yeah, it worked," he said, smirking at the witch. "I didn't know you liked me so much."

She scrambled off his lap and wiped her bloodied hands on his shirt. "*You wish.*"

He undid the top button and pulled the fabric aside, and they all watched as the gaping hole in his chest healed.

Blue handed Drew a clean tea towel as Finn dragged himself out from behind the bar.

The fae picked glass out of his dreadlocks and surveyed the scene before him. "Well, that was a performance. I didn't even get a chance to use my magic."

"We had no hope," the shifter groaned and pressed the tea towel over the gash on his temple.

"He took Hardy," Blue said, his hand still on the butt of his shotgun.

"And my spell is screwed," Vera added, picking up the bloodied crystal off the floor.

Joseph dragged himself to his feet and stumbled towards the bar. Reaching over, he grabbed the nearest bottle of alcohol, which was a Jim Beam and cola pre-mix, and unscrewed the lid. Blue didn't stop him as he chugged the whole thing.

"He's got a hostage now," the vampire said, dropping the bottle into the sink. The glass clattered loudly. "And we've lost the element of surprise."

"So why didn't he kill you?" Finn asked.

"He almost did," Joseph replied. "If it wasn't for Vera, I'd be brown bread. I'd like to say Darius doesn't miss, but the chap has gone all sloppy like." His accent had deteriorated into something that Vera recognised as a thick London cockney.

"Brown bread?" Drew asked, screwing up his nose.

"It's cockney rhyming slang." His near-death experience had obviously gotten to him and his mask was slipping. The real Joseph Cheapside was bleeding through—no pun intended. "We need to rescue Hardy," Vera went on. "I'm not going to leave him at the mercy of that man. Kyne or Eloise wouldn't want it."

"Darius won't kill him," Joseph said, his gaze moving to the door. "Not yet, anyway. We've got a bit of bird lime."

"Oh no you don't," Vera warned, stepping in front of him. "You're not going up there guns blazing until Eloise and Kyne get back."

The vampire snorted. "From their magical mystery tour? You seriously think they're going to find all the answers in some old woman's cave?" He pointed towards the door. "Darius has Hardy, and I know the kinds of things daddy dearest is going to put him through. It's nothin' but Barney Rubble. He won't wait until your elementals get back from their honeymoon, and he certainly ain't going to rabbit and pork. The only language Darius understands is violence."

"I don't understand half the things he's saying," Drew muttered sourly. "But I reckon I get the gist of it."

"The only cockney slang I know is Khyber Pass," Blue said.

Finn perked up, suddenly interested. "What's that?"

"Your arse," Wally told him.

"Shut up!" Joseph shouted, slamming his fist onto the bar, which let out a loud crack. "Don't you people take anything seriously?"

"Careful there, mate," Blue growled, "that's my bar you're breaking."

"Of course, we take things seriously," Finn said with a scowl.

"We do things differently around here," Vera said before things deteriorated. "We're not vampires, and we're certainly not prone to violence. Hardy wouldn't want us rushing in there to save him at the cost of our own lives...not unless we had no other choice."

Joseph threw his hand into the air. "So you're just going to sit in here and wait?"

"Yes," she told him. "I'll forgive your anger, Joseph, because you're new around here. You don't know us and the things we've already been through to protect the seal. I've seen the things Eloise has done since she's arrived, and I trust when she says Andante has the answers."

"*Might* have," Drew muttered.

"If there's a way we can rescue Hardy without putting the entire world at risk," the witch went on, "then that's the route we're going." She narrowed her eyes and lifted her hand. Briny blue magic pooled in her palm and she pointed at Joseph. "If you try to screw things up for us and Hardy, I will stop you. I don't give two flying fruitcakes about your revenge."

The vampire snorted and eased back against the bar. "Spoken like a true witch." He nodded to the bloodied crystal she'd set on the table. "So, is there anything you can do with that in the meantime?"

Vera sighed and picked it up, turning over the beautiful piece of cloudy white quartz. It was one of her favourites. "Yeah," she said, setting it back onto the table. "Actually, there is... Anyone got a hammer?"

"I do!" Finn declared and slammed his fist down onto the quartz, which shattered, splitting into five almost equal pieces.

Vera stared him open-mouthed. She'd felt his magic for the first time and was shocked. The fae camp had a barrier of its own around it, but she knew it was an illusion—something Unseelie fae were masters of —and a trick wouldn't have kept Darius out.

"How long have you been able to do that?" she asked.

Finn smirked. "Oh, for about a thousand years or so."

CHAPTER 20

Eloise looked up at the boab tree and thought about Coen.

Kyne stood beside her as they waited for the Indigenous man, his expression grim.

"Have you noticed that Hardy's speaking all proper since Joseph arrived?" she asked.

"Yeah, I have. He sounds like all my essays in high school," Kyne mused. "I'd put all the 'don'ts' as 'do nots' to up the word count."

Her mouth fell open. "You didn't!"

"Nah, yeah, totally did."

Eloise smirked and looked up at the boab. "I did, too."

Kyne took her hand. "I knew you were a rebel."

"Hello."

Eloise jumped, her heart lurching, and looked up. Coen sat in the branches of the boab, his eyes sparkling with mischief as he grinned down at them.

How he even got up there, she didn't know. The boab trunk was smooth and wide, but everything he did was mysterious. It was best not to ask questions unless she wanted to have her mind blown with a cryptic answer.

"Coen," Kyne said with a wave. "How's it going?"

"It goes," he replied. He looked to the north, his brow creasing. "And you?"

"That's why we're here," the miner told him. "We're running out of time."

"We need to speak to Andante," Eloise added. "Can you help us find her?"

Coen nodded as if he expected her to ask and pointed to the east. "Make paths by walking."

Kyne made a face. "Just walk east? Are you sure?"

"Of course, I am," he said with a chuckle. "You are both elementals. The Dreaming calls to you." He poked Kyne in the chest. "Even you can hear through the rocks in your head."

"I'll pretend I'm not offended by that," the miner grumbled.

"The vampire lingers, but he won't see you," Coen added. "Walk and you will find her. East, in the dark spaces between the stars. It's time she woke up."

Eloise blinked, wondering if it was Coen's way of saying Andante needed to come out of her cave. She hoped so.

"So, we just walk and we'll find the cave?" She looked up, but the Indigenous man was gone.

"Sometimes I'm not sure if we should take

everything he says literally, but then, at times like these..." Kyne nodded to the east. "We better get a move on."

They headed into the scrub, weaving through the gum trees and dodging clumps of spinifex. Kyne showed her the way, using the sun to guide them. The vegetation thinned the farther they went from town, but it was still a winding maze and it was easy to get turned around without a point of reference. Eloise had learned that the hard way.

The land was flat, the outback stretching into a plain of red and sunbaked green. A few rocky outcroppings littered the horizon, rearing like jagged shards of rusted metal, but none of them looked like they harboured an invisible cave.

Eloise was just wishing they'd brought water with them when a flash shone through the scrub.

"Did you see that?" she asked, tugging on Kyne's arm.

"See what?"

She pointed as three golden lights emerged in the distance, peeling away from the scant shadows and began bobbing through the scrub.

"The Min Min," Kyne said.

"In daylight? I thought they only came out at night." Eloise watched the orbs dance about, transfixed as they flared brighter, then dulled. She remembered them in the darkness when she was lost and was glad there wasn't a kadaitcha—a vengeful shadow spirit—

lurking out there. There'd be a lot of snakes sunbaking on rocks this time of day, but thankfully, she'd seen few of those.

The miner looked around and breathed deeply. "I don't think we're in our own world anymore."

Eloise tensed and peered at the sprites. Had they stepped onto a path that led them to the Dreaming? She wasn't sure she should be here, all things considered, but Coen had pointed the way. He trusted them—if he didn't, she was sure the way would've remained shut.

"Do we follow them?" she asked.

"Normally, I'd say no. The Min Min have a habit of leading travellers astray...but I reckon we're good." He kept walking, allowing the sprites to guide them along the path.

They'd been following the lights for about fifteen minutes before they darted around wildly, buzzing like busy bees, then flew straight up, disappearing into the heavens.

As Eloise looked around, she gasped as the air shimmered, revealing a large rock formation rearing into the sapphire sky. The veil cast by Andante's magic fell away like a clear gossamer curtain, the spider-like webs sparkling in the sunshine.

"Now that's some magic," Kyne murmured, holding his hat in place as he looked up at the rust-coloured rock. His eyes flared amber as he reached out with his elemental power. "It's quartz sandstone, eroded over millions of years, to form cone karsts."

Eloise stared up at the rock formations in awe. They looked like giant beehive-shaped towers, each made of banded stone in yellows, oranges, and browns. Another remnant of the ancient coral reef that gifted them with the opal that built Solace.

"I've seen these before," Eloise said. "They're the same as the Bungle Bungles."

"Purnululu," Kyne said with a nod, speaking the Indigenous name for the famous rocks in Western Australia.

She took one last look before she started walking. "C'mon, let's keep going."

They found a dark opening at the base of the formation, their path leading them where they wanted to go. Coen was right as usual—all they had to do was walk with their destination in mind and their elemental powers would guide them to the bullseye. Handy, even though that kind of magic came with zero fanfare.

"We're looking for a cave, so..." She stepped into the tunnel, leaving the heat of the day and submerged herself in the cooler interior of the karsts.

"What is this place?" Kyne asked behind her, his voice hushed. "It doesn't feel...*right*." It must be his latent elemental affinity for ether that spoke to him, or he was feeling the disconnect between the cave and the earth it should be attached to.

"A place locked away in space and time," Eloise replied. "Which is why no one in Solace has ever found it."

They emerged in a small cavern, finally reaching a landscape she was familiar with.

A hole in the roof let in a beam of warm light and a campfire crackled in the centre of the 'room'. A lumpy mattress lay to one side and a variety of baskets woven out of strips of dried bark sat against the cave wall, but there was nothing else of note, other than the runes carved into the banded stone.

An old woman emerged from the shadows, her eyes narrowed at the elementals. She'd woven her wiry white hair into a long plait, her clothing looked handmade, and her feet were bare, but her eyes shone with an intelligence that made the two elementals hesitate.

"I'll be stuffed..." Kyne said, taking off his hat. "You were right."

"Of course, I was," Eloise huffed. "This is Andante."

"If you're here, then you must be in trouble," the old woman said, not offering a hello. "Otherwise, that thunder cloud wouldn't have told you where to walk."

"Coen?" Eloise asked.

"That's the one." She reached out and slapped Kyne's hand away from the wall. "Don't touch that."

He snatched his am back and screwed up his nose. "Why?"

"It'll fry your brain, that's why," the old woman snapped. "Sit down before you hurt yourself."

The miner looked at Eloise. "It's just a rune," he said. "A Norse rune."

"It's not," Andante said.

Eloise frowned and looked around the cave. It was covered with carvings—runes and other symbols she didn't recognise—and they seemed to make her powers tingle. The last time she was here, she'd been on death's door, dehydrated and not one hundred percent sure she was in her right mind. Now that she had a handle on her magic and understood the supernatural ways of the world, she was positive Andante's cave held more than just a few scratches on the walls.

"I think you should sit down, Kyne," she said. "Andante owes us an explanation."

"I don't owe you anything," the old woman said, sitting by the fire. "You're the ones who knocked on my door."

"You rescued me from the outback all those months ago, then dumped all those ominous warnings into my lap," she retorted. "Now I'm in my right mind, I have the right to ask questions."

Andante let out a *humph*. "Then sit before I change my mind."

"You never said she was grumpy," Kyne muttered, earning himself a swift kick in the shin.

The elementals sat, crossing their legs. Eloise didn't

think it was best to push, so instead, she waited for the old woman to explain what she would.

"My people are the Druids," Andante said. "An ancient arcane race of travellers with the power to bend space, time, and the fabric of nature itself."

She held out her hand and the elementals watched in stunned silence as bright blue magic pooled in her palm like metallic liquid...then began to grow. Shimmering strands emerged, forming lines and turning corners, creating a complex geometric shape that shone with purples, greens, and blues that reminded Eloise of holographic cellophane.

The runes on the walls began to glow, responding to the rush of magic and charging the air with static. She was right to warn Kyne away from them. They were anchors for her magic, like the sigils Vera used in her spells.

In that moment, as they watched the threads grow, Eloise realised Andante wasn't an old hermit scratching out a living in the dirt. She lived like the mobs who'd called this place home for thousands of years before Australia was colonised. She lived in harmony with the land, sky, and spirit. Her cave lay within a strand of what she called space and time, but what the Indigenous peoples called the Dreaming. The dark places between the stars where Coen told her he looked to the ancestor spirits.

Andante's magic went beyond their world and into places Eloise could only barely touch. Her elemental gift was unique, but the old woman's was boundless.

"I have travelled far, across many worlds, and have been hunted along with my people for a thousand years," Andante went on, shaping her magic.

"Hunted?" Eloise asked. "By whom?"

"Darkness…" she murmured, "and the things that live within it."

"Is that why you hide here?" Kyne asked.

"The Druids are watchers," she snapped. "We do not interfere. *We are not warriors.*"

"You're pacifists," Eloise murmured. "That's why you haven't come to Solace. You know what we face there."

She nodded curtly. "I do."

"If you watch, then you know the danger we're in," the elemental added. "You've seen Darius and what he's done to those *EarthBore* workers…and what he plans to do to the seal."

Andante nodded again and allowed her magic to solidify.

Kyne snorted, his temper rising. "And still you won't come out of your cave to help us?"

"There are more dangers to worry about than vampires," the old woman said, scowling at the miner. "Many more."

The druidesses magic flared and gained form and colour until she held a bouquet of flowers—daisies, pansies, and cornflowers.

"Tell us," Eloise urged. "If you've been watching us, then you understand how close we are to calamity. That's the word you used, remember? *Calamity*."

Andante let the construct dissolve, the flowers falling away in a shower of glittering sparkles.

"You remind me of my niece," the old woman said. "Of Gilhana. She was just as spirited as you. She made the ultimate sacrifice for our people, remaining behind to protect those who remained."

"I'm sorry..." Eloise murmured. "Do you know what happened to her?"

"I do not know. She... She took up the mantle when I would not."

Her heart sank and she glanced at Kyne. Andante had refused to help her own people and her niece had stepped up in her place. Maybe that's why she remained here, as some sort of penance.

"Andante," Eloise murmured, reaching for her hand. As her fingers brushed her cold, wrinkled skin, Andante looked up, her eyes glowing with the threads of her magic. "Will you help us now? Will you tell us what we face so we can understand it?"

The old woman pulled her hand back and looked at Kyne, who'd been sitting stoically beside Eloise for most of their meeting.

"I don't claim to understand anything you've already told us," he said, "but maybe this is a chance to make up for old regrets. It won't change the past, but maybe it can help you find some peace with your future."

Andante's face softened but she remained silent. For a while, the three sat beside the fire and listened to the crackling logs. Eloise's anxiety rose, knowing what they'd left behind in Solace—Vera was casting her boundary spell, but it was only a temporary fix—and the longer they sat, the closer Darius got to the hidden 'key' within the iron ore.

Finally, Andante drew in a deep breath.

"In this world, it was called the heart of the ocean," she said, gazing into the fire, "but its threads weave through many curtains, stretching outwards like the roots of a great tree."

"The tentacles." Eloise glanced at Kyne, Andante's words conjuring the vision of the mountain they'd seen on Valentine's Day.

"Yes," the druidess said. "Thread, tentacle, root... They're all just words describing the same thing."

"Then what is it?" Kyne asked. "The thing under the seal...the mountain? What are they?"

"My people, the Druids, call them the Old Ones. Entities as old as the universe itself, neither living nor dead. Made from the particles that created everything, they exist between worlds, between space, between time...just out of reach to all but a few." Her gaze moved to Eloise.

"My powers," she whispered, a chill running down her spine. "That's why I... That's why I see it."

Andante sighed, a sadness creeping into her expression. "It calls to you. The mountain."

"I dream about it almost every night." Her hand found Kyne's. "He's seen it, too."

"Why?" Kyne asked. "Why is it looking for Eloise?"

The old woman shrugged. "I do not know. There is no way of knowing until she stands before it."

Eloise swallowed hard. She'd never go to that mountain if she had any say about it.

"I'm guessing your people have a history with these things," the miner said to Andante.

"Unfortunately," the old women told him. "Our leader made a pact with an Old One. We were hunted by the Darkness and faced our extinction. Our only hope was to return to our ancestral home, but in order to stop our enemy from following, we needed help. The entity would guard our home world in exchange for the souls of the unworthy." The runes on the wall flared dully. "The Darklands are a black, crystalline world that all Druids must travel in order to reach home."

Kyne snorted. "Let me guess, only 'the worthy' make it."

"The Old Ones have no emotions. They feel no joy or sorrow...they know no mercy. They have no benevolence for biological life, thus they cannot be reasoned with."

"And one of those things is buried underneath Solace," Eloise murmured, her heart sinking.

"And lives within your black mountain," Andante said, effectively dropping the mic.

"Of course, there is," Kyne said with a heavy sigh. "Soon we'll have Old Ones coming out of every orifice."

Honestly, Eloise still found herself confused about most of what Andante had revealed. What did the Old One want? To destroy worlds? Or was it just what they did, like a natural predatory response like a vampire needed to hunt to survive? At the thought of these entities needing to devour worlds like a juicy hamburger, she shivered.

"Whoever trapped the Old One under your town, did so long before I arrived," Andante said. "Quite a long time."

"And it's different from the Old One in the mountain?" Kyne asked.

"It seems so."

Eloise watched Andante as she spoke, and knew she had her suspicions about who'd sealed up the heart of the ocean, even though she wasn't voicing them. Maybe it was important they found out who had imprisoned the Old One and why, but for now, it was more pressing to stop Darius from opening the seal and letting it out.

"The vampire is digging," she said. "He's looking for something buried in a mass of iron ore north of Solace. Do you know what it is?"

Andante shrugged. "A key, perhaps? I do not know

anything that would be worthy enough to bury inside iron that deep."

"We have the key to the seal. I hid it myself," Kyne said. "It has to be the key to the mountain."

"You won't know until you dig it up," the druidess added.

"Uh, hell no." The miner shook his head. "It can stay down there."

Eloise was only half-listening to their exchange. Her mind was full of all the things Andante had revealed about the Old Ones, especially the mountain. If she was dreaming about it, was it calling to her? Her visions had led her to Solace, where her van had promptly broken down, her magic grew, and... It was all beginning to feel like one huge cosmic manipulation, and she was not going to stand for it.

"Andante," she began, leaning forwards, "you've given us so many answers, but we didn't just come here to talk. We came here for help."

The druidess narrowed her eyes and said nothing.

"Is your magic linked to your life?" she went on. "Does it fade if you're gone?"

Andante shook her head, her lip curling. "I know what you ask, child."

"Then you see the sense in it."

"The Old Ones stretch over hundreds of worlds," the druidess said. "I cannot contain it all."

"Then just hide the part that reaches into ours,"

Eloise pleaded. "If we can't help the entire universe, then at least we can safeguard what we can."

"A little is better than nothing at all," Kyne agreed.

Andante's lips thinned. "We have been given extraordinary gifts, but we are not masters of nature. Do not fall into the trap of believing you have total control over the forces you shape." She made a point of looking at Kyne. "Both of you should remember that."

Eloise's shoulders sagged. She was saying no.

"So you won't help," Kyne hissed. "You'll just keep sitting here in your stupid cave while your Old Ones erase our world."

"They're not *my* Old Ones," the druidess said. "They cannot be defeated."

"Andante, *please*," Eloise pleaded. "We don't know what to do..."

The old woman said nothing. She didn't even move. It was becoming obvious she'd given all the help she was willing to while taking the Druids' role as pacifists to a whole new level.

"We need to get back to Solace." Kyne stood and glared down at Andante. "We've sat on our arses here long enough. She won't come, so let her rot."

"*Kyne*," Eloise hissed. She stood and looked down at the druidess. "Andante? Will you come with us?"

Silence was her only reply.

"C'mon." The miner tugged on her hand. "We don't have much time left. If we want to stop Darius, we have to go now." He pulled her across the cave.

Eloise looked over her shoulder as they stepped into the tunnel, her heart heavy. To say she was disappointed by Andante's choice was an understatement. At least they knew what they were protecting now, never mind how ambiguous it all seemed. A new piece of the puzzle had slotted into place, and they would return with a renewed sense of urgency...but they'd have to take on Darius by themselves. Andante's magic was powerful, they could do with her help, but they couldn't force her.

"There are so many things I don't get..." Kyne said as they clambered back through the cave. His temper had seemed to ease now that he was away from the glowing runes. "Are these Old Ones at war with one another? And who locked them up in the first place? Are we just collateral damage?"

"All I know is that we're trying to hold back forces too powerful for people like us to stand against. We're a grain of sand on a beach the size of a grain of sand compared to these things, and that's being wildly generous." *Old Ones.* Even the name sounded ominous. "Whatever they are or what they want seems irrelevant. They'll destroy our world for no particular reason, and it'll be all *no hard feelings, that's just how the cosmos works.*"

"When you put it like that, it's frustrating as." Kyne took her hand, helping her over a rough outcropping of rock. "It feels like they're waving their hands at us and saying they want to destroy us all because... 'reasons'."

That was exactly what they were doing. Mulling it over wouldn't help them, not now, not later, and not ever. The only thing that seemed reasonable was to keep their access points plugged—and that meant keeping the seal closed.

As the elementals left the shadowy cave and stepped into the burnished afternoon sun of the outback, Eloise felt a stab of melancholy in her heart.

"I can't help feeling sorry for her," she told Kyne.

"Why? It's her choice to sit in that cave."

"I guess..." She looked back at the rock formation, but it'd dissolved, disappearing into the illusion of Druid magic. "But...she's all alone."

"Also her choice." Kyne wasn't budging on his assessment of the old woman. "We reached out to her and she declined." That was a loaded statement, but she didn't have it in her to bite back.

She wondered how long Andante had lived in her cave amongst the karsts, and how long it'd been since she'd seen her niece Gilhana. Perhaps it'd been a thousand years or maybe more, just like the number of all the worlds she imagined the druidess had visited in that time. Maybe her niece was long gone.

She'd wanted to ask, but as they moved west across the outback, Eloise knew there were some stories that weren't for her to know. They belonged to other people, in other worlds far away from her own.

But her story, and that of the Exiles, was still unfolding. Safeguarding them and the world at large was her only concern right now.

Eloise sighed, knowing Joseph was about to get his wish. A reckoning was coming for Darius, and not a moment too soon.

CHAPTER 21

It wasn't the first time Hardy had his neck snapped. It'd snapped so many times in his early years as a vampire, it was a wonder it hadn't come off entirely.

As he came to, he felt a dull ache in the base of his skull. It bloomed outward, twisting around his vertebrae and down his spine and up through his brain and into his temples. The magic that'd created him had a cruel way of letting him know he was still alive.

Hardy jerked awake, his eyes flying open, and his arms and legs met with resistance. His skin hissed as the ropes burned into his flesh, sending a sharp throb of pain through his body. The bonds were wet with... What was it? Acid? He didn't know of anything else that would eat into his skin like that.

He sat on a chair, his ankles and wrists bound, and around him was the khaki-coloured canvas of a tent. Outside, the sounds of men and machinery clashed and banged. He must be in the *EarthBore* camp.

The chair wasn't fixed to anything, and he was about to try and break it when the tent flap swept back, letting in a bright shard of sunlight.

A shadowy figure strode in and the canvas fell back into place, plunging the tent into shadow.

Hardy blinked, his eyes adjusting enough to make out Darius standing before him.

"It's such a shame," the vampire said, looking down at him. "You showed so much promise, Frederick. *So much*."

He pulled against the ropes, but whatever they were coated with not only hurt, but sapped his strength. "What do you want with me?"

"You are collateral," Darius replied, turning away. "I can't afford any more interruptions."

Hardy said nothing. He looked around the tent, but it was bare. There was nothing he could use as a weapon or use to escape.

"Your witch was putting up a barrier spell," the vampire went on. "Next, it would've been an all-out attack. I can't have that."

"They won't stop fighting," Hardy rasped. "Jo—"

"Joseph?" Darius laughed. "You think he can kill me? He's been following me for centuries and he still hasn't managed it. He was a pathetic creature when I turned him, and he's still a pathetic creature now. He was a *waste*." He smirked, an evil glint sparking in his eyes. "I wonder if any of them had the guts to pull out that stake. Is he still alive? Or are they burning his corpse out the back of that tin shed they call a pub?"

No! Hardy snarled and jerked against the ropes. It only caused his flesh to sear even more, and his expression twisted as the pain reached an almost unbearable height.

"I put him out of his misery," the vampire went on. "Which is what I'll do to you once I've got what I want. I'll be doing you a favour."

"There has to be another way," Hardy hissed. "This can't be the only way to open a portal."

"It is the only way," he murmured. "I've been searching for it my entire life, but I never understood until now. A thousand years in this world and a thousand more in another."

Hardy stared at him. Two thousand years was more than he'd suspected, which made Darius even more dangerous than they'd anticipated. It was a suicide mission before, and now...? What was worse than that? There wasn't even a word or concept to encompass it all.

"I've heard its call and I'm inches away from finding the key to unlock it all," Darius went on. "I will set it free, and when it breathes the air of this pathetic world once more, it will send me home."

It was that moment that things began to click into place. Darius had been sought out by the entity—just like Eloise had been sought out by the mountain. He was being manipulated, but how much of it was true?

If he going to be rewarded or not was still up for debate.

Hardy knew enough about what lived underneath Solace to understand it would never bargain. All it wanted was to be set free. There would be no time to open any portal because they'd be swept away. The entity was using Darius and the vampire was too blind to see.

"It's corrupted you; can't you see that?" Hardy shook his head in disbelief. "It won't help you. How can it?"

"How can it not?" Darius knelt before him and smirked. "The creature you contained under your pathetic town exists over multiple worlds. Once I break the chains of its prison, it will be able to go where it pleases...and take me with it."

"No, it won't. You'll die with the rest of us."

"Let me go," Darius said. "Then you will have this world all to yourselves."

"That's not going to happen," Hardy rasped. "To get out of this world, you have to go through a lot of people I care about and then some. I won't let it happen."

"Oh, Frederick..." Darius said, his eyes darkening, "who said you had a choice?"

Hardy was sure the Exiles would come for him, and Joseph wouldn't give up a chance to exact his revenge on Darius. If he was trapped here, then the least he could do was try to buy them a little time.

"Just tell me one thing," Hardy said, trying to stall. "Why did you choose me?"

Darius looked down at him, his eyes black and unfeeling. For a moment, Hardy thought he wouldn't get an answer, that he'd live out the rest of his immortality never knowing, but the vampire smiled, his lips pulling into a vicious curl.

"You're not special, Frederick...far from it. You were a wretched whelp on the verge of death. You were a nobody. *Nothing*. You weren't chosen, you were *convenient*."

The blow didn't hit as hard as he expected, and it didn't change anything. Frederick Marmaduke Hardy was still the same man he was thirty seconds ago. He supposed he'd always knew this would be Darius's answer. Hearing it...well, it was just a full stop on one long, tortuous sentence.

"If you'd given me a choice..." Hardy muttered. "If I'd understood what you wanted to turn me into, I would've said no."

Darius chuckled. "You say that now, after all this time, but you and I both know that's a lie. The broken man I remember laying in that filthy hole would've done anything to get out. You would've said yes."

Hardy shook his head. "You think you know everything, but you're wrong. I didn't want to leave."

"Not even to go back to your family?"

"No, not even that."

The vampire snarled, shot forwards, and grasped Hardy's head.

As they stared at one another with unmasked hatred, Hardy realised that Darius thought he'd saved him. That he'd given him a *gift*. That's why the vampire was so beaten out of shape when he'd escaped.

Darius *did* care about something, but it wasn't Hardy. It was his legacy.

"Then you're just as delusional as all of them," the vampire snarled...then twisted.

***

Darius emerged from the tent wiping his bloodied hands on his handkerchief. It was a tad old-fashioned to carry the little square of fabric around, but he'd never seemed to have let go of the habit. Besides, they were useful in these kinds of situations.

A man wearing a dusty high-vis *EarthBore* uniform walked up, seeing straight through the blood. He tipped the edge of his hardhat and said, "The machinery is ready to go."

"Good. How far do you estimate it will blast?"

"Another dozen metres, I reckon."

Darius pondered the figures. One blast wasn't enough, but he had enough power to get to the depth... and by sunset, he'd have the key in his hands.

"Our guest?" the man asked, looking towards the tent.

"He won't be bothering anyone," Darius said. "I will deal with him this evening. Tell the men to steer clear of the tent until then."

The man nodded and scurried away, the compulsion Darius had woven in his mind driving him to his next task.

He approached the edge of the pit and tucked his handkerchief into his trouser pocket. What had begun with a small core drill had now expanded into a ditch twenty metres wide. The *EarthBore* employees had constructed a ramp so the excavator could get in and out, then reversed the truck with the Caldwell drill down so they could drive farther into the iron ore. It was slow going, but they were nearing the key.

He stood at the lip of the hole and looked down. A brushed silver orb hovered at the bottom, lazily rotating counter-clockwise.

It was too bad Frederick and his band of outcasts had spoiled his plans. Darius hadn't wished to use the orb, but push had come to shove. Truthfully, he was eager to see what it could do.

A thousand years had brought him to his moment.

Once, Darius couldn't have even imagined such an expanse of time, but now that he'd lived almost twice as long? It seemed like it was all over in a blink of an eye.

He would never forget the day he was sent to this place, a world that was so like his own, but not.

He'd been fighting with the Saxons against the

Danes during their second invasion of England in the eleventh century—an event which had transpired in both places but had ended much differently in each. Here, the Saxons won, defeating the Norwegian king Harald Sigurdsson outside of the city of York. In Darius's world, the Danes prevailed.

Vampires played their own roles within the chaos, using the instability to further their own agendas. They fought one another, factions splitting between the new breed of demons and those loyal to their bloodlines. Darius was one of the latter, but in defeat... many had died. Many he'd cared about.

He hissed at the memory of the Viking witches and their *blóði fjölkyngi*—blood magic. Sacrificing everyone and everything to their so-called *gods* and playing with ancient power they didn't understand. The coven had torn him apart, spilled his blood over their sigils, and sent him into the void.

Did they know he would arrive here? He'd had a long time to dwell on it, and he'd concluded that no, no they didn't.

Darius had not only survived their punishment, but he *thrived*. There was no guarantee his enemies— vampire or witch—still lived in whatever new world they'd created, but go back he would.

The orb's humming sounded like triumphant music, a herald for his imminent homecoming. A reckoning was approaching, and Darius would deliver justice where it was deserved.

The compelled man had returned while he was lost in thought and lingered just outside his field of vision.

"Activate the device," Darius commanded. "It's time to end this."

The rugged outback scrub parted as Eloise and Kyne made their way home.

Her heart was heavy, not only with the revelations of the entity underneath Solace, the Old One—but Andante's story. The life the druidess had left behind, the fate of her people and the pact they'd made, her niece's sacrifice, and her regret over not stepping up when it counted.

Eloise had hoped their fight with Darius and the seal was Andante's chance for closure and to make up for her regret, but she'd chosen to remain in her cave. As she and Kyne reached the town limits, she wondered if asking the old woman to help was a little selfish on their behalf. Their fight wasn't anything like the battles the Druids had faced. The Exiles were just a bunch of random supernaturals, why would she?

She sighed as they left the scrub. The boab tree loomed before them and she looked at Kyne, realising they'd passed into town without smacking into the invisible barrier Vera had been working on.

The air felt like it always did—hot and dusty—and there was no sign of any magic...not even a tingle.

"I thought there was supposed to be a barrier," Eloise said. "I can't feel anything..." She paused. "Hang on, am I *supposed to* feel something?"

"We shouldn't have been able to walk back into Solace, if that's what you mean," Kyne replied, his brow furrowed. "Vera should be here to let us back in."

Now that he mentioned it, Eloise thought it was a little too quiet. Solace was usually a tumbleweed kind of place, but it felt as if the intensity had been turned all the way up. Maybe it was the weight of all the things they'd learned from Andante, or perhaps it was the looming threat of Darius. She shook her head, wondering if it was just her mind playing tricks on her. It wasn't every day that people learned their town was built on top of a multi-dimensional spirit-like thing that was probably as old as the universe itself.

The thought of it conjured an image of the tentacled darkness living inside of the black mountain and she shivered.

"Something's not right," Eloise said. "I don't know if I'm just creeped out or..."

"I feel it, too," Kyne said, looking up at the boab. "If the spell went wrong, the others will be waiting at the pub."

Something had gone wrong. Darius had come back

and this time, he'd drawn blood. She felt it in the air. Her skin prickled and her head turned towards the highway. "*Oh no.*"

"Don't jump ahead of yourself," Kyne told her. "Not just yet."

They hurried along the track behind the *Outpost*, keeping away from the highway in case it was being watched. Darting across the side road, they slipped around the back of the opal shop, then into the yard at the rear of Blue's pub where they skirted the building to the front.

Kyne rattled the door, but it was stuck. He thumped his fist on it. "Hello? Anyone there?"

"You didn't say knock, knock," Finn's muffled voice came from within the pub.

"Just open the door," Eloise called out, shifting her weight from foot-to-foot.

The air shimmered, splintering with shards of steely blue magic as the door opened and Vera appeared.

"We were getting worried about you two," she said, letting them inside.

"What happened to the barrier?" Kyne asked. "Why is it only on the pub?"

Eloise was the first to step inside and she jerked to a halt.

Joseph and Drew were covered in dried blood, a broken chair was pushed into the corner, the glass-fronted fridges behind the bar were shattered, and all the tables were up against the walls. It must've been one hell of a spell.

"What happened?" Eloise asked, her gaze moving to a mop and bucket propped against the bar. The whole pub smelled like cheap pine lime disinfectant. She scanned the room and didn't spot Hardy. "Where's Hardy?"

"Darius paid us a visit before I could finish the spell," Vera said glumly. "He gave Drew a nasty concussion, staked Joseph, ruined my barrier...and took Hardy hostage."

A twist of fear wrung at Eloise's heart at the thought of Hardy being back in the clutches of the vampire who had ruined him. *They had to get him back.*

"Staked Joseph?" Kyne narrowed his eyes at the vampire, who was seated at the bar.

"Your little witch pulled it out before I kicked the actual bucket."

"*What?*" Kyne exclaimed.

"I'm fine, thanks for asking," Joseph drawled. "Did your old cavewoman give you any answers? Because I'd like to go up there right now, tear Darius apart, and get my friend back."

"Depends on what kind of answers you were hoping for," Kyne said with a grimace.

"Bloody hell, here we go," Drew muttered. "At least the old bat exists."

Eloise hung back as Kyne told them about the Old Ones. Hearing it all again made her head spin, and at least eighty-five percent of it sounded completely bonkers.

Everyone stared at them in stunned silence until Finn leapt up onto a chair and declared, "Hands up who thought it was a person and *not* a tentacle monster!"

The Exiles and Joseph all thrust their hands into the air.

Kyne frowned at Vera. "You've seen it and you still thought it was a person?"

The witch shrugged. "There's some real whacked ghosts out there, *just saying*."

"So, your old woman was a bust," Joseph said. "I hate to say I told you so, but—"

"We learned some valuable information," Eloise snapped, her anxiety getting the best of her. They were talking about the Old Ones when they should be devising a plan to rescue Hardy. "It may not help us beat Darius, but we understand *exactly* what's at stake now."

"Do you?" the vampire asked. "Because it all seems a bit la-di-da to me."

"I wouldn't count Andante out just yet," Kyne said.

Eloise turned. "What makes you say that?"

"I pressed all her buttons. Hopefully one of them worked."

"It's nice that we know about these Old Ones and all," Vera said, "but it doesn't help us right now."

"You're right. Nothing's changed." The miner

sighed and turned to the Exiles. "The mission is still the same. Protect the seal at all costs."

"And Hardy?" Wally asked. "We can't just leave him there."

"We'll get him back," Kyne said, looking at Joseph.

The vampire narrowed his eyes. "Now can we do things my way?"

"What do yo—"

BOOM!

The ground shook and glass bottles clattered behind the bar, sending the Exiles reeling. Eloise almost jumped underneath the table, but she clutched Kyne's arm instead, her eyes widening.

"What in the blue blazes was that?" Blue exclaimed.

"Darius…" Vera said. "He's blasting."

"Blasting with what?" Drew exclaimed. "A nuclear bomb?"

Finn coughed and put up his hand. "Fae trickery, that is."

Eloise gasped as she saw the droplets of blood on the fae's palm. "Finn?"

"That's one of those magic trinkets Darius has dug up, I reckon," he said with a shrug. "If I'm feeling it, the others are for sure. Siora's going to be *mad*."

"What others?" Joseph demanded.

"The other fae," Finn told him with a shrug. "They don't get out much."

"This town is the gift that keeps on giving," the vampire drawled.

Kyne placed his hand on Vera's shoulder. "I don't know what's going to happen out there, but you might be our last line of defence. Can you put a barrier around the seal?"

The witch nodded. "I can, but I'm not sure how effective it'll be."

"Anything is better than nothing," he murmured.

"I'll stay with you," Drew said. "I'll shift and keep watch."

Blue picked up his shotgun. "I ain't no match for vampires and fae explosives, so I'll cover you, Vera."

Wally nodded his agreement. "Another vote for this old dog sticking with the town."

Kyne turned to Eloise.

"No way," she said, crossing her arms. "I'm coming with you to get Hardy. I won't argue about it, so keep your trap shut, Kyne Brady, and let's go already."

Finn sniggered and backed towards the door. "You heard the little desert pea. Let's get this show on the road before I get blown to bits. Blue's already running low on disinfectant."

"Hang on," Joseph said. He picked up the broken chair and smashed it against the wall. Gathering the splattered pieces, he handed them out to the elementals and the fae. "You can't go up there empty-handed. Stab him in the heart with this and it'll all be over."

Finn flipped his bit of chair over in his palm and grinned. "Cool."

Eloise held her chair leg and stared at the jagged point. She hoped she didn't have to use it...but if it came down to it, she'd shove it into Darius's cold, dead heart.

"Let's go," she said, shoving the door open.

"When did she get so bloodthirsty?" Finn asked behind her, but she wasn't listening—her thoughts were firmly on Hardy.

Hang on, she thought as she strode towards the highway. *We're coming.*

One of the first things Joseph had learned about Australia was how vast the distances were. The *EarthBore* camp didn't seem so far from Solace on the map, but it took them thirty minutes at top speed to reach minimum safe distance.

He pulled the silver hire car off the highway—voiding his insurance—and into a secluded thicket of gum trees slightly south of the *EarthBore* dig site. Kyne was sitting in the front passenger seat and pressed his palm against the dash to brace himself as the car jerked to a halt. The tyres slid in the loose dirt, spitting gravel out behind them.

Finn and Eloise sat in the back, and both had been silent the whole way up here.

Explosions continued to rock the whole area, the length between the detonations shortening. The last one felt like it'd gotten down to fifteen minutes. The one prior, twenty.

Finn felt them all, though he kept it to himself. He was as strong guy, but it was clear he was on the edge of an agonising end.

He cast a fleeting glance at the fae, who was looking increasingly worse. To Darius, the bomb was a way to blast deeper into the iron ore deposit, but for Finn, it was a weapon of mass destruction, one capable of mass genocide.

They got out of the car and made their way up the rise, weaving through the scrub. A plume of rust-coloured dirt marred the impossible blue of the sky, but the sun still beat down on their shoulders, hot and relentless. As they reached the top, they crouched low, silent as they looked down on the scar Darius had opened up across the outback.

Joseph surveyed the dig site, his gaze flying across the tents, to the machinery, then to the pit. It sank into the ground like a meteor crater, the dust and debris kicked up by explosions coating everything in a layer of red. The yellow excavator had turned a muddy brown and the khaki tents sagged as the falling dust gathered in the dips and creases of the fabric. Joseph tasted the grit on his tongue and spat, though it wasn't the dirt that had him worried.

"Hardy's in the tent in the middle," Joseph said.

"How can you tell?" Kyne asked, keeping his voice low.

The vampire narrowed his eyes. "I can smell blood. Lots of it."

Eloise tensed beside him. "We have to get down there."

"I'll say," Finn muttered, holding his side.

"We need to split up," Joseph said. "I'll grab Hardy and go after Darius."

"You can't do both those things," Eloise told him. "I know vampires can heal, but if it's as bad as the look on your face says it is, you're going to need help." Joseph looked at Kyne, but she scowled at him. "I'll go with you."

Kyne shook his head. "Eloise—"

"*No*," she snapped. "You and Finn should go after the bomb. I owe this to Hardy. I told him I'd be there no matter what, and I won't let him down…not now."

Joseph felt a pang of jealousy as he felt the full force of the little elemental's ferocity. It'd been a long time since someone had gone to bat for him like that. A few centuries pursuing the immortal megalomaniac that had murdered his family and spending a couple of decades of being mercilessly tortured had left little room for much else. If he was being honest, he didn't know who Joseph Cheapside was without his revenge plot.

Another explosion shuddered through the ground and the magical shockwave hit them all at once. For

Joseph, it felt like a wave of static electricity, but Finn doubled over and coughed, spitting droplets of blood over the ochre dirt.

Eloise put her hand on the fae's back in an attempt to soothe him.

"We've got about ten minutes," Finn said, wiping the back of his hand over his mouth. "I reckon it might be the last one. My insides feel like slime."

"Then we go," Kyne said. "Finn, you're with me." He shot a warning glare at Joseph. "I'm trusting you with her."

Eloise sighed and turned towards the *EarthBore* camp. "I can look after myself."

"C'mon," Finn said. "Our little desert pea will be fine. Me, on the other hand...I'd like it if I didn't turn into pink mist in the next nine minutes."

"Watch out for the humans," Joseph said. "They'll be compelled, so don't bother trying to reason with any of them."

"Don't worry about us," Finn rasped. "I've got some tricks of my own."

Kyne nodded his agreement and turned to Eloise. "Be careful."

"I will." She smiled. "Love you..." Her gaze moved to Finn, "both of you."

"*Wow*," Finn said, backing away towards the pit. "Love you too, desert pea."

Joseph led Eloise down the side of the hill, following the natural growth of the scrub. She stumbled a little in the scree and he steadied her before she landed on her backside. When they reached the last scrap of cover, he held up his hand.

He scanned the camp, looking for *EarthBore* workers and listening for movement. All he could hear was the rumbling over in the pit—the tents cast out an eerie silence that made him pause.

Darius wasn't anywhere to be seen, but that didn't mean they were in the clear. He just hoped Kyne and Finn would get by undetected. Then, once they got Hardy out, he'd search out his maker and draw him away from the pit. Then he'd finally get his chance to kill him.

"Where are all the *EarthBore* workers?" Eloise whispered.

"The pit, probably." He wasn't looking a gift horse in the mouth.

They skirted around the camp, keeping their heads low. The smell of blood rose with each step, along with the burn in his throat—his vampire side rearing its ugly head like an allergic reaction. They reached the main tent and the smell intensified.

"Stay behind me," he told Eloise. "I'll go in first."

He didn't wait for a reply. Sweeping back the tent flap, he saw Hardy and his stomach dropped.

The vampire was laid out on the ground, his arms over his head and his legs splayed, both wrists and ankles impaled with rusted bolts and hooks. The metal kept Hardy's wounds from healing, allowing his blood to drain, taking his strength with it. The ground was soaked, the metallic reek of it thick in the air, and Joseph had to hold his breath for a moment.

Eloise gasped behind him, "*Oh my God.*"

Joseph put his hand on her shoulder. "Stay back. I'll get him down."

"But—"

"Eloise," he interrupted, "he's been drained of most of his blood. When he drops, he'll start to heal, and that takes..." He coughed. "Well, he might not be able to control himself."

Her eyes widened and she nodded. "O-okay."

The metal had to be connected to another of Darius's magical artefacts. There wast nowhere near enough reinforcement in the earth to hold anyone in place, especially not a vampire.

He knelt beside his friend. "Hold on there, old chap," he murmured. "Let me just unhook you."

He grasped the first bolt and snatched his hand back. His flesh sizzled and he hissed.

"What is it?" Eloise asked.

"Magic," Joseph told her.

"Can you undo them?"

He nodded. "I can. It'll just hurt like hell..."

Hardy moaned, his eyes cracking open. Joseph grimaced and grabbed the bolt again. He twisted, his flesh burning, and pulled it free. He moved to the second, the third, and the fourth as Eloise looked over his shoulder, the sound of her anxious heartbeat thrumming in his ears.

When the final bolt twisted free, Hardy's eyes flew open and he gasped, his back arching as he clawed at Joseph's arm.

"Hold on, old fella," he said.

"The seal," Hardy rasped. "It's got into his head. It's corrupted him."

"I don't doubt it, old fella," Joseph said. "Just wait until you hear what that crazy old woman told your friend here." He rubbed his thumb over one of the wounds. It was healing, but much too slowly for his liking.

It all seemed a little too easy...but Darius had been counting on it, hadn't he?

Hardy's gaze flew to Eloise. "What are you doing here? You can't—"

"I can and I will," she told him. "I promised you."

"You don't understand," Hardy said, trying to sit. "He wanted you to—"

The tent flap opened with an abrupt *whoosh*, letting in a shard of sunlight...*and Darius.*

Eloise yelped as Joseph grabbed her arm and yanked her behind him. Hardy *might* feed, draining her of all her blood, but Darius would *definitely* kill her. She was much safer within Hardy's reach.

"Joseph Cheapside," Darius drawled, his eyes turning black, "it's about time you made your move."

CHAPTER 23

A rust-coloured haze billowed out of the pit, muddying the brilliant sapphire summer sky.

Kyne and Finn made their way around the edge of the *EarthBore* camp and headed towards the hole.

It was buzzing with activity. A worker was driving the excavator back towards the truck where another man was preparing the tray, clanging chains noisily. Another man stood on the Caldwell rig, messing with the hydraulics. Another appeared to be walking the perimeter of the pit, his bright yellow hardhat bobbing through the haze.

Darius was nowhere to be seen.

Finn pressed his closed fist against Kyne's chest, holding him back as the yellow hardhat passed. Once the man's back was to them, the fae stepped out into the open and made a beeline towards the pit, leaving Kyne no choice but to follow.

They'd made it halfway when Finn skidded to a

stop. An *EarthBore* employee stood a dozen paces away, staring straight at them. The man's white hardhat had turned a dull shade of rust, and his high-vis overalls weren't so reflective anymore.

Kyne tensed, his muscles coiling as he readied himself to leap, but the man straightened his hardhat, turned, and walked in the opposite direction.

"What the...?" he muttered. "He was looking right at us. There's no way he didn't see us."

"I'm an Unseelie fae," Finn told him. "I like to charm beasts, but my real talents lie with illusion magic."

"You could have told me. I almost pissed my pants."

Finn sniggered and made his way to the edge of the pit.

"That's how you hide your camp," Kyne said, following him. He already suspected that was the case, but the fae had never explained it. It was best that he didn't, all things considered. Secrets lost their power the more people who knew them.

"I can make people see what I want them to... within reason." Finn looked over his shoulder. "But they can still hear us, so as much as I like having this deep and meaningful conversation, we best zip our lips."

They stood at the edge of the pit and looked down into the dusty crater. The ramp Drew had told them about had been obliterated by the explosions, so they were forced to slide down the side. Their boots skidded in the scree—which changed colour as they descended through the top layers and into the iron ore—and kicked up a thick cloud of dust in their wake.

Kyne's heartbeat sped up and he looked up towards the rim. No one had spotted them or called out their presence...*yet*.

"Here's the culprit," Finn said from below.

Kyne reached the bottom and coughed as dirty air filled his lungs, but when he saw the silver ball hovering a metre and a half off the ground, his expression fell. He'd never seen anything like it in his entire life.

It rotated slowly, an unmistakable static charge building up around it. He thought he could see some kind of symbols or writing etched on the outside, but he wasn't certain. His power flared, his earth magic sensing silver, quartz, and something else he couldn't quite put his finger on—a foreign material from another world, most likely.

"What is it?" he asked.

"That's an *ash'strad*," Finn replied. "Nasty business is what it is. In my homeland, the fae have been through some pretty nasty civil wars. War is bad enough but when magic is involved, you get things like this."

"Yeah, but what does it do?"

"It's a bomb."

"Of course, it's a bomb."

Finn made a face. "Then why'd you ask?"

Kyne resisted the urge to snap. Sometimes Finn's dryness really got on his goat, but since they were standing before a primed magical explosive, he took a breath. "What does it do?"

"It'll keep going off in increasing waves of intensity until," Finn clapped his hands together, "*boom*. It will blow the ground apart like a meteor crashing into the Earth, and every fae within a five-kilometre radius will go splat." Kyne's eyes widened. "It's the magic, you see. That's why they're called *ash'strad*."

"I don't know what that means," Kyne said, his temper rising. They didn't have time for this.

"It literally means death star," the fae told him. "And yes, I've seen *Star Wars*."

"What do we do now?" He moved around the spinning orb, the buildup of magic making his bones rattle. "Can we shut it down?"

"Nope."

The miner's expression faded as he realised what it meant, not only for Solace and the seal...but for Finn.

"There has to be a way," he said. "It can't end like this."

"It has to end sometime," Finn told him, and for the first time Kyne thought he saw what looked like fear in the fae's silver eyes.

"*No*." He grasped Finn's arm and wrenched him away from the bomb. "Not today."

The fae stumbled, then steadied himself. He'd gone quiet...too quiet.

"*Finn.*"

"I think…" His brow creased. "I think I can trap the explosion around the orb. It'll contain the shockwave and make the device implode." He clicked his fingers. "No, I know it will." He lowered his hand. "Wait…"

"Which is it?" Kyne asked. "You think or you know?" They only had a few minutes to decide.

Finn bit his bottom lip and looked at the *ash'strad*. It rotated in a serenely menacing way, making Kyne's hackles rise along with the hair on his arms.

"I can do it," the fae said.

"Finn," Kyne grasped his shoulder, "will you survive this?"

He shrugged. "Maybe. Probably… It's hard to say."

"Then there has to be another way."

"Yeah, nah," the fae said. "There isn't, but my magic is the only thing that'll contain the blast. We *are* on a timer, you know."

Kyne grimaced and grasped Finn's shoulder. There wasn't anything he could do to stop the device or dampen the blast. Even if he could cover in the pit with his elemental magic, it wouldn't be enough. The shockwave was the real danger, and no amount of rock could stop it from tearing Finn and the other fae apart.

He shook Finn to get his attention. "I know you think you always get the rough end of the stick, but you've always been part of our family."

Finn smiled and grasped the miner's shoulder in return. "*Ashlar an lor, shride lei an val'ash.*"

Kyne didn't know what that meant, but it sounded a lot like goodbye. "I'll see you soon, *okay?*"

"Go," the fae told him. "I like to think I'm amazing, but there is a margin of error. Our little desert pea will kill me if you kick the bucket."

"You're very noncommittal, you know that?"

Finn chuckled. "I like a good surprise. Save one of Joseph's party poppers for me?"

"You got it."

Kyne scurried up the side of the pit, using his elemental power to steady the scree. When he reached the top, he cast one last look downwards but couldn't see the bottom through the dust.

"Good luck, mate," he said, then made a run for it.

As Kyne disappeared over the top of the crater, Finn closed his hands around the *ash'strad*. He focused his magic, allowing it to surface and cover the orb in thick layers, the rush of power familiar, yet alien to the touch.

It'd been a long time since he'd called on this much magic. When he'd first been exiled to this world, he'd made a promise to never call upon it again. It was too much trouble.

He'd stuck to simple things, like making friends with snakes and lizards. He'd hidden the camp out of necessity, but compared to the magic he was weaving now, that illusion was a drop in the ocean.

You give so much for them and this isn't even your world, Siora's words echoed in his mind. She'd be angry knowing he was here. He'd helped save Solace and been a victim of the chaos surrounding the seal, but where else would he go?

Finn thought of Eloise, Kyne, and the other Exiles —they were his family now, even Vera.

His home world was a distant memory. This place, this red heart dusted with opal, was his home.

And he'd protect it.

The orb stopped turning and cracked open like a sliced orange, letting out brilliant shards of icy blue light. His body began to quake, making his limbs turn into jelly, and he knew he was in trouble.

Big trouble.

Finn tightened his hands around the orb and called on every last scrap of his magic, pouring it around the device.

"You piece of *za'adei* filth," he cursed. "Not today. *Not today!*"

The *ash'strad* clicked and his eyes widened as the buildup of power began to discharge.

Then...it exploded.

Hardy looked up at Darius as Joseph faced off with their maker.

Eloise knelt beside him, her gaze moving from him to the two vampires and back again. She had a haze around her that blurred the edges of her being. He blinked, but it didn't go away.

He didn't feel so good.

"It's taken you three hundred and fifty years, but here we are," Darius drawled. "Joseph Cheapside, still *cheap*."

"If you were going for a pun, you fell short, old chap," the vampire retorted.

Hardy groaned as Eloise helped him sit. She wrapped her arms around him, her warmth seeping into his cold flesh.

His blood soaked into the fabric of her trousers, staining the navy material black. The thought of blood made his throat sear and his gaze latched onto her neck.

"Don't," he murmured. "I'm starving... I..."

"Please do," Darius said with a sneer.

"You'd like that, you salty old bastard," Joseph said. "You lost faith in Hardy, but I haven't. He won't hurt her."

Darius narrowed his eyes. "Perhaps not...*but I will*."

He bared his fangs and lunged, but Joseph shoved his shoulder into the vampire's stomach, forcing him to a grinding halt. Their boots scraped in the blood-soaked earth as they wrestled.

Eloise yelped and held onto Hardy, her fingers biting into his arm. He tried to move, but he felt sluggish, and his veins rasped together like sandpaper—he'd been on the verge of desiccating.

"*Hardy*..." she murmured, her voice tinted with fear.

The two vampires continued to wrestle until Darius wrapped his hand around Joseph's neck and began to push.

Joseph's eyes widened as he grunted in pain, his neck reddening as Darius tried to tear his head from his body.

"Eloise, you have to get out of here," Hardy rasped. If she stayed, she'd die. If she ran, she'd at least have a chance.

An image of his sister appeared in his starved mind and he choked back a sob. Her frail body curled up in bed, her chestnut hair tangled across the pillow, her wet coughs, the blood that spotted her hands.

Mary.

He couldn't save her, but he could save Eloise. *He had to.*

"*That's it*..." Her expression changed so quickly, he barely caught it.

"You don't understand...he wanted you to come," he rasped. "He wants me to kill you."

"*No*," she hissed, grasping his bloodied face. "*He doesn't understand.*" Her gaze burned into his and he felt her elemental power flare. "You drink my blood, Frederick Marmaduke Hardy, and you *drink it now*."

His eyes widened as the haze around her glowed amber, the colour swirling into her eyes. He didn't know if it was a hallucination or her elemental power, but she looked so much like an angel he almost started praying.

Eloise forced her wrist to his mouth, and he couldn't hold himself back any longer.

She flinched as his fangs tore into her flesh, but didn't pull away. Rich, coppery blood filled his mouth and he swallowed.

As her blood filled his veins, a warmth spread through him like he'd never felt before. His body came back to life, humming with a strange magic. He felt the rivers of time brush up against him and the flutter of the curtain that separated their world from the vast expanse of all the universes beyond their own. He felt so small in the face of it all, but her blood showed him the way forwards.

*Make paths by walking...*one of Coen's favourite lines.

Hardy loosened his grip on Eloise's arm and finally understood. The mountain, her arrival in Solace, why Coen liked her so much, why things had escalated with the seal, and why she was so special...

Darius had hoped the Exiles would come and save him, but he hadn't counted on this. *Eloise Hart.* She was the key.

He bared his fangs and stood, peeling himself out of Eloise's grasp. He moved with a speed he'd never possessed before and shoved Joseph out of Darius's grasp. But before he could turn, a deafening explosion boomed in the distance.

It was now or never.

Hardy lunged towards the vampire just as the ground quaked underfoot, the earth rising and falling like a tsunami wave.

The vampires collided as the shockwave slammed into them. They fell as a shower of rock, debris, and metal shrapnel tore apart the tent.

Then everything went dark.

CHAPTER 24

I t was over in a matter of seconds.

Something heavy pressed down on Eloise and she squirmed, her ears ringing.

Opening her eyes, she saw Joseph staring down at her. He winked and lifted himself off her, grunting in pain, and revealing the dusty sky above. The explosion had blown the tent away, *literally*.

"Joseph?"

He fell back on his arse and looked over his shoulder. Blood soaked through the remains of his shirt and dripped onto the ground.

"Shrapnel," he said. "I'll be fine, but that fellow..." He nodded across the ruined tent.

Eloise's heart twisted and she sat up, her gaze finding the aftermath of not only the explosion, but the fight between the vampires.

Darius's withered corpse was laid out on the ground. His skin was all grey and wrinkly, and a gaping hole tore apart his chest—a blatant cause of death if she'd ever seen one. Hardy stood over the desiccated vampire, a thick layer of crimson blood coating his hand and wrist.

She stood, though her knees felt like rubber, and swallowed hard. "Hardy?"

"I'm okay," he said, though he clearly looked shellshocked. "I'm okay."

Eloise looked at Joseph, who'd begun plucking shrapnel out of his back.

"You gave up your revenge to save me," she murmured.

"Hardy kind of pushed me out of the way." He winced as he plucked a piece of metal out of his shoulder. "But it doesn't matter. He saved my life...and you saved his. That's a better way."

She pressed her palm against her temple. "You could've turned back."

"You a therapist in training?" Joseph chuckled, then winced as he pulled out another piece of shrapnel.

"No, I just want to understand."

"Well..." He reached his arm back and felt his torn flesh for more bits of metal. "Killing Darius wasn't going to bring my family back, and the satisfaction of dealing the blow wasn't worth letting you die. Sound about right?"

"Sure." Eloise rubbed her filthy palms on her trousers, but only smeared the dirt further. "I'm going out to find Finn and Kyne. They were in the pit." She nodded towards Hardy, who was still standing over Darius, his expression frozen. "Look out for him."

Joseph mock saluted her. "Aye, aye."

Eloise picked her way over the ruined remains of the tent, trying to keep her emotions in check. They had to have gotten out before the blast. If they didn't… She didn't want to think about what might've happened to Finn and the other fae. The increasing explosions had caused him so much pain, and that last one was the biggest yet.

She stumbled and caught herself on the edge of a dirty 4WD, her fingers smearing through the ochre dust. The air was still thick with grit, the cloud obscuring everything as it began to settle.

Coughing echoed through the haze and she squinted. Where were all the *EarthBore* employees? What'd happened to them? She'd forgotten to ask about their compulsions. Darius was dead, so did that mean they were free?

"Kyne?" she called, her voice sounding far away through the ringing in her ears. "Is that you?"

Another cough, this time followed by the faint outline of a person a handful of metres away.

She stepped forwards, pushing away from the 4WD. "Hello?"

A dirty, disoriented Kyne stumbled out of the dust cloud and she let out a strangled cry of relief.

"Eloise, *thank God*." He fell into her arms and they

embraced, clapping together like a pair of chalk dusters. "Darius?"

"Dead." She looked past him, but he was alone. "Where's Finn?"

The elemental's expression turned grim, and he glanced over his shoulder.

Her heart skipped a beat. "*Kyne...* Where's Finn?"

"He stayed behind..." he managed to say. "He tried to stop the explosion."

Eloise's expression fell. "He... *He was in the pit?*"

"He said he could—"

She pushed past him and broke out into a run. "Finn!"

Her boots thudded on the broken earth, her head throbbing and her ears ringing, but she didn't care. He had to be okay.

"*Finn!*"

<hr>

Leaving her cave was difficult, but it was time to face her fear.

Andante peeled apart the edges of her reality, pushing through the veil and stepping into the sunlight. She blinked, holding her hand up to shield her eyes.

The runes etched on her arms pulsed, shimmering like metallic gossamer threads as they connected to the power of the land once more. This place was special and her connection to it ran deeper than any other place she'd ever been.

The Old Ones had scarred this place a millennia ago, and she still felt the reverberations of their meddling. Her stomach churned, the unfamiliar sensation calling out to her—the pact her people had made with the cosmic entity calling to her.

As her courage began to build, she walked, her bare feet burning on the baked earth, her toes sinking into the red soil.

She walked the path, finding her way to the iron ore the elementals had told her about, but she cast a furtive glance over her shoulder, watching for the *èildear*.

Coen had always been lurking around her prism, sniffing around the edges like a hungry spirit. He wanted her power, they all did. The Dark, the Old Ones...everyone envied the Druids' control over space and time, but Andante was a coward, so she remained inside her cave where it was safe. No one bothered her there, and she was able to forget her past mistakes.

She'd managed quite well until she'd seen the elemental girl stumble through the outback. Eloise Hart.

She reminded her of her niece Gilhana, and her regrets rushed forth like a tidal wave of icy water, the coldness freezing her in place, the despair bearing down upon her.

Andante's greatest regret was turning her back on her people.

The path led her to a pit, the gaping hole a blight on the pristine outback landscape. A rust-coloured cloud billowed out of it and into the air, smearing across the brilliant blue above.

This wouldn't do.

Waving her hand, Andante manipulated the current around her and stepped into the crater. There she found a curious glowing silver and blue ball and a fae man who looked worse for the wear. Blood spotted his lips and his silver eyes glowed with a mysterious hue. He hummed with a strange magic she hadn't encountered before, but one glance told her it wouldn't be enough to stop what was coming.

She cast a prism around the shining orb as his startled gaze met hers...then the device clicked.

It detonated and ignited her power, her construct flaring in a shower of violet and indigo sparks as magic collided with it. It didn't stop all the explosion, but just enough.

The shockwave tossed the fae through the air and he slammed into the wall of the crater, flailing as rock shattered around him.

Andante's magic coiled around the silver orb, tightening until it contained the device. The blue light faded and the metal retracted, then the entire thing fell to the ground, landing with a dull thud.

The fae coughed and pushed away from the

crumbled rock, staggering to his feet. "You're Andante," he managed to rasp. He spat, a glob of blood landing a few metres away. "What did you do?"

"Saved your life," she retorted, glancing at the orb. "Your device is quite dead now. It won't trouble you or your seal."

"Finn!" Eloise's voice shrieked in the distance. "*Finn!*"

Andante glanced towards the sound. "It's time for me to leave."

"They would welcome you," the fae said, taking a step towards her. "Come back with me."

She shook her head. "Druids aren't warriors. I'll do what I can, but I'm not the key."

Finn said nothing, but his expression did the talking for him. He didn't quite understand, but that didn't bother her. The destination wasn't important...it was the journey that mattered.

"This place is a beacon," she told him. "I will snuff out its light, but the door will be one way."

The fae nodded. "I understand."

"Go. Be with your friends."

"Family," he corrected. "They're my family."

***

Finn scrambled up the side of the crater, his boots skidding in the loose rocks and dirt.

"*Finn!*" Eloise shrieked again.

"Calm your farm, desert pea," he said, clawing at the lip of the pit. "Give us a hand, won't you?"

Kyne emerged from the haze and grasped the fae's outstretched hand, hauling him up the last metre.

Finn rolled onto his back and coughed as Eloise rushed forwards.

"I was scared you were dead," she blurted, helping him sit. Her hands cupped his cheeks and she tilted his had from side-to-side, checking for gaping wounds.

"I'm fine." He swatted her away and cast a fleeting glance over the edge of the crater, but he couldn't see the bottom through all the dust. "What about the vampires?"

"Darius is dead," Eloise told him. "Hardy took care of it. Joseph's with him."

He coughed and shook his head, dislodging a shower of grit and gravel. "Could've been worse, I guess. At least he's fine."

"Fine is a relative term," Kyne said with a grimace.

Finn looked around the dig site and spotted a group of *EarthBore* employees huddled by the excavator. "What about them?"

Kyne followed his gaze and sighed. "I'll rustle up Joseph. They'll have to be compelled."

Finn pressed his palms on the ground and sensed the old woman's strange magic at work. The web that had woven around the orb reminded him of the sacred geometry scholars of his homeland studied—the shapes and patterns that lived in all living things. He looked up at the elementals and knew Andante's powers were deeper and more connected to the universe than they could ever imagine. She could help him go home.

"Do it now," Finn said, his gaze moving to the dazed humans, "because there won't be any coming back to this place."

Eloise stared at him, her smile fading. "Andante?"

He nodded. "I was never going to stop that explosion on my own. She saved us all." He grunted, his lip curling. "Took her sweet time about it, too."

The elemental laughed and threw her arms around his neck, almost making him fall backwards.

"Careful, desert pea," he murmured, embracing her, "I'm still feeling a little squishy."

CHAPTER 25

Eloise sat on the weathered wooden table outside the pub, watching the sunset. She never tired of the colours flaring above her, even though the vastness of it all made her feel insignificant sometimes.

The sapphire blue of the summer day, the flames of the setting sun, the darkness giving way to the glitter of the Milky Way stretching from horizon to horizon. The outback was stunning in its harshness—a beautiful wrapper for what lurked below.

Sighing, she looked to the north, her thoughts on Finn and the fae. Whatever they were going through was a mystery to her and the other Exiles. They'd chosen to remain apart, but yet again, the chaos surrounding got seal had dragged them into a life and death situation. First, the Nightshade and now the *ash'strad*. There was only so much they could take before it caused trouble—the bomb might be the last straw.

Eloise sighed again, knowing there was nothing she could do about it, though she worried for Finn. What had happened in that pit hadn't dulled his dry sense of humour, but even as she hugged him, she knew he was different.

A door banged in the distance and Joseph and Hardy emerged from the opal shop. They closed the space between there and the pub in a second, appearing in front of her.

"Well, if it isn't the little desert pea," Joseph declared with a grin.

"Hey," she said. "If it isn't the pincushion."

"*You're welcome.*" The vampire smirked lopsidedly and headed towards the pub. "Coming in for a drink?"

"Yeah, in a sec." She glanced at Hardy.

"Go on," he said to Joseph. "We'll be in in a moment."

The vampire nodded and disappeared inside, the opening door letting out the sound of music—a song from one of Blue's famous mixed CDs of Aussie pub rock classics—before it slammed closed again.

"How are you?" Eloise asked.

Hardy shrugged and ran a hand through his hair, slightly dislodging the artfully messy man bun at the base of his neck. "As well as I'm able to be."

Eloise smiled. "Well, that's a good sign, I suppose."

"I thought I would feel satisfied, but…" he trailed off with a shrug.

"It ended with a bang, but felt more like a whimper?"

"Something like that."

Eloise smiled and pushed off the table. Her boots hit the ground with a thud, and she looked up at the vampire. "The sun always rises after 'the end'," she said, "and we keep on living. I don't think any chapter in life ever feels finite." She clapped her hands together.

Hardy grinned. "Are you sure you're not a vampire? You just explained it perfectly."

"Yeah, nah," she tapped her temple, "I just think a lot."

He regarded her for a moment, then nodded towards the door. "Coming in?"

"Yep."

Inside, the pub was full of the smells of good home-cooking. Blue was whipping up an epic spread, and the kitchen was a beacon that made Eloise's stomach rumble.

She slipped into the chair beside Kyne and kissed his cheek. "Hey, you."

"Hey yourself." He glanced at Hardy. "All good, mate?"

The vampire nodded and reached for the jug of beer. "All good."

Finn wasn't anywhere to be seen. Eloise knew he wasn't going to be here, but she looked for him anyway, his usual perch by the bar awfully empty.

"What about the *EarthBore* employees?" Vera asked, resuming their conversation. "Did you help them?"

"Yeah," Joseph replied. "Patched them all up, did a bit of light dusting, then performed a little trick with my eyeballs, and they packed up what was left of their gear and rolled off into the sunset."

"As far as *EarthBore* is concerned, the core sampling was a bust," Kyne said with a nod. "They won't be coming back here."

"They won't find anything, anyway," Joseph added. "That old lady you all bang on about came and did some magic spell and hid it all. Not that anyone saw it." He grunted. "I still think she's a figment of your imagination."

The Exiles chuckled and Vera held up her wine glass.

"Faith can be a tricky concept," the witch said. "Sometimes you've just got to let go and accept it."

"Hear, hear," Blue declared.

"Why didn't she hide the seal?" Eloise asked, voicing the one question that'd been plaguing her since the chaos at the pit.

"The old bag didn't want to help us," Drew said. "She was screwing with us the whole time. No wonder she was hiding in her cave."

"No," Kyne told him. "I don't think it was that cut and dry."

"Maybe it can't be contained," Vera said.

"Huh?" Drew asked. "What do you mean?"

"When we were down there, I felt its power reaching through my barrier spell," she explained. "I can't remember much from when the Nightshade possessed me, but being able to access its power at all is a sign that it can't. If we take everything about the Old Ones at face value, we're literally messing with the fabric of the universe. Someone plugged that hole, but..."

"It still leaks," Wally muttered.

"Finally, something older than you two fossils," Drew proclaimed, holding up his pint glass.

"Which two fossils are you referring to?" Joseph asked, raising his eyebrows.

Vera snorted. "Take your pick."

The Exiles laughed and clinked glasses.

"Now," Blue said, reaching up to the bar. He picked up a stack of papers and waved them at Hardy. "Before I give you this, you have to promise you won't get mad at me."

The vampire frowned. "What is it?" He reached for the papers, but the publican snatched them back.

"*Promise.*"

"I promise."

Blue shuffled the stack and coughed. "I researched your family tree," he admitted. "I had the approximate dates and an inkling... I was gunna keep it hidden until you were ready, and you seem ready."

Eloise's heart skipped a beat. "You found them?"

"Found who?" Kyne asked.

"My brother and sisters," Hardy murmured in shock.

The Exiles fell silent, glancing at each other. Drew shifted, his chair creaking, the sound breaking Hardy out of his daze.

"My sister was sick," he told them. "We couldn't afford medicine, so I... It's why I was sent to Port Arthur."

"*Strewth*," Wally said.

The vampire took the papers, folded the pile in half, and stuck them in the rear pocket of his jeans.

"You're not going to read it?" Joseph asked.

Hardy shook his head. "Not yet."

A minute of awkward silence followed.

"On that note," Drew said loudly. "Is dinner ready yet? *I'm starving.*"

Blue chuckled and clapped the shifter on the shoulder. "Should be. Come give us a hand."

The Exiles lingered after dinner. Joesph was taking great pleasure regaling them with tales of Medieval England and all the gruesome and gross things humans had to endure in the big cities.

Hardy sat back from the group, his expression closed. When he caught Eloise staring at him, he leaned towards her.

"I wanted to talk with you," he murmured. "Outside."

"Sure." She nodded.

The sun had long set and the stars shone overhead in the clear sky. The lights from the pub didn't dull their glow at all, their little blip on the map passing by unnoticed...by most people at least.

They sat on the wonky table again, but it was Eloise who spoke first.

"Can I ask... What did you do with Darius?"

Hardy sighed. "We took him into the pit and buried him. Even after all the horrible things he did to us, it didn't seem right to just leave him exposed like that. For better or worse, he was the father of all vampires in this world."

And in the end, he just wanted to go home. It was a sobering notion, that all bad people wanted many of the same things as the good ones did. A home, family. It humanised the villain when it was easier to see them as all one thing.

Eloise nodded. "And that's what separates you from him." She placed a hand on his arm. "You were never going to be the monster he tried to turn you into. He underestimated who you really are, Hardy."

"And he underestimated you," the vampire told her.

Her expression faded. "How?"

"You understand why the mountain calls to you," he explained. "I felt it when I drank your blood."

Eloise bit her bottom lip and remembered the moment her true power had ignited. She'd seen Kyne do it before, how his eyes had glowed amber in the darkness of Black Hole Mine, but the thought had never occurred to her that she could do it, too. At least not until the universe had given her a shove in the right direction.

"I didn't until that moment," she admitted. "It was something Andante said. *You won't know until you dig it up.* I was sitting there with you in my arms, and I felt my power… I felt it…" She waved her hands before her. "It rose like a flame. I don't know if it was the magic from the bomb or the exposed iron ore, or if it was another current of space and time brushing up against me, but it filled me up and *I knew*."

Hardy said nothing, but she knew he'd felt it, too. Her blood had given him the power to stop Darius, a two-thousand-year-old vampire.

"The Old One in the mountain called to Darius, like it calls to me," she went on. "There is no key in the iron ore, Hardy. There never was."

"Because you are the key to the mountain," the vampire murmured.

And what that meant for her, she didn't know. That fact that it could reach out to her was enough proof that whatever prison held the Old One in the mountain was eroding. Maybe she did have to find it, if only to make sure the door remained locked.

"It wants to be set free," she said. "And it will do anything in its power to make it happen." She sighed, her heart heavy. "It'll come for me again."

"Do the others know?"

Eloise shook her head. "I'll tell them...just not today." She tapped the papers sticking out of Hardy's jeans pocket. "You gunna read that?"

"Maybe later." He smiled, shrugging. "There's something I want to do first."

Eloise tilted her head to the side, but he wasn't in the sharing mood.

"Cool," she said. "Let me know if you need any help."

Hardy chuckled and wrapped his arm around her shoulders. "Deal."

<hr>

Hardy knelt on the rusty earth, loose stones digging into his knees. He set the last stone in place, angling it so the light caught the seam of black opal potch just right.

The memorial was complete, and he looked over his handiwork and smiled.

Kyne had helped him retrieve a slab of rock from Back Hole Mine, helping him solidify the crumbling layers and preserving the slash of potch running through the middle. It reminded him of the standing stones of ancient Britain, the jagged edges rising out of the ground, the monoliths calling to mysterious magic long-forgotten.

Then Hardy had spent all day and night chiselling

away in his workshop, fixated on completing it as soon as he could. He'd etched the names of his siblings across the face, remembering the good times they'd had growing up in London. For almost two hundred years, his memory had been clouded by the night when he'd been caught at the apothecary and all that'd followed.

No more.

Around the stone's base, he'd placed more rocks, leaving a space for a glass jar where he could place flowers, even though they'd wilt in the middle of summer. Wildflower season was fast approaching, and he knew his sisters would love the colourful blooms that sprung up in the big wet. He'd ask Vera where he could find some and bring them back here.

Hardy traced his fingers over the chiselled stone, his heart aching. *Mary, Thomas, Elizabeth.* Their memory had been pushed aside for too long.

The settlers' cemetery sorely needed tending to, and now he'd erected the memorial to his family, his thoughts were turning to restoring the entire plot. A new fence, some weeding, a plaque, and repairing the broken headstones belonging to the pioneers of Solace. A tribute to the Indigenous peoples could stand by the gate, acknowledging their plight, and he'd add their names to the obelisk by the highway.

The story of Solace wasn't always a pleasant one, but it deserved to be remembered.

"Looks good."

Hardy looked up at Joseph, then to the car keys in his hand. "Are you leaving?"

"Yeah," the vampire said. "It's about time I rocked and rolled outta here."

Hardy rose and dusted off his jeans. "You can always stay longer. The others won't mind."

"I know." He shrugged. "All I've ever known is pain and revenge. It's time to figure out who I am without all of that."

"That's deep." He clapped a hand on his friend's shoulder. "I'm proud of you."

"And I'm proud of you." He grinned and nodded towards the memorial. "Are you going to read those papers Blue gave you?"

"Yeah, actually. I'm going to in a minute. You don't want to stick around and see how it all ends?"

Joseph shook his head. "I don't need to. I know it'll all work out."

Hardy chuckled. "Eloise really did a number on you, didn't she?"

The vampire let out a heavy sigh and ran his hand through his hair. "You've got a special one there, old fella. Kyne's one lucky bloke."

"We're all lucky," Hardy murmured. The day her van broke down should be turned into a national holiday as far as he was concerned.

"Oh, before I forget..." Joseph reached into his shirt pocket and pulled out a party popper. "Give this to Finn, would you? I promised to save one for him."

Hardy grinned and took it. "Sure."

"Will he be all right?" the vampire asked. "He was pretty churned up from that bomb."

"He will be. We'll look out for him and his people." It would take some convincing, considering the fae's offhand approach to Solace, but he'd make sure they heard it. "And don't be a stranger or wait another hundred years before you call."

Joseph chuckled. "I'll do my best."

The vampires embraced one last time.

"You were always the best of us," Joseph murmured into his ear. "And don't you go forgetting it."

They parted and Hardy stood by the side of the highway as the vampire got into his silver hire car. As it peeled away, the tyres kicking up a cloud of dust before they hit asphalt, he raised his hand in a wave.

Joseph was more well-adjusted to life than he gave himself credit for, and he knew his friend would find himself out there. He had faith.

Turning, he walked back to the memorial. There was one last thing he needed to do before it was complete.

Hardy plucked Blue's research out of his back pocket. It was the closure he was missing. The whimper was turning out to be a bang after all.

He unfolded the papers and smoothed out the creases.

The first page was the death certificate for his sister, Mary. It listed the cause of death as consumption, dated November twenty-first, 1831. Three months after the night he was arrested.

Three months after he was sent away.

It was a long time and knowing how she must have suffered, he lowered his gaze to the headstone. He'd been at sea, almost at the end of his tortuous journey to Port Arthur on that foul tall ship…but that was nothing compared to what Mary had endured.

"Rest in peace, little sister," he murmured.

The next two papers were marriage certificates, and his heart sped up.

Thomas Hardy, age twenty-three, occupation: carpenter. Mary Wallace, age twenty, occupation: maid.

Elizabeth Hardy, age twenty-one, occupation: seamstress. William O'Connell, age twenty-six, occupation: clerk.

Hardy's hopes rose sharply as he shuffled to the next pages. *Birth certificates.* Elizabeth had three children and a fourth who'd died at birth. *Oh, Lizzy…*

Tom had six children with his wife, and with the absence of more printouts for them, he assumed they'd all lived.

The final two pieces of paper were death certificates. Hardy looked up, not daring to look at the dates just yet. They'd both had entire broods of kids, there'd be no way they would've died young.

Thomas Hardy. Died 1884, age seventy-two.

Elizabeth Walker. Died 1878, age sixty-nine.

They'd lived long lives, gotten married, had children, and found their place in the world.

Hardy folded the papers back up and clutched them tightly, his gaze returning to the memorial.

They'd *lived*.

Reaching out, he traced the chiseled letters of Mary's name.

It was finally time for him to do the same.

CHAPTER 26

Coen lounged in the branches of a windswept gumtree, his legs dangling in the air.

Below, *Marlu* gazed into the distance, her warm brown eyes searching out the barrier between them and the Druid's hidden home. Her joey peeked out of her pouch, mimicking his mother's movements and the Indigenous man chuckled. The little 'roo had a big heart.

Above, the Milky Way had long set, the yearly rotation of the stars bringing the great emu down to the billabong to rest. He took care of all the animals—the kangaroos, the wombats, the little bilbies, the lizards, the snakes, and all the creatures of the land—while they sheltered from the heat of the sun. But soon the emu would rise, and he would take flight once more, bringing sweeping rains across the outback. It was the way of things.

The wet would bring life to the dry, coaxing green

things to grow while washing away the billowing dust of the summer. But the rains would also bring danger, for peace could not exist without it.

Sunset came and the earth stilled, calmness returning to the currents sweeping past him. Yes, all was as it should be.

The curtain billowed and the old woman appeared, her bare feet a whisper as she approached.

"You finally came out to meet me," Coen said, grinning. "Hello!"

"You're quite persistent," Andante told him, "annoyingly so."

"You know why I'm here." He leapt out of the gum and landed before the druidess.

"Eloise."

"I knew she would draw you out," he said with a chuckle. "You see the same thing in her that I do."

Andante nodded.

"There are many who can see, but very few who can see *beyond*," he went on. "She is one...and so are you."

"The Old One calls to her like it did the vampire," she said, "but you already knew."

"Yes."

"Why didn't you say anything to her?"

Coen laughed. "That's a very direct thing for a Druid to say."

"I think we are past that, don't you?" Her

expression darkened. "I know you feel them. They are returning. Breaking through their bonds."

The Indigenous man nodded. Of course, he did. It wasn't the first time. The creatures had marked this world, but Coen saw the potential in the living things here. There was beauty amongst the suffering—one couldn't live without the other—and it shouldn't be a reason for a final end.

This place deserved a chance to flourish.

Andante's wrinkled brow creased as she frowned. "When I look at you, I see…"

"Best not to think about it," he told her. "There is a long path behind me, but all that matters now is the trail ahead."

"Through what you call the Dreaming?"

Coen nodded. "It is all around us. It is all things. Up, down, side-to-side. The sun, the wind, the rain. It is you and me. It is how we live our lives. It is our morals. It is memory." He smiled and tapped her on the temple, their beings connecting with a sharp *crack* of electricity. "You feel it every time you call on your magic."

Andante jerked backwards, blinking. "I understand."

"They will need your help before the black heart wakes," he told her. "Will you go if they call?"

Andante looked towards the horizon, her eyes shining with a mysterious blue hue. It was the colour of the threads she wound into structures she called 'prisms'. Coen saw them in the barrier surrounding the karsts where she made her home. They were pretty things, sparkling like the crystals the witch Vera used in her spells.

Finally, the old woman nodded. "And what will you do?"

"For many years I have made my own paths..." Coen grinned and pointed to the east. "I will follow the tracks left behind. There is wisdom to be found there."

The druidess's smile faded. "The mountain lingers in the east."

"And yet, east I must go."

"Are you sure?"

"The rains are coming," he said, turning towards the mountain, "and when the clouds bruise the sky, the great emu will fly."

ABOUT NICOLE

Nicole R. Taylor is an Australian Urban Fantasy author.

She lives in the western suburbs of Melbourne dreaming up nail biting stories featuring sassy witches, duplicitous vampires, hunky shapeshifters, and devious monsters.

She likes chocolate, cat memes, and video games.

When she's not writing, she likes to think of what she's writing next.

Follow Nicole Online:

Website: www.nicolertaylorwrites.com
Facebook: facebook.com/nrtaylorwrites
Newsletter: www.nicolertaylorwrites.com/newsletter
Email: nicole.this.is@gmail.com